Praise for Rashid Darden's
A Peculiar Legacy

"His story and characters are funny, poignant, illuminating, surprising, tragic, bawdy, and redemptive. I wept reading the last chapter."

Steve Chase, author of *Letters to a Fellow Seeker: A Short Introduction to the Quaker Way*

"Rashid Darden excels at crafting richly layered characters with unwavering resilience…The voices in Slope feel intimately familiar, resonating with a powerful message of hope."

Kia DuPree, author of *Shattered* and *Disentangled*

"With *A Peculiar Legacy*, Rashid Darden shows that he is at the top of his writing game. Indeed, a spectacular novel."

Frederick Smith, author, *One and Done* and *Down For Whatever*

"Set against a backdrop of risk and revelation, Darden crafts a novel as bold as it is immersive. This book lingers long after the final page—unsettling, moving, and utterly original."

Peterson Toscano, artist and co-host of *Quakers Today* podcast

"Darden has woven an amazing literary tapestry of lives shared and shaped in a DC enclave filled with tragedy, forgiveness, learning, acceptance and a commitment to community. An exceptional novel filled with memorable and relatable characters."

La Toya Hankins, author of *K-Rho: The Sweet Taste of Sisterhood* and *SBF Seeking.*

"Through masterful storytelling, Darden peels back…layers and reveals the very soul of [Slope], and how its soulfulness and devotion to each other help it during difficult times."

Gar McVey-Russell, author of *Sin Against the Race*

"A lad…takes us on a 'Peculiar' journey of prayer, migration, and maturing in a DC quite familiar to me. The 'Legacy' calls us to a journey of self-discovery and meditation fixed on a Slope whose folks invite us in. I want more of this community."

Rev. Raymond B. Kemp, Georgetown University.

"*A Peculiar Legacy* investigates the question, 'What if there were a community that truly embodied the Quaker belief in "answering that of God in everyone?"' The story paints a picture of embracing the principles of beloved community even when faced with injustice and oppression."

Lauren Brownlee

"Like *Black Fire: African American Quakers on Spirituality and Human Rights*, Rashid Darden's *A Peculiar Legacy* will open eyes to the fact that Quakers are a diverse group of people."

Audrey Greenhall,
Manager of QuakerBooks of FGC and QuakerPress of FGC.

"I love this book…especially its dramatic climax. Fiction exists to take us to other worlds, to see through other eyes, and in that, the book amply succeeds."

Mitchell Santine Gould, author of *Kelson of the Creation*

"Rashid Darden invites readers to explore a vision of diversity within the Religious Society of Friends, offering a much-needed lamp post for the ongoing conversation regarding the future of Quakerism."

Lynette Davis, SFCC, writer for *Illuminate*; contributing author of *God's Grace: Comforting, Guiding, Supporting*

"*A Peculiar Legacy*… reveals useful traditions that are both community-led and intergenerational."

Loraine Hutchins, PhD
bisexual Washingtonian who helped put the "B" in LGBTQ

"*A Peculiar Legacy* begins with a murder, but it is not so much a story about death but rather about how we live—how people come together in challenging moments—and how love stays alive in the midst. It is a beautiful story."

Steven Cleaver, author of the award-winning novel *Saving Erasmus*.

"The text also offers an intimate glimpse of the Quaker religion, specifically as experienced by people of color. It moves you to seek your own path to spirituality and listen through silence."

Ja'Sent Brown

A
PECULIAR
LEGACY

Rashid Darden

Old Gold Soul   Conway, NC

Old Gold Soul

www.oldgoldsoul.com

First Edition

Cover Design by Sarah Katreen Hoggatt,
Book Layout Biz (BookLayoutBiz.com)

ISBN: 978-1-7347228-4-0

For Talib and for Kiyana,
and for all who thrived.

Acknowledgements

To God be the glory!

I thank my wonderful mother, Carolyn Darden-Stutely, for being everything I needed when I most needed it.

Thank you to my friends Angela, Sahira, and Lola Stepancic, not only for their enduring friendship, but for allowing me to borrow "Slope" as the background for this story.

To my good-good girlfriend from Da 'Ville, Jordyne Blaise, thank you for being my champion, cheerleader, and confidante. To my Brothers Rodney Frank, Chris Moore, and Tremaine White, thank you for getting me through when I could not make it on my own.

I would like to thank my many spiritual guides, companions, and elders on the long journey toward completing this novel: Regina Renee Nyégbeh, Lori Patterson, Lee Andrew Sayles, John Skinner, Lori Piñeiro Sinitzky, many Friends of Color at various Friends General Conference events, Transatlantic Friends, and the meeting to which I am a member, Friends Meeting of Washington. You have created for me and with me a community of strong, intelligent, and spiritually deep people who are ready for the next generation of Quakers.

To the staff of Friends General Conference, as led by Barry Crossno: Thank you, too, for seeing me as a whole person, capable of doing the work and writing the story at the same time.

Thank you, also, to the staff of Pendle Hill, for creating a wonderful, spiritual place to write a chapter or two.

To my friend Tiana Beard, the greatest editor I could ask for: thank you for knowing my intentions and redirecting me toward them. You have guided my hand as I chisel the story of Slope out of rough stone. My gratitude also to Jennifer Samson and Tranise Robinson.

To my Beta Readers Betsy Bramon, Gina Bulett, Rachelle Gardner, Elaine Wilson, Jim Fussell, Loraine Hutchins, Archelle Lincoln, Zoila Primo, Tara Proctor, Trenile Tillman: thank you for being brave enough to be among the first to read this story and thank you for your valuable feedback.

The Care and Clergy Writing Group, led by Minister Blyth Barnow of Femminary, was an invaluable part of my journey toward completing this work. Thank you for seeing my work as ministry and welcoming me into your circle. Thank you also to the writing group of the Fellowship for Quakers in the Arts, for creating a space where we may share our various goals and hold one another accountable.

Last, but not least, thank you to the many people who have given unselfishly as my patrons to ensure that the writing still happened. Your financial support over the years made this book possible:

Alex Montgomery, Angel Brown, Anice Schervish Chenault, Ayana K. Domingo, Barbara Gosney, Becky Britz, Belén Ramirez, Carolyn Darden-Stutely, Chris Rutledge, Cicely Garrett, Claire Finn, Corey Boone, Danielle Barrios, Deonne Cunningham Nauls, Dwayne Steward, Edwina King, Elyshe Voorhees, Erica Danielle, Erika Gunter, Evan Oxhorn, Florence J. Davidson, Fred Davis, Gary Chyi, Gaven Mayo, Geniro Dingle, Gil Shannon, Henry Marx, Ja'Sent Brown, Jamie Wilkins, Jeanné Lewis, Jeff Marcella, Joe Alexander, Josh FromThrall, Bibish Kazadi, Katherine Steadwell, Kathleen McDaniel, Katie Branagan, Kelly O'Shea, Khalila Lomax, Krista Robertson, LaToya Hankins, Latoya Mitchell Hodges, Laura Grothaus, Tony Lamair Burks II, Lesa Jeanpierre, Leslie Rogers, Lisa Green, Lisa Hinton, Lori Lincoln, Lori-Ann Gregory, Markia Williams, Mary C. Garvey, Michelle Freeman, Muhammad Salaam, N. Rashad Jones, Nikki Richards, Patty Deneen, Robert Donigian, Shaunica Pridgen, Shonte M Harrell, T.N. Tillman, Tanya McCaine, Christopher Jaramillo, Tiana Beard, Tina Suliman, Will Saunders, Yea Flicker, and Zoila Primo.

To anyone I have omitted, please charge it to my head and not to my heart.

Prescript

Prologue:
Thursday, August 4, 2022

Jordan and Rahman would probably never own a house in the country. Jordan craved quiet but couldn't bear to give up the convenience of the city. Rahman, on the other hand, couldn't stand the quiet, and couldn't live someplace without hustle and bustle, as well as easy access to his children, who were now both in college back in New York.

DC would do. Rahman had always liked DC when he visited for fraternity meetings or conferences, or when he'd carve out time to see his favorite person, despite having a wife. In his wildest dreams, he pictured himself in a house with Jordan, finally able to be who he wanted to be, not who he was expected to be, optics be damned.

Rahman sipped his Moscow mule and stared at Jordan while he typed away on his laptop. This was the life he wanted with the man he wanted. Not a country cottage, but a modern farmhouse on a hill, separated from a couple dozen other such homes. Each house had a porch, some supported by wooden posts. Most of the neighborhood's homes had vinyl siding, in drab yellows and off-white. Theirs, though, was one of the few brick houses on the street. It was painted gray, and their porch was only accessible from inside the house. Their front door was on the side.

Jordan tapped away from that porch, his usual office space in good weather, rattling off an email to his colleague at the Smithsonian Institution, where he'd worked for decades now. His eyebrows furrowed into a fisherman's knot; his nose flared with his latest disgust.

"I done told this b—"

"You been working all day," Rahman interrupted with a laugh. "Have your drink."

"I don't know how many times I have to approve the posting. I need to fill my vacancy right now. I've been without a coordinator for *three months*."

"It's after six in the evening. Is she even going to be logged in?"

Jordan looked into Rahman's eyes, annoyed. Then, he melted, in that way only Rahman could make him melt. He closed his laptop, put it on the wooden coffee table, and sipped his matching Moscow mule.

"It's good?" Rahman asked hopefully.

"You never miss," Jordan said.

The breeze through the oak trees cooled the August heat. They could have been in Virginia, North Carolina, or Georgia, but the muffled sounds of far-off street bikes and faint tunes from radios unknown told the truth. They were not where their fathers were from. They were from cities, and finally, after decades of tension, the school principal and the museum curator—the son of the Bronx and the son of Dorchester—were at peace in their own home. This was the last do-over for them. Their house on Slope would be their forever home.

"Hey Google, play Mingus radio," Rahman commanded his speaker. Jordan smiled. Mid-century jazz was his love language, and the combination of Charles Mingus and a good cocktail rendered him particularly susceptible to Rahman's advances.

Rahman, the elder by two years, rose and walked to his husband with the intention of initiating a massage. His gait was interrupted by a scream.

The men's eyes locked in a millisecond of confusion. Jordan stood and hurried to the waist-high railing. Up the hill, a petite young woman stood at the corner, wailing the timeless song of unimaginable grief, known well to the mothers, sisters, and daughters of Slope. Rahman and Jordan knew this song, despite growing up elsewhere. It was a heartbreaking elegy, calling forward the regal woman across the street in her colorful caftan; the shirtless youth down the street, with his sleeveless t-shirt in one hand and his phone in the other; and even old Pops, who sat on his porch around the corner, leaning forward to hear whether the song of hopelessness announced the death of a Black man he knew or raised, or at least tried to.

"Fuck!" the youth shouted. His blond, shoulder-length dreadlocks angrily swirled about him as his body twisted in agonized frustration. Sweat and tears dripped from his face to his waist, moistening the royal blue band of his boxer briefs.

More youth and more elders came out to the center of Slope to hear the news, to scream, to cry, to curse, to ask why, to hold, to rock, to be still, and to stew.

"Naw, man. Not Gino."

"Shit ain't right."

"Where his people?"

From their white porch with deep gray brick walls, Jordan and Rahman Gaffney-Bruce mourned for the young man they had not met, their neighbor Gino Powell, who was loved by those assembling at the quiet intersection of 57th Street and Burr Place NE.

Only the United States Census Bureau knew for sure how many families lived in Slope, the tiny sliver of the District of Columbia known as Grant Park to some, "over by Deanwood" to others, and "you might as well be in Maryland for all that" to a few. The post office knew them as part of 20019. Slope knew what it meant to be counted, yet still be dismissed.

The reason it was called Slope was obvious: the neighborhood sat on a hill, crowned by about a dozen houses on Bale Street. 57th Street bisected the neighborhood, and if you followed it down the rather steep hill, past Burr Place and then Caine Place, you'd go straight into Watts Branch, a woody creek snaking through DC and Prince George's County. A footbridge connected Slope to the neighborhood called Northeast Boundary, but skirmishes between crews decades ago had seeped into the community's DNA, and very few people ever took that particular shortcut out of Slope.

Slope had a heartbeat. What was once a barren wasteland no sane person would have built a house on was now a community of ninety families in seventy or so houses and apartments. Slope lived, from Pops, at 90 years old with a mind as sharp as it was the day he had escaped to Slope from the unforgiving South; to the newborn in the house overlooking Watts Branch. Slope breathed, with memories from every movement that touched DC and the world. Slope worshiped, and believed, and came together every Sunday under an ancient sun, to perform a rite that had no name, but that gave to them an indomitable spirit that lived in each of them.

Slope had a soul, that now mourned with the death of Gino Powell, its favorite son, yet swelled with the promise of new life, despite the blood-stained pavement of Washington's streets.

That night, Rahman held Jordan a little tighter, even as the mourners' wails faded to leftover fireworks and gunshots into the sky. In a few more days, they would observe, for yet another week, that peculiar rite, and finally be curious enough to accept Miss Sandra's standing invitation to her weekly family dinner.

Miss Sandra:
Sunday, August 7, 2022

It was hard to say who was more handsome between Jordan and Rahman Gaffney-Bruce. Rahman was tall, dark, and smooth, like Miss Sandra's first husband, Billy. He was the more dapper of the two. Early in the mornings, he'd come out of his house in his dark suit, put on his expensive sunglasses, and strut to the car in his driveway. He had a swagger like Billy, too. Around his third time driving up the hill, he decided to smile and wave at the woman in her flowing caftan. She hadn't known how obvious it was that she'd been staring at him and daydreaming of her first love.

An inch shorter than Rahman with a wild afro and full beard, Jordan looked much more like Miss Sandra's second husband, Tommy. No matter how intense he looked while working from home, tapping furiously on his laptop on his front porch, he was still adorable, like a soft Frederick Douglass, or like a Monchhichi toy her children played with in the 80s. Adorable, but sexy. Both men were athletic, and she could only imagine the acrobatics they got into after hours.

When she saw them together, sweating profusely during their mid-summer move-in day, she knew not only that they were a couple, but that they *belonged* together. There was something about the way they looked at each other, especially when they thought the other wasn't looking: Rahman, like he was the luckiest man in the world; Jordan, like he still couldn't believe he'd gotten away with whatever he had to get away with to be with this man.

Miss Sandra trusted her gut—her *discernment*, as Miss Jennie once taught her. It was more than what she guessed or presumed. It was, instead, those feelings inside her that were already so complete and powerful that God must have put them there.

A few weeks after the two had moved in, that discernment led her to put one foot in front of the other and ring their doorbell. She had a bottle of vodka in hand. Her kids convinced her Ciroc was what the fancy people drank, but she wouldn't know—she was sold out on Rémy Martin since 1976.

The one who looked like Frederick Douglass answered the door.

"Oh…well hi!" he said. He was more jovial than Miss Sandra would have pegged him for.

"Hi! I'm Cassandra Lassiter, your neighbor across the street," she announced.

"Jordan Gaffney-Bruce," he said, extending his hand.

So formal, she thought.

"I noticed you and your…well I noticed you two moved in a few weeks ago, and, well, you know, back in the day we would have brought over a cake or a fruit basket, but people be just so…you know…*funny* about folk all in your business, so I said to myself 'Now Sandra, leave them people alone, it's a new day.' But I just don't have it in me, cuz we know each other around here on Slope, you know?"

"Slope?"

"Yeah, that's what we call this neighborhood. From the bottom of the hill up to the houses on Bale, and Burr in the middle. I bet the real estate agent called it Grant Park, or tried to tell you this was Deanwood."

"Well…yes, that's exactly what she said," Jordan laughed. "To be honest with you, Ms. Lassiter, I was hoping anybody would come say hi, but especially you."

"Me?" she giggled.

"I see how all the kids around here respect you. They're loud, but they hush and tighten up when they walk past your porch. And the older ones…I'm not a parent, but I can tell they adore you, too."

"All this in just a few weeks of observing?" Miss Sandra blushed behind her chestnut brown skin.

"I work from home. Some folks watch the stories, I watch people. Hope that doesn't make me sound like a stalker."

"Chile, who's the one ringing a stranger's doorbell?" Miss Sandra laughed. "Anyway, this is for you. I hope you don't mind me presuming y'all are drinkers."

She extended her hand and presented Jordan with the slim bottle of Ciroc Summer Watermelon.

"Oh, indeed we are. Thank you so much for this! Better than a bottle of wine, that's for sure. Won't you come in?"

"Is your…is the other one home?"

Jordan cracked up on the inside. The nice older lady with gray cornrows did her best to be welcoming but still couldn't find the fortitude to say "husband" or even "partner" without potentially offending.

"The other one is Rahman. He's my husband. He's still at work."

"Oh, I thought so, chile. I just don't know what people are saying these days, and now I gotta learn extra pronouns, too. I'm a she/her, by the way. Chile, help an old lady keep up. I don't mean no harm. Anyway, no, I think I'll come back when he's at home. Don't want him to walk in and think I'm putting the moves on you."

She winked.

"Then I'll see you later, Ms. Lassiter."

"Oh, Miss Sandra will do," she sang as she floated away. He was devastatingly handsome, up close. Twenty years ago, with some persistence, she would have done everything she could to make him her next husband. But those days had passed. She'd entered her crone years with grace, as Miss Jennie had demonstrated years ago.

She thought of Miss Jennie often as she contemplated life in her retirement years. Even though the old lady was old when Miss Sandra was a girl, and she had been dead since the early 90s, it still felt like way too soon. She'd done so much for so many in so many ways that Sandra felt like she'd never be able to keep Slope together like Miss Jennie had.

She twisted her wedding bands while she walked, remembering what the lady had said to her after her second husband died.

"You've got choices, Cassandra, and leadership is always one of them. You don't have to be a President or a CEO. You don't have to be a General or an Admiral. But you do have to push through and prove to God that you can lead your family, despite this terrible loss."

"Why do I have to prove anything to God, Miss Jennie? Why can't I just be sad?"

"You don't *have* to prove anything to God. But…why wouldn't you *want* to?"

All these memories and not a single damn photo, Cassandra mused.

At 9:50 a.m. on Sundays, Miss Sandra walked out of her house and stepped ever-so-carefully down her wooden porch stairs, which were worn and slightly warped by the elements. Her seven children were long grown and mostly far away, with their own lives now, leaving her with her own sense of balance to trust as the stairs got more and more perilous with every passing year. She wasn't in bad health, and she wasn't falling apart, but she did notice the stiffness in her knees lasting longer and longer these days.

Her black and gray caftan whipped around her like a cyclone as her legs pumped up the hill. She covered her gray cornrows with a white turban and her gold bracelets jangled against each other. She carried a folding chair with her.

At the intersection of 57ᵗʰ and Burr Place, several of her neighbors were already assembled, seated in their own chairs. She nodded at the Jones family, with old Pops in his black suit and sophisticated wooden cane flanked by his daughter, Earnestine, and granddaughter. Pops nodded back and the women smiled.

About half a block up Burr Place, the baby of the family, Peek, pulled a metal barricade from between two houses, placing it in the middle of the street. The scrape from the metal against the asphalt echoed past the intersection, as Ziggy did the same. Peek was the spitting image of his great-grandfather: tall and lean with a sharp nose and piercing brown eyes, except Peek was a deep brown. Pops, in comparison, could pass for white under other circumstances. They both had soft, short curls, even though Pops' hairline had receded back to the civil rights movement, let his daughter tell it.

Peek sat behind his family, legs splayed and arms folded. Ziggy, who usually sat with his mother, joined Peek. Ziggy's hair was long, his bi-tone dreadlocks turning from black to blond as they passed his ears. He'd had a "fuckboy" haircut at the beginning of the pandemic: short at the sides, long on top, curly, and colored, but his discomfort at the risk of COVID infection at barber shops led him to take matters into his own hands, giving him a less polished look. He'd gone from mumble rapper to rock star in about two years: narrow hips, perpetual five o'clock shadow, and locs that hid his eyes depending on which way the wind blew.

Miss Sandra noticed Korey was still missing, as he had been since Gino died. It was bad enough the Gang of Four was now permanently three, but Korey's absence disconcerted her.

The Flythes shuffled to the square forming in the intersection under the sunny August sky. Close by them were the Warrens, the Pierces, and the Lamberts, with their stairstep children in front. They nodded and took their seats.

Miss Sandra looked at her Fitbit as 9:59 became 10:00. She looked up and locked eyes with Peek. She nodded.

He shook his head and looked at his lap. She continued to stare at him, so hard, in fact, that Ziggy looked up. He nudged Peek with his elbow. They both returned Miss Sandra's stare.

Bring your ass, she mouthed.

Peek sucked his teeth and exhaled. He rose, and his gangly limbs moved him from behind the second row of folding chairs like a brown praying mantis. He stood at a corner and stuffed his hands in his denim pockets.

She cleared her throat. Peek took his hands from his pockets and adjusted his posture.

"Slope gathers here…" The words caught in his throat, and he stopped, both in an effort to remember the words said at the beginning of their time together and to try and forget that the man who'd most recently said them was now dead.

"Take your time," Miss Sandra whispered. But Peek didn't want to take his time. He wanted to fast forward through this meeting, past the funeral rites, past his GED graduation—whenever that would be—and past everything until he was no more and would have to think no more about anything, much less the horrors of his life, known and yet to be known.

He squinted, blinking dust or pollen or sadness from his eyes. One of the new gay dudes on 57th Street stepped out to his porch to water his plants. He didn't know him yet, but he liked him. He looked like the kind of dude who would answer the door to trick-or-treaters and play touch football with the boys on the block. He bet that dude knew where he came from, and because he did, he wouldn't try to change Slope just because he moved in.

Focus, dummy, he commanded of himself.

"Slope gathers here, at the intersection of our neighborhood, under the watchful eye of God, to experience His love directly. We sit in silence to wait on what God is saying to us. Preachers don't tell us what God means. We listen to Him. The Bible gives us a road map, but we know—as everybody in Slope knows—that our understanding of God evolves every day. What we knew yesterday may be different tomorrow. Just like…just like the people we love who were here yesterday might be gone tomorrow…so please, wait in silence with us, and speak if God is trying to tell you something."

Miss Sandra beamed with approval. Peek's shoulders slouched and he returned to his seat.

The meeting was completely silent that day, to no one's surprise. The grief's humidity hung in the air like molasses, making the hour together feel longer and heavier than it needed to. Sandra spent a lot of time thinking about old Miss Jennie, and what she might have said if she was here, but she found that she could not, as things were never this bad when Miss Jennie was alive.

A few hours later, after hands had been shaken and families departed to enjoy the rest of their Sunday, Miss Sandra cooked a meal fit for kings back in her empty house. Her many children, spread throughout the country, called and FaceTimed her to check in and hear the latest gossip.

"Say hi to Grandma," her youngest son, Qiang, said to his tribe of kids. They babbled in unison from Qiang's Upper Marlboro backyard. He stopped coming to Sandra's house so he could see all his children at one time at his own place, once a week.

"Aww, Grandma's babies so cute," she cooed. They quickly disengaged from their father's arms and continued their loud playtime on their dad's acre of lush lawn.

Qiang's high cheekbones hid his eyes. His smile was widest when he was with his kids.

"And you don't know nothing about what happened?" Miss Sandra asked quietly while stirring a pot on her stove. His smile faded.

"Nothing, Ma. Streets is quiet. Them kids ain't in nothing that would be on my radar."

"Ain't nothing gon' be right until we find out who did it, Qiang." Her son knew by the usage of his full name, not 'Key' and not 'Baby Boy' that she was serious.

"I know, Ma. Gino deserved better. I know he was your favorite."

"Ain't got no favorites. Just lights that shine bright enough to notice." Qiang smiled.

"I'll see you Thursday, Ma. And be careful out there."

"You be careful, too. Love you."

As soon as she ended her call, a knock rattled the bars of her front storm door. She wiped her hands on a dish towel and hurried to the door.

Another woman would have been scared to see a man in a black hooded sweatshirt peering into her house, but she knew it was Korey.

"Hey," she said softly.

"Hey Miss Sandra," he replied. His eyes were on fire, but then again, they always were. Korey could very rarely hide his true emotions from anyone, even his friends.

"I'm glad to see you. Come in." She unlocked the door and let Korey in. He pulled his hood down and revealed his unshaven face and silver stud earring. He'd seen better days, but she wouldn't dare say so.

"How you holding up?" she asked. He shrugged.

"It's okay to be sad."

Korey rolled his eyes. He took out his phone and scrolled through Instagram. Miss Sandra couldn't see what he was looking at or looking for. She was used to these kids using their phones as security blankets. Miss Sandra leaned against the railing of her staircase and stared.

"I'm not sad," Korey finally said, looking into her eyes.

"Okay. Why not?"

"I don't wanna talk about it, and I ain't staying." He shrugged again.

"Korey, stay."

"No."

"It's family dinner."

"I don't care about none of that. Not now."

"I know you miss your friend."

"He wasn't my friend. He wasn't never my friend. If it's one thing I don't do, it's that fake shit."

"Korey, don't be this way. Y'all were inseparable. 'Gang of Four,' right? That's just the pain talking."

Korey walked to her.

"I gotta get outta here. I can't breathe. And I don't wanna see none of their fake asses. Bye, Miss Sandra."

Korey pecked her on the cheek and quickly turned around. He left the house, and breezed past Jordan and Rahman on the steps.

"'Scu'me," he muttered, minding his manners even in his agitated state.

Jordan and Rahman looked at each other, shrugged, and climbed the remaining stairs to Miss Sandra's porch while Korey hurried down the street.

"Don't mind Korey. He was friends with the boy that got killed. He just need to get his head together," she explained.

"Understood," Rahman said softly.

"Miss Sandra, this is my husband, Rahman," Jordan said. Rahman smiled, showing off years of orthodontic work and a meticulous teeth whitening regimen.

"Do you hug?" she asked.

"We got all our shots!" Rahman announced.

"Me too, chile! Make sure y'all get that monkeypox one, too. Shoot, if it ain't one thing, it's another, ain't it? Miss 'Rona finna get two legs and start walking if we ain't too careful."

She hugged both men.

"I baked a cake!" Jordan said, one note shy of being pleased with himself.

"Now I said you didn't need to bring anything!" Miss Sandra playfully chastised.

"I think you'll like my pound cake. It's my mother's recipe," he said.

"Well shut your mouth and keep on talking," she said, salivating at the prospect of a sweet treat for dessert. She beckoned the men inside her house. Jordan immediately noticed all the graduation photos decorating the off-white wall, leading from the foyer all the way up the staircase. So many photos of children in caps and gowns adorned the wall that Jordan presumed she might have been a teacher in a former life.

Rahman noticed the framed photos as well but quickly turned his attention to the pristine living room, unironically decorated in mid-century modern furniture: wood end tables and a coffee table bent in futuristic, smooth shapes; a love seat, sofa, and chair in matching velveteen green. The carpet was shag, in a shade of orange that reminded Rahman of the Tennessee Volunteers.

"You like it? My parents spent a whole paycheck trying to get a modern living room. Finally did it right before I went to secretary school. I wanted to replace it after they died, but by the time I got around to it, this was back in style."

"Crazy how that works," Rahman remarked.

"Yeah. Finally took the plastic off last year."

Jordan stifled a laugh.

"Hey look, we still Black, right?" Miss Sandra laughed.

"We sure are," Jordan said.

"Bring me that cake and y'all sit down to the dinner table. You early. Kids be through shortly." She grabbed the cake from Jordan and took it to the kitchen. Jordan and Rahman followed her and stopped in the dining area. She leaned over the partition between the rooms.

"Everybody feeling a little raw since Gino got killed, you know. But I figure it's still a good time for y'all to come by. These kids need to see more, you know?"

"See more of what?" Jordan asked.

"This neighborhood…it's good, you know? I know you know. Y'all wouldn't pay as much as you did for a house in a *bad* neighborhood. It's good, but these kids don't have a lot of role models right here. A lot of the men with any sense leave. All my sons did. They want more for themselves. They want a real yard, room for their own kids to play, access to good schools. Ain't no incentive to stay in their parents' house in Slope. So, folks die, and they sell."

"But you didn't sell. You're still here," Jordan said.

"The Spirit say so, chile. I just can't leave. Can't afford to fix the place up enough to sell it. And where could I go, anyway? I can't get enough on this house to live how my son living out Upper Marlboro, or my daughter down Atlanta. But this home anyway, you know? God said stay put, so I stay put."

She disappeared and pots and pans rattled for a few moments. Rahman leaned over and whispered to Jordan as he put his hand on his thigh.

"God say stay put, heard?"

Jordan smiled and brushed Rahman's hand away.

"Y'all from here? Prolly not, huh?" Miss Sandra called out.

"The Bronx and Dorchester, Massachusetts," Rahman shared.

"Lemme guess…you from the Bronx and Jordan is from Dorchester."

"You got it! How did you know?"

"New Yorkers got they chest puffed out all the time. I see you walking around the neighborhood all confident."

"Well damn, read me then," Rahman laughed.

"That ain't a bad thing! You just got a little swagger, that's all. Now Jordan—he's got that true northerner, mind-his-own-business vibe. Relaxed. Stays in his lane. But I know you don't miss a beat."

"Read me, too," Jordan laughed.

"So how did Dorchester and the Bronx end up in Slope?"

"We met in college," Rahman said.

"Oh! Where'd you go?"

"Penn," Jordan said.

"Oh, that's nice! My baby girl got in there, but she said she ain't wanna be in the snow in the winter. She went to Spelman instead. So y'all been together since college?"

The temperature in the room dropped a degree and Jordan and Rahman's shoulders tensed up.

"Rahman was a few years ahead of me," Jordan began, trying to explain the long version of the story.

"The timing was wrong. Until it wasn't anymore," Rahman said, rushing to the abbreviated conclusion. Jordan rolled his eyes just a few millimeters, but Miss Sandra caught it.

"But y'all got it together. All's well that ends well, right?"

Jordan nodded slowly.

"How many kids do you have, Miss Sandra?" Rahman asked.

"Dozens, if you count the Slope kids. But seven of my own, between two dead husbands and a deadbeat baby daddy. You?"

"Two. Both in college in New York. One's about to finish and the other just started."

"Oh, so you a daddy and Jordan a stepdaddy!"

Jordan shook his head vigorously.

"I'm just Jordan."

"Hmm. Not sure why I'm getting all this daddy energy from you," she said.

"Well, I call him—" Rahman began.

"So, what's for dinner, Miss Sandra?" Jordan's tight jaw and raised eyebrows begged for a change in subject. Miss Sandra obliged.

"Barbeque chicken wings, ham, collard greens, string beans, candied yams, macaroni and cheese, and cornbread. And some of your poundcake for dessert!"

"I approve of that." Ziggy's lazy baritone cut through the air as he entered the house. A bevy of teenagers and young adults came through the open front door, led by Ziggy, wearing a plain white sleeveless t-shirt and low-slung skinny jeans, with a sparkly belt and high-top sneakers. He wore a custom baseball cap with puffy silver glitter paint spelling out NEDC on the front.

"Well, I'm glad you approve, Mr. COO. Now where the CEO at?"

"CEO dead, ma."

"You know what I mean, chile," Miss Sandra sighed.

"It's the CEO, Chairman of the Board, COO, and CFO. Gino was always the CEO. Peek is the Chairman of the Board. I'm Ops and Korey the money man."

"Okay, chile, okay. Where is Peek?" Miss Sandra received hugs and kisses from the half-dozen young folks crowding her house.

"On the way with Pops."

"Okay, good. Now say hi to Mr. Gaffney-Bruce."

"Which one?"

"They both Mr. Gaffney-Bruce."

"They don't look like brothers."

"They *married*, Ziggy."

"Oh. Why you ain't say that?"

Ziggy sauntered to the dining room while Jordan and Rahman rose.

"Hi. I'm Ziggy." He extended his hand.

"Jordan Gaffney-Bruce. This is Rahman Gaffney-Bruce."

The men exchanged handshakes. Unlike many of the students Rahman worked with, Ziggy had a tight grip and a presence akin to confidence. He knew immediately this guy would have been Jordan's type back in the day: something between Quavo and Basquiat. If Jordan hadn't been so possessed with his own sense of morality, he probably could have bagged Ziggy, if either were willing.

"Y'all just moved into that house across the street, right?" Ziggy asked.

"Sure did!" Rahman said, trying to quell his jealousy even as Jordan loosened. His mind had wandered to the place where he'd lost his husband, again. Jordan was usually the insecure one, but the mood struck Rahman occasionally.

"Oh, my bad, let me introduce you to my girls. That's Audree, Pooh, Laurie, La'Naya, and Twinkie."

"Heyyyy," they purred in unison, then giggled. Jordan couldn't figure out whether Ziggy was "in the life" as the old gays said, or if this was his harem. Gay men and pimps both had a penchant for surrounding themselves with beautiful women, and so far, he couldn't tell.

"We're so sorry to hear about your friend," Jordan said.

"Thank you, Mr. Gaffney-Bruce," Ziggy said. "That means a lot. Gino was one of a kind."

"I'm hongry, Miss Sandra," Twinkie purred.

"Now you know we don't start 'til Pops get here. You might as well gon' out back and do what you do 'til he get here. Y'all know better to come this early anyway. This the grown folk's hour."

"Miss Sandra, everybody here over 20! Come on, now!" Twinkie argued.

"Mmm-hm, over 20 and not a diploma among you."

"Not yet. You know we all close," Laurie said.

"Almost don't count. I need to see GEDs and degrees. Now go on out back and chill out. I'll let you know when we ready to eat."

Rahman noticed the jay Ziggy produced from behind his ear. He led the way to the small backyard beyond the kitchen.

"Ain't that something?" Miss Sandra asked anyone who would listen.

"At least they respect you," Rahman offered.

"Ain't nobody else left to respect. That's what I was getting at earlier. These kids…their parents ain't shit. Most of 'em grew up in the 80s when this city was a damn war zone. Dodging bullets on the way home from school. Crack pipes in the streets. The lucky ones got out. The unlucky ones got pregnant early and didn't know how to raise kids, so they didn't.

Ziggy mother on that heron. Father been dead now longer than he was ever alive. A knucklehead. But shit, so were my husbands."

Miss Sandra began putting the food on the table. She shooed Jordan and Rahman away when they offered to help, so they sat there patiently.

"I grew up here, in this house, knowing that my parents wanted more for themselves than what they came from down Virginia. DC meant everything to them. Opportunity. Culture. I got all that. But there's that other side to DC that comes with all the opportunity. Something faster. Something bigger. Something more. We all just want a love like the movies."

She sat her pristine Corelle serving dishes on silver warmers. Steam rose from the vegetables.

"I think that's what y'all really got. I can tell."

"Maybe so," Jordan said wistfully.

"You're so lucky. I was young and dumb. Marrying men with big cars and big money and not stopping to think or ask questions. But they made me feel good. But the 80s, man…the 80s."

"How did your kids make it out?"

"I had my foot on they neck! I accepted nothing less than As in my house. And I never had to beat my kids, either. I got beat. I had worse things than that done to me. But I knew there was another way. God told me. And I did what He said. Gave them tough love, but love regardless. And now, between my seven kids? Eleven degrees. My oldest is a PhD. Qiang got a degree, too, even though he running these streets at his big age."

"Qiang?" Jordan asked politely.

"My two babies are half Chinese. Once I was done with the hustlers, I called myself falling in love with the man who ran the corner store. He ain't never tell me about his wife. That's my excuse for Mei-Hui. He ain't never tell me he was married, and he never wore a ring. No excuse for Qiang, though. I knew by then and didn't care. I guess that's why he turned out how he did. Oh, he smile in my face and bring me gifts. But I know he be out here."

"You are a fascinating woman, Miss Sandra," Jordan said.

"Chile you just as charming as you wanna be, you betta stop before I steal you away from your man."

"If anybody could, I bet it would be you," Rahman laughed.

The iron storm door rattled, and Pops entered with Peek. They shared the same down-turned nose, high cheekbones, and broad shoulders. Pops wore a dark suit and wide-brimmed straw hat. He walked with a cane but didn't appear to need it much. He took his hat off, exposing a balding head of soft and curly salt and pepper hair. Peek's hair was similarly soft, but thicker, crowning a much darker shade of brown than his great-grandfather's "high yellow" skin.

"Hey, Pops!" Miss Sandra exclaimed.

"Hey, sugar!" Pops said. His honey-coated southern drawl had been dragged along a gravely road, but he was spry and glad to be in the number.

"Hey, Miss Sandra," Peek said softly.

"Hey, my baby." She hugged him tightly. "You did so good at worship today," she said.

"Thank you. Oh, hey," he said with a small wave as he noticed the Gaffney-Bruces.

"This is Mr. Jordan Gaffney-Bruce and Mr. Rahman Gaffney-Bruce. They the ones bought the house across the street."

"Oh, okay. Nice to meet you." He shook their hands.

"Same to you, young man. Very sorry to hear about Gino, by the way," Rahman said. Pained at the mention of his friend's name, Peek mustered a head nod as he backed away.

"You heard that, Pops?" Miss Sandra asked in an elevated voice. "This is the couple that moved in across the street, the Gaffney-Bruce family."

"Say what now?" he asked.

"These men bought the Franklin house. They're married."

Pops paused and gave the men a once-over glance.

"Oh. Well, God bless America."

"Nice to meet you, Mister…"

"Jones. But everybody calls me Pops, so I guess you can, too. Or Mr. Jones. Or Tyrone. Getting too old to be worried about it either way. What's for dinner, sugar?"

Miss Sandra repeated the menu as she guided Pops to the head of the table.

"Peek, Ziggy and the girls are out back. Could you go get them and then come say grace?"

He sucked his teeth.

"Ain't gonna be too many more clicks, Peek. Time to take the lead."

He grumbled, and then leaned out of the kitchen door, calling on his friends to come eat. They filed back in, red-eyed and hungry.

"Hey, Pops," they said, greeting the patriarch of Slope.

"We used to hold hands and pray, but we just stand quietly now, since corona," Peek explained to Rahman and Jordan.

"Heavenly Father, we thank you for allowing us to be together one more time. Bless this food and the hands that prepared it. In Jesus' name…"

"Amen," everyone said in unison.

As dinner progressed, Jordan giggled at how all of the people who smoked simply rocked in their seats and savored every bite in silence, while Pops and Miss Sandra bantered about. Rahman noticed Peek was in his own world, neither engaged in the grown folks' conversation nor paying any attention to his friends.

"Do your kids ever come to Sunday dinner?" Rahman asked Miss Sandra.

"Nah. Christmas, sometimes, but the house isn't big enough to fit everyone. I go to them, mostly. But Qiang comes by every Thursday. Our little tradition. Have your kids come to see you yet?"

"They're not keen on DC," Rahman answered quickly. Jordan thought he imperceptibly rolled his eyes, but once again, Miss Sandra caught them.

"I see," she said softly.

"Everybody likes DC, especially when you're college age. They just don't want to see me," Jordan said.

"That's not true," Rahman rebutted.

"Okay." Jordan's "okay" was never the end of an argument, but the beginning of a cold war that could last days if Rahman didn't play whatever diplomatic game Jordan needed him to play that day.

"It's a nice house. Your kids will love it, especially if the basement is still what I remember. Them Franklins could throw down back in the seventies. A full bar in the corner. Enough room to have a real house party. You remember them days, Pops?"

"Mmm-hm, sure do. Used to have to drag Earnestine out of there by her ear…then come back so I could drink my damn self."

Miss Sandra laughed heartily and then sighed.

"Those were the days," she said. Peek put his fork on his plate and made enough noise that Rahman noticed.

"I'll be back," he said. He excused himself from the table and stepped out the front door, carefully closing it behind him.

"He'll be okay. He's just hurting," Miss Sandra said.

"He wants to go to Westhampton," Pops announced.

"Westhampton County? Why he wanna go there? Y'all never took him before. Hell, you talk so bad about it—"

"Hush. He wanna go. He can go. Let him learn." Pops had a tone which suggested that this subject was closed.

"Is there a funeral for Gino scheduled yet?" Rahman's question broke the silence.

"We don't do funerals around here," Twinkie said.

"No?"

"Nah," Ziggy interjected. "No funeral, no bodies, and absolutely no preachers."

"Then how do you say goodbye?" Jordan asked.

"Same way we do things on Sundays—you ain't been to worship yet?"

"Is that what you call your prayer meetings?"

"I mean I guess so. We say worship. It's prayer. It's church without the church. We just be together. So, yeah. This Friday evening. You'll see."

"Then we'll be there," Jordan declared.

"Fo' sho."

Yet another figure opened the door. Her formal Metropolitan Police Department uniform stretched against her hips. Her dreadlocks were tied in a bun at the back of her head.

"Hey y'all, sorry I'm late! The press conference ran over, of course. You know your mayor likes to talk. And then the line at the Shoppers was crazy, as usual."

"Hey Royce!" Miss Sandra said. Rahman tensed a little at the sight of law enforcement.

"How you doin', I'm Royce," the officer said to Jordan and Rahman. They began to push their chairs back.

"Nah, please. Don't get up. I'm the late one. Welcome to Slope—I've seen y'all around."

"Thank you," the men said in unison.

"Peek not joining us? I saw him outside on the corner."

"What was he doing?" Miss Sandra asked.

"Nothing, really. Minding his business like he be doin'."

"That's the best we can hope for, I guess. All things considered," Pops said.

She was glad Royce came. Her ability to be the grand dame of Slope had petered out and the small talk nearly killed her. The language of the young folks got louder as it dripped with their own urban dialect, becoming more foreign to Miss Sandra with each passing day. What was "bumpin'" in her day was now "bussin'"—which used to be what guns did just a decade before. And somehow, guns were now "glizzies," but hot dogs were "glizzies" also.

Gino would have been hip and would have translated for her.

"Not hip, Miss Sandra. *Sharp*," Gino would have said. She giggled to herself.

Gino was dead. Korey was in the wind.

Her giggle stopped as reality set in. She floated through the evening, even as the Gaffney-Bruces got more comfortable in their learning all about Slope and the various families. She laughed, she looked, and she checked in, but she was no longer present.

Peek quietly came back in and picked at his plate some more.

"When we gon' talk, Peek?" Royce asked softly.

"Ain't nothing to say," he mumbled. Royce wiped her mouth.

"Thank you, Miss Sandra," Ziggy said. His harem knew it was time to glide to the corner, to hang out, to start using more cuss words, to play music on their phones, and to remember. Peek would join them, eventually. Pops sauntered off to the living room to watch the baseball game.

"I guess we should call it an evening, too," Rahman announced.

"Everything was lovely, Miss Sandra. Truly," Jordan said.

"Same time next week?" She asked hopefully.

"I'd like that," Jordan said. He noticed Miss Sandra's eyes glistening. Something more than sorrow hung heavy in the air, but he couldn't put his finger on it. It felt like a family dinner, truly, but it was also like she was begging them not to go at all.

Royce was already on the stoop, leaning against the post while Peek stole away from the house, like a cat. He walked up the hill to his colleagues. The heaviness hit them all now and wrapped itself around their necks like the August humidity.

Miss Sandra saw the young adults as themselves, then as people, then as paper dolls, then as her own children, then as ghosts—things pretending to be alive but were quite dead in almost every way that mattered. She was not alive, but she was, but then she wasn't again. This neighborhood, a utopia for so many, for so long, now was little more than a graveyard.

Peek looked back at the four adults on the stoop. Royce, the warrior. Miss Sandra, the mother. Jordan and Rahman. Who would they be? He stared, then turned his attention back to his friends, trying to feel alive for one second more.

"For the hours they in school, they ain't dead. They ain't dying. For the hours they with me, they ain't dead. They ain't dying. I pray to God every day to cover these babies, but sometimes I think the prayers only stretch two blocks. Maybe that's why ain't been no murders in this neighborhood for decades. Look it up. You'll see. Some of the safest blocks in Washington besides 1600 Pennsylvania Avenue. But when they leave these blocks…"

Miss Sandra choked up. Royce rubbed her back and the tears fell.

"I'm sorry," the matriarch whispered.

"There's nothing to be sorry about," Jordan said. "We're here."

He didn't know why he'd said it. But they were here, just trying to breathe like everybody else.

Stardust:
Friday, August 12, 2022

Ziggy knew how to find the silence. It might be as challenging as a *Where's Waldo?* book, but in time, he always found the silence.

His earliest memories were of Sunday mornings in Slope, when he would squirm out of his mother's lap and sit on the asphalt playing with an old GI Joe action figure he'd inherited from his Uncle Mike. He knew even if he couldn't sit still, he could play silently and not bother anyone. That silent time went by quickly as he imagined Destro and Cobra Commander squaring up against Duke and Shipwreck.

He was the son of a flower child who had played music throughout her pregnancy. Kara Blackford was always a little bit off. Raised in a small house at the top of Slope, the only time she wore shoes was in school. Her classmates from Kelly Miller and H.D. Woodson remembered her as the slut who never wore a bra and came to school reeking of weed. Even though she loved marijuana and hated undergarments, she was in fact a virgin until her prom night, and in truth disliked sex enough to have it just once every ten years.

Ziggy was conceived that night. Throughout Kara's pregnancy, she craved watermelon, iced tea, and rock & roll. She barely took off her headphones for the whole time she was pregnant, from class at UDC, to her part-time job at Family Dollar, to her barefoot walks around Slope. She listened to Led Zeppelin, the Beatles, The Who, and David Bowie, while she glided and danced across the neighborhood.

The elders never understood where they had gone wrong. Kara had had both her mother and her father in the home, who themselves had been raised on Slope and were there even when the church burned in 1968. Her three older brothers had gone to college or the military and had done well for themselves, so what was it about Kara's upbringing that made her the one in the streets with a big belly and sagging titties?

Her father would roll his eyes and sit in his easy chair with a glass of bourbon, numbing himself to his own embarrassment, while her mother would try to convince herself at least Kara wasn't hurting anyone, despite how offbeat she had been.

Kara took one look at her baby, born on February 6, 2002, and despite it being Bob Marley's birthday, decided to name him Ziggy Stardust

Blackford. On her shortlist were Johnny Ramone Blackford and Revolver Blackford, but when the evening light hit Ziggy's face just so, Kara was convinced the room had filled with stardust, making her choice clear.

Luckily for Ziggy's job prospects, his grandmother intervened and decided the boy's name would be Kevin, because if it was good enough for the Costners and the Bacons, it would be good enough for the Blackfords, too. Ziggy would be a middle name, as a compromise, and because even Mrs. Blackford thought the initials K.Z.B. were cool.

"Kevin Ziggy Blackford, back again," the detective said. The interrogation room's metal door slammed behind him. Ziggy never looked up. All detectives looked alike to him: white, antagonistic, and ready to retire.

Ziggy rubbed his fingertips together. His eyes half-closed, he imagined his hand-me-down G.I. Joe's and the rough asphalt under his legs.

"Take your hat off, man. Ain't you got no respect?"

Ziggy had forgotten the other detective was even in the room. He raised his eyes and scoffed at the Black detective, who wore a nearly identical gray suit and puke-patterned necktie like his colleagues. Ziggy continued to inspect his fingertips, even as the white detective pushed a Sprite and bag of Cool Ranch Doritos toward him.

"I know you're hungry after a long day of selling weed, friend. Here. Enjoy."

"I'm not your friend," Ziggy said defiantly.

"Why, because I'm not from Slope? That's what everybody from Slope calls each other, right? But not outsiders. Nah, only Slope can be your friend."

Ziggy rolled his eyes and popped the tab on the Sprite can. He sipped the cool drink and smacked his lips.

"Nothing like a cool pop," the Black detective said.

"It's soda," Ziggy yawned. He was tired and annoyed. That weed they confiscated was going to be cash to help with the repast. Those ounces could have been 70, 80 dollars easy.

"Listen man, we're not trying to stop your hustle, but we gotta do our jobs. Muriel trying to crack down..."

Ziggy was back on the asphalt. Cobra Commander had the advantage, but Duke takes him out with a drop kick. An old lady across the intersection rose and spoke.

"Praise the Lord. He's been so good to me, but I'm so scared for the babies. Seem like it gets worse and worse out there. Look around. Where are the men? Used to be dozens of men around here raising families. Now it's just widows and women raising boys. What are we gonna do? How we gonna preserve the way we do things for the next generation? What's he gonna do when he's grown?"

The old lady locked eyes with Ziggy and a shiver went through his body that stayed with him through his adulthood, tightening his jaw even as the detective tried to reason with him.

"We just want to know what you saw that day. We wanna bring justice to Slope. To Gino's family. To you."

Ziggy closed his eyes. He was at 53rd and East Capitol Streets on the Southeast side, where they always are. Right next to the carry-out so they could get some wings if they get hungry. Far enough from home to make it feel like they went somewhere, but close enough to still feel safe, to run.

What was there to remember to even snitch about? They hung out, waiting, making money, talking, being stupid, being immature, cussing, being who that old lady didn't want them to be.

He shivered.

On the corner, he looked at his phone. A text message from Netta flashed: COME SEE ME, THEN.

He smiled.

"Ole sprung ass nigga, go see your girl," Gino growled through a grin.

"I be back," Ziggy said. He walked around the corner, to the alley where he always met Netta. Never in public. Always alleys, basements, and dark porches after sunset. He didn't know where Peek was. He didn't know where Korey went. All he knew was he wanted to see his baby Netta.

She stood there about fifty feet from him with her arms folded over her bosom. Her thick thighs filled out her tight jeans, but she was still narrow in the hips.

"What's up?" she asked in her typical falsetto.

"What's up with you? Why you standing like you mad at me?"

He came up to her, stood on his tiptoes—just a tad—and kissed his Amazon queen.

"I ain't mad. Korey said you wanted to see me."

"When he say that?"

"Like ten minutes ago."

"Something ain't right," he said.

"Well don't go yet…let me show you something." She grabbed him by the belt buckle and pulled him to her. She dropped to her knees and gave him a few minutes of what he'd hoped for.

"Ziggy, snap out of it," the Black detective said. Ziggy blinked.

"What?"

"You were there when Gino got shot. What did you see?"

Ziggy's jaw clenched.

"I ain't see nothing."

"You had to. You and Peek were there when the ambulance arrived. You had to have seen something. Heard something."

When Netta was done, he kissed her, tasting himself.

"You nasty," she said.

"You love it," he replied.

"You love me?" she asked.

"Don't start, Netta."

"I'm just saying, Ziggy, I'm not trying to be somebody's little secret forever. It's guys out here that ain't ashamed of girls like me."

"I ain't ashamed of you. I ain't ashamed of nobody I be with. I just don't feel like hearing everybody mouth."

"Aight. Well holla at me when you feel like being more than a cum dispenser."

"Yeah, holla at me when you feel like being more than a hole, bitch," Ziggy said.

"Wow. Okay, faggot," Netta said, storming off.

"The fuck you think that makes you, freak?" Ziggy shouted back.

She'd be back. She always came back.

Bang! Bang!

What?

Bang, bang, bang, bang!

"Ziggy, what happened?" Netta shouted.

"Go in the house, right now!" Ziggy yelled back. With his hand on his nine, he ran down the alley and toward the carry-out.

A shadow raced across East Capitol Street away from the carry-out. Ziggy took his weapon out. The shadow looked familiar, and even though he was inclined to follow him, he knew he had to check on the men he'd left behind to go see Netta.

"That ain't…nah…that ain't him." He convinced himself that the shadow was a stranger.

As he approached the carryout, he noticed Peek running from another direction. A long, Black body, encircled by a growing pool of blood, flailed on the ground. He grasped at the air, due east, trying desperately to move.

"Gino!" Ziggy shouted. Peek and Ziggy locked eyes in horror.

On television, Ziggy knew these moments would play out in slow motion, with moody music playing over the muted, frantic shouts of him and his friend. But in real life, it wasn't so simple. There would be no silent tears and a quick cut to a hillside cemetery with a headstone already carved. To Ziggy, it felt like an unforgiving, hyper-real, neither too-slow nor too-fast scene he'd simply have to live through in order to get to the other side.

"Call an ambulance!" Peek yelled at Ziggy. He put the gun back in his belt and fumbled with his cell phone, struggling to call 911 through tears.

Netta showed up in seconds, screaming.

"I told you to get in the fucking house," Ziggy fumed.

"What happened?!" she shrieked.

"He got shot, Netta!" Peek said, irritated. Ziggy dialed 911.

Gino stopped grasping at the air. He huffed and puffed but could not speak. Finally, he looked at his friends. His eyes watered and he smiled.

Then he died.

A blast of warm air blew through them. A blinding light filled Ziggy's vision for a moment, like a migraine was coming on, then it went away.

"No," Peek said. Netta and Ziggy were stunned into silence.

A handful of people who had been in the carry-out filed out and stood back, giving the trio their space while still preening their heads to see if they knew the body.

"Gimme the glizzy," Netta whispered.

"What?" Ziggy asked.

"12 gon' think you did it when they show up. Gimme the gun."

Ziggy surreptitiously handed over his gun to Netta.

"You too," she said to Peek.

"I ain't packin'," he said.

"Fuck," Ziggy said. "Nothing we could have done anyway, then. Go, Netta. And thank you."

Netta fled from the scene. The police were there five minutes later.

"I saw my friend on the ground, bleeding. I heard him gasping for air. I saw his spirit leave his body. I didn't see who did it. I told y'all this the night it happened. Why you asking me the same questions?"

A knock at the door punctuated Ziggy's demand.

"Because we want to know if there's anything you missed, or we missed, that's letting this dude run free. We can't have a killer on these streets, Ziggy."

The Black detective opened the door and sighed heavily when the defense attorney with the short afro came in.

"Detectives, we meet again. Ziggy, you kept your mouth shut as usual, didn't you?"

Ziggy nodded.

"So this is what y'all wanna do?" Denise asked the detectives. "You gonna play Barney Fife and detain this young man on the day of his best friend's funeral? What a shitty thing to do. An absolutely shitty thing, bereft of any sort of morals or compassion. You charging him?"

The white detective shook his head.

"He's free to go. But I wouldn't leave town if I were you, Ziggy," he said. Ziggy grunted, using all his self-discipline to stifle a snappy comeback about surrendering his passport to Waldorf.

"Why didn't you call me, Ziggy?" Denise asked Ziggy as she buckled her seat belt. She was annoyed with him—still, or again. Ziggy couldn't tell which.

"I was fine."

"No, you weren't. One of these days, a cop is gonna make you slip up and say something that's gonna put you away for a long time. You're not a juvenile anymore."

"I sell weed, Denise. Not crack. Not pills. Weed. Only difference between me and the man down Georgetown is he got a license."

"Only difference between you and that man is your African ancestry. Don't forget that."

Ziggy sucked his teeth.

"Never be fooled by this city. You see Black folks and think you home. You ain't home. None of this was built for you. It was built *by* you, but it ain't *for* you."

"Then where *I'm* suppose to go, Denise?"

Denise sighed.

"I think you're supposed to go wherever you want to. Wherever Spirit leads you. I don't think none of this is right, Zig. It ain't right that Gino's dead. It ain't right you gotta go through this. It ain't right you out here selling weed to gentrifiers and Georgetown kids when you deserve to be right there in those classrooms with them. You damn sure smart enough."

Ziggy gritted his teeth and watched DC fly past his window as Denise hurried across town.

"I wouldn't wanna go to no dry ass Georgetown no way. I'd be playing football up Shepherd or Marshall. In the mountains. Away from here."

Denise fell silent as they crossed the Anacostia River. It was getting so clean now that people were thinking about swimming in it again.

"What's wrong with you?" Ziggy asked, sensing a change in her energy. Denise sniffed and wiped a tear from her eye.

"Just sad."

Ziggy's chest tightened.

"You know I didn't see who shot him, right?"

"Would you tell me if you had?"

"Hell naw. I would have dealt with it myself by now."

"I think it was—"

"Don't. Don't say it."

"Okay," Denise said, retreating from the conversation.

The barricades had been pulled out by the time Denise parked in front of her house at the top of Slope. Black bodies dressed in all white silently trickled into the intersection in small groups.

Miss Sandra sat in a chair in the northeast corner of the intersection. Ziggy thought, for some reason, that this might be an intimate affair—that a dozen or so folks would show up, weep, then leave.

He was wrong. Two dozen people were already in the intersection, with more trickling in by the second.

"Hurry up and change, Ziggy. I'll see you there." Denise walked up the steps to her house, keys jangling in her hands all the way. Ziggy lived next door, in the basement of his grandparents' house. His mother Kara sat on the front porch in her white sundress, dragging on a blunt

"Thought you might not be coming," she said.

"Po-po had me. Thought I knew something about Gino."

"They used to send detectives to funerals when somebody got themselves killed. Now they can't even be bothered to leave downtown."

Ziggy hurried inside. His mother never said the right things—always using a motherly moment to criticize the government, or white supremacy, or capitalism—which, to Kara, were all the same thing anyway. The times where he wanted a hug or a warm wish, Kara was there, smoking and signifying.

He put on his white denim jeans, slashed haphazardly at the knees and thighs. He pulled a silver-studded white belt through the loops and tightened it to his slim waist. He kept his sleeveless t-shirt on, but put on a white linen, short sleeved shirt on over it. He kept it unbuttoned, for the look and for the weather. His jewelry remained the same: a silver crucifix around his neck and various silver rings on his fingers and thumbs, like the rock star he was in his heart. He slid on his white Jordans and hurried back upstairs and out of the basement.

His mother and grandparents were all on the porch now. Mrs. Blackford wore a white, short-sleeved blouse that revealed a little piece of arm fat. A wide-brimmed sunhat covered her short, relaxed hairstyle. Her long, pleated skirt, a slightly dimmer shade of white, came to her mid-calf. She wore heeled sandals but had the good sense to go no higher than an inch at her age. If she fell down Slope, she might tumble clear into Watts Branch and be the laughingstock for generations to come.

Her husband, Mr. Blackford, wore a white suit, white shirt, white tie, and white alligator loafers with a gold buckle. A white, straw fedora covered his balding head. He was sharp.

Djembe drums began to echo across Slope, from the intersection to every hearing ear in a four-block radius.

"It's time," Mr. Blackford announced. He descended the porch stairs with his wife, and Kara followed. Ziggy was close behind. His feet moved one step in front of the other, but his heart and mind were in two different places. His head hurt, right behind his eyes.

In a few moments, they were at the intersection, where many chairs had already been laid out for the occasion. A small table sat in the open space in the middle. Miss Sandra had laid out a white tablecloth and white carnations on top. She sat in silence while Mr. Boardall played beats on his djembe, as he always did during memorials on Slope. Mr. Boardall lived in a house by Watts Branch and only came to Sunday worship occasionally, but Ziggy knew him. He waved slightly and Mr. Boardall nodded in return.

Peek led Pops to the intersection and sat him near Miss Sandra. The rest of the Jones family followed: Peek's mother, Jacquetta; his grandmother, Earnestine; and his great-aunt Deborah's family, down to Dana Jones, Peek's cousin—and Gino's girl. Dana clutched an 8x10 photo of Gino in a silver frame close to her body. She stoically placed it on the white table and took a seat near Peek.

Mr. Gaffney-Bruce and the other Mr. Gaffney-Bruce came. That made Ziggy happy but he didn't know why. He didn't know these gay dudes on the block from the man in the moon, but their presence made him feel like somehow, everything was going to be alright. The slimmer Mr. Gaffney-Bruce—the artsy one—had on a white linen shirt and pants set, and sandals, like he was going to that beach up north that Ziggy'd heard the rich Black people go to. Martha's Stewart? Martha Washington? Something about an Inkwell, but Ziggy couldn't put all the pieces together in his head. The other Mr. Gaffney-Bruce, the sporty one, had on white slacks, a white dress shirt with no tie, and a white vest. He looked vaguely like a pimp.

The husbands exchanged head nods with Ziggy. They held hands, not even caring they were in public. Ziggy wondered what everybody would say if he held Netta's hand in public. She sat behind the Gaffney-Bruces, dabbing her eye with a tissue, not even looking up at Ziggy.

This is so fucked up, Ziggy thought. He didn't want to be there. He didn't want to be in all white in the sun, saying goodbye in silence to his best friend and big brother. On that, everyone in the intersection agreed. Peek, Netta, the girls, the parents, the elders. Nobody wanted to be saying goodbye to the best the neighborhood ever offered.

And he wasn't even from Slope, quiet as it was kept.

About a minute before the hour, the drumming slowed. Mr. Boardall's son and one of Peek's male cousins flanked Mrs. Powell—Gino's mother. There was no body, and there would be no body. That's not what happened on Slope. She clutched her son's ashes in a simple silver urn. The worst of her crying had been done at the morgue. They were the heaving, ugly sobs of a woman who never knew her son.

She knew to go to Miss Sandra after Gino had died. Mrs. Powell's sister, Patricia, knew Gino must be handled in the same way as all others on Slope. He was their son, even if he wasn't born there.

Mrs. Powell fussed. She argued. She didn't want a cremation for Gino. She wanted a church funeral. She wanted everyone to see her finest creation one last time. She cried.

"Mrs. Powell, nobody doubts you loved your son," Miss Sandra said at the funeral home. "We all know you sent him to Slope so he could get a better chance. And everybody feels terrible about his passing. But like it or not, your son was grown. He lived here for five years. Maybe the best five years of his life. He became a man here. Came to worship on his own. Adopted our ways. I promise you this is what he wanted."

"No. I'm his mother. This is my decision," Mrs. Powell said sternly, wiping snot from her nose. Miss Sandra sighed and glanced at her son Qiang, who raised his already high eyebrows.

"Hey, um, Mrs. Powell?" Qiang asked.

"Yes?"

"Gino was a fine young man. Everyone here loved him—and he was known and respected beyond Slope, too. He was like a little brother to me. I felt like my mom was safe with him. Like I could go live my life and not have to worry about leaving my mom in the city by herself. I trusted my mom and my 'hood with Gino.

"But he's gone. And to tell you the truth, Mrs. Powell, the man I knew was not the boy that you left to fend for himself when he needed you the most. Maybe a more mature woman would have known how to handle a teenage boy who just wanted to be somebody someday. Maybe a better woman would have hugged the hell out of him rather than beating the shit out of him until her arms got tired. And he never once hit you back. Now I bet you wish you had hugged him a little more, lived with him a little longer before you gave up and sent him to your sister. A mature woman might have found a way. But Gino didn't have a mature woman for a mother. He had you.

"The decision has already been made. Gino is going to get sent off like a true son of Slope, in the way we have always done things. You're sitting in the funeral home we've always used. They know us. They know what we want. And I'm paying for it, okay? That's what I do. We all have a part, and paying for it is mine. Ma is going to take you to get your all-white outfit, and you are going to look beautiful. And we're all going to remember Gino that evening, and we're going to see you, and we're going to pity you, and we're going to cry with you. But never once—not for one moment—will we believe you. You're an actress to us. No, not even that— you're a prop—a piece of furniture pretending to be a mother for the hour we'll be together. And then, after it's all over, you'll never have to come back. You won't be welcome anyhow. Do you understand?"

Mrs. Powell's tears stopped, and her red eyes betrayed a seething rage.

"Do you understand?" Qiang shouted at the shell of a woman.

"Yes," she whispered.

"Then I'm stepping outside for a smoke. I'll send Mr. Hunter in to finalize the arrangements—in the manner of all Slope funerals."

Qiang touched his mother's shoulder as he stepped out. Mrs. Powell slouched in her seat while the slightest of smirks crept over Miss Sandra's face.

At the memorial service, Miss Sandra wiped the corners of her mouth, now relaxed, with a white handkerchief. She nodded at Peek, who rose, cleared his throat, and spoke.

"We gather here today to honor the life of our friend, our brother, our son of Slope, Gino. We do this the same way we do everything else: by letting God talk to us through our silence. If you feel moved by God to say something in celebration of Gino's life, you're welcome to speak. Please leave a little time in between messages so they can hit us the way God wants them to.

"As for me? Gino was my friend. One of my best friends. One of the best to ever do it. And I'm gonna miss him."

Peek quickly sat and closed his eyes.

A few silent moments passed, punctuated by Mrs. Powell's occasional sob, weeping from friends, birds chirping in the trees, and latecomers filling up the sidewalks.

Dana finally rose, quaking with nerves.

"What I want people to know…is that Gino was good. He wasn't perfect. But he was good. He treated people right. He treated me well. And I loved him. I was looking forward to many more years with him, but what I got was what I got. And what I got was good. I'll miss him."

She sat. Her comments opened the floodgates of memories for many of Gino's family members, acquaintances, and school mates, who stood and gave their own testimonies and toasts to Gino. There were funny stories, poignant moments, and many recollections of how Gino had done something kind without expectation of reward.

Netta also rose.

"Gino really did treat everybody the same way or whateva… Like, he really accepted me for who I am. And I think because he set the tone, you know? Like, he was a leader, and how he acted set the tone for how everybody else around here and around the way acted toward me. And I love him for that, I really do."

She sat and wiped away another tear.

Ziggy remembered a conversation he'd had with Gino, on a cold day in February, half a year before this memorial. They walked down the steps at Alternative Futures, on busy 16th Street in Northwest DC. They crossed the tree-lined boulevard as a MetroBus came to a stop at the intersection.

"G, man, I got a problem," Ziggy announced solemnly.

"We all got problems," Gino quipped.

"This one big. I like…Netta."

Gino took out a cigarette, lit it, and took a big drag. He passed it to Ziggy.

"Do she like you back?" Gino asked. Children laughed across the way at a childcare center. They walked around an old man, drunk or strung out and sleeping across the sidewalk.

"Yeah. She do."

"It don't sound like you got no problems."

"But she…you know…"

"A girl. Netta is a girl just wanna be loved like any other girl. Anything else is between you and her. Fuck what people say, aight?"

"Respect, bruh."

Ziggy's heart threatened to burst out of his chest and he felt lightheaded. His hands trembled. The street was quiet and still. He stood.

"My mans…is gone. But he was here. I remember being a kid, playin' with toys while the grown folks prayed. And a lady stood up and talked about how she was worried wouldn't nobody be around by the time I got grown. She said 'where are the men?' and she pointed dead at me. It felt like a curse, almost. But it woke me up a little bit. I ain't have a father, know what I'm saying? But I had my grandfather. And I had Pops—we all have Pops, right? And I had my friends. Korey and Peek and me. But we weren't complete until Gino came. He was here. He walked with us to school, until we all got kicked out from regular school. Then he walked with us to alternative school. He might have made the same mistakes we all made, but he was here, with us. And I ain't never gonna forget what he went through before he got here. And I ain't never gonna forget how he was the best of us knuckleheads. I ain't never gonna forget the kind of friend he was to me when I needed one the most. God as my witness, that motherfucker showed me what kind of man I really wanted to be. And now I know what that old lady meant when she started off her words with 'God has been so good to me.' Cuz no matter what is happening right now, no matter how sad I feel that my mans is gone, God was good to me to send me Gino for as long as he did. So…long live Gino, man. He was here. He was here. He was here."

Tears streamed down Ziggy's face as he sat.

Audree, one of the girls in the harem, sang softly.

"We are…
Climbing…
Jacob's ladder.
We are…"

Pooh, Laurie, and the rest of the girls echoed the first and second lines and harmonized on the third.

"Climbing…
Jacob's ladder.
We are…
Climbing…
Jacob's ladder.
Soldiers of the cross.

Keep on…climbing…we will make it
Keep on…climbing…we will make it
Keep on…climbing…we will make it
Soldier of the cross."

The girls continued singing as the hour ended. The drummer started once more, giving this slow hymn a livelier, even joyful beat. Gino's mother was led to the altar once more to retrieve the urn and take Gino for his last walk down Slope. She clutched the urn to her chest and then shook her head.

"I can't," she whispered.

Miss Sandra dug deep into her soul to find compassion for this woman after all she'd done to her son.

"Are you sure?" she asked.

"Yes," she whispered.

Miss Sandra grabbed the urn herself and walked behind the drummer, down the hill to Watts Branch. Ziggy and Peek followed close behind her.

The sun was low. Pale blue skies turned fiery orange. Though the processional squinted through sweaty brows and broken hearts, they marched with pride to the little wooden bridge that connected Slope to the rest of Northeast. Dozens and dozens of people, most dressed in blue jeans and black t-shirts, lined the north bank of Watts Branch. As the residents of Slope approached the slash in the earth that divided their territories, the people from the other side of the bridge removed their hats and bowed their heads in reverence.

Ziggy locked eyes with John Owens, a dude who'd gone to H.D. Woodson with him. A bully. Someone who had pushed him into lockers on a good day or gotten into bloody fights with him on a bad day. Even John nodded his head, his eyes full of sorrow. Ziggy nodded his head in return.

Miss Sandra lifted her sandaled feet carefully over the rough pavement on the way to the bridge. Ziggy and Peek held her steady while Gino's mother walked behind them. The bridge creaked a little as they stepped on it. It was old, but it was sturdy.

Miss Sandra waited for the people in white to finish crowding the grass near the bridge. Mr. Boardall finished his drumming and Miss Sandra held the urn high over her head.

"All go to the same place; all come from dust, and to dust all return," she quoted Ecclesiastes. "Gino, we love you. We miss you. We'll see you again."

She lowered the urn, removed the lid, and poured Gino's remains into Watts Branch. The gray dust, flecked with small fragments of Gino's bones, poured like sands from an hourglass into the glorified ditch, masquerading as a creek. Some of the ashes rose into the sky and dissipated.

The block was silent. For some, they had never been close enough to the bridge to see someone's remains go back into the earth and into the sky. Some didn't expect the bone fragments. And those who looked skyward, rather than downward, noticed those same flecks of light Ziggy's mother claimed to see when he was born. It was a phenomenon that could have been explained by simple physics if anyone cared to look it up, but Ziggy decided those flecks of light were Gino's sign to them that everything was going to be okay.

"Long live Gino!" Ziggy shouted, breaking the silence. The others joined him, repeating their chant until every bit of ash had left the urn. Miss Sandra passed the urn to Peek, who passed it to Gino's mother. It was the last time anyone on Slope saw her.

The families and the friends slowly broke away from the footbridge and walked back up the hill. The various repasts would begin all over the neighborhood now that the worst part of the day was over. Nobody had enough food for the crowd of now well over 200 people, but everyone had a little. It was close to eight in the evening and the golden sky had turned indigo. Streetlights flickered on. Ziggy and Peek were the last ones standing on the footbridge. They stared into the dark water, now barely visible in the shadows.

"Korey ain't come," Ziggy said.

"Nope," Peek said softly.

"Twelve ain't come, neither. Guess they ain't really looking, huh?"

Peek shook his head.

"It's two days I ain't never gon' forget, Zig. The day he died and the day we said goodbye. Nothing could get worse than this."

"Nothing," Ziggy echoed.

"I had a dream last night. I was in this boat. Like a rowboat in the ocean. Pitch black water, boat tossing every way. All I could do was hold on. Then arms came up out the water and grabbed onto the boat. They got longer and longer and tried to grab me. I fell backward in the boat. I looked up and all I saw was stars. Then I woke up."

"Damn, Peek."

"What you think it means?"

"I don't know, man. I think it just mean you sad."

A million hands in the ocean trying to take you down was a pretty good symbol for sadness, Peek thought to himself.

"We can't let him get away with what he did, Zig."

"But we ain't no snitches. That ain't what we do. Pigs had me detained today. But I ain't say shit. This ain't for them to solve. Let them worry about the rest of this city. We deal with Slope our way."

"It ain't happen in Slope, though."

"It's don't matter, Peek. This is ours. Not theirs."

"Fuckin' sucks, yo." Peek's shoulders sunk low, and he sucked his teeth.

Two young kids ran to Peek and Ziggy with foil-protected hot dogs in their hands.

"Aye, y'all gon' get you some hot dogs?" one of the boys asked.

"Where y'all get hot dogs from?" Peek asked.

"The faggies up by Miss Sandra got a whole truck, giving away hot dogs!" the other boy said.

"Hey, watch your mouth!" Peek said, his already deep voice lowering an octave.

"Them dudes are nice," Ziggy added. "Don't you ever call nobody out they name when they been nice to you. Would you want some crackers calling you 'nigger' if you was down in Georgetown?"

"Sorry," both boys said in a pitiful unison before they ran away.

"You down for a glizzy?" Ziggy asked Peek.

"I could eat," he said. For the first time in a week, he was a little hungry. The young men sauntered off the bridge, through the grass, and across the street. Sure enough, halfway up the hill was a food truck, passing out hot dogs, chili dogs, and half-smokes. Mr. Gaffney-Bruce and the other Mr. Gaffney-Bruce stood on their porch, supervising the scene and welcoming people over.

"Peek! Ziggy!" the more effeminate one called.

"Come eat!" the butch one said. Peek and Ziggy smiled and nodded. The line of about a dozen people parted and pushed the pair to the front like they would have any of Gino's family members. They both got hot dogs, nice and burnt on the grill, with a little relish and ketchup.

They walked up to the sidewalk in front of the Gaffney-Bruce house and began to eat.

"Would you like to join us up here?" Ziggy seemed to remember that the softer one was named Jordan.

Ziggy looked at Peek and they both shrugged. They knew this house didn't have street access to the porch, so they walked around to the side of the house, where the mailbox was, and arrived at the barred screen door. Ziggy turned the knob, and the door opened. The butch one emerged and beckoned them in.

"Always keep your doors locked, Mr. Gaffney-Bruce," Peek said sternly.

"Oh, we knew you—or somebody—would need to come in, so…"

"No matter how safe you feel, this is still DC. Ya dig?"

"Yes, sir," Rahman said, startled at both Peek's decisiveness and his own carelessness about not locking the screen door.

Ziggy looked around the house and concluded that it was a vibe. They had a huge television mounted on the wall—as big as the display sets he'd seen at Best Buy in Columbia Heights. They had brown leather furniture that reminded him of *Mad Men*. And their floors were wood, and shiny. They really took care of this place.

They walked through the living room and to the porch door. Jordan begged them to take a seat. They chose the rattan sofa on the far side of the porch, while Jordan and Rahman took chairs. Ziggy and Peek continued to eat.

"This all must be really hard," Rahman said. "But you both did great today. I didn't know Gino, but I've gotta believe he'd be proud of you."

"Thank you," Peek said.

"And Ziggy, those words you delivered—that sermon—it may have been the best thing I've ever heard at a memorial. 'He was here.' My God today. He will never be forgotten, that's for sure," Jordan gushed.

"'Preciate it," Ziggy said softly. They finished their hot dogs in no time, but despite the silence between the four men, the younger pair was in no hurry to leave, and the older pair were of no great desire to push them out.

"Where y'all from?" Peek finally asked, breaking the silence.

"I'm from New York," Rahman said. "He's from Massachusetts. We met in college."

"I came to DC right after college. Been working at the Smithsonian ever since. Except when I went overseas for grad school," Jordan said.

"Where you went?" Ziggy asked.

"Paris. I studied art."

"You be painting and shit?"

"Nah, not really. I studied art history."

"I ain't even know you could do that," Peek laughed.

"Art history," Ziggy mocked. "You a real big nerd, huh?"

Jordan, gobsmacked, could not speak. Rahman snickered.

"Close your mouth, Mr. Gaffney-Bruce, before something fly in there," Peek said with a laugh.

"I…I…I mean he's the one with the doctorate!" Jordan said, as though he had accused his husband of a mortal sin.

"I sure do! And I bet you wish you did, too!"

"No, thank you. The best thing I ever learned about myself was that, at the end of the day, I really don't like school. Like at all," Jordan announced.

"Yeah, school some bull," Peek said.

"But I understand you're not finished yet," Rahman said.

"Nope," Ziggy said. "Damn near none of us around here finished."

"Nobody? Nobody at all?" Rahman asked.

"Long story short…we all went to H.D. And they kicked us all out, one at a time. Fighting. Smoking in the stairwell. Absences. It's like we couldn't get no second chance on nothing. Some folks tried Job Corps, and that wasn't shit. Now we all at Alternative Futures, in and out, at least," Peek explained.

"I've definitely heard of Alternative Futures," Rahman said. "I've met the Head of School, too. Kyren Towers, right?"

"Good ole Mr. Towers," Ziggy said. He reached into his crossbody bag and pulled out rolling papers. "Do y'all mind? I ain't smoked all day and if I don't start now, I ain't gon' be able to sleep later."

Jordan and Rahman looked at each other.

"Oh, come on. I walk past your porch and smell that herb when it get dark out. Y'all be smokin'. Don't act like y'all church deacons."

Everyone laughed.

"Alright, alright. Blaze if you got 'em," Rahman said. Ziggy produced all of his tools from his white bag and intently got to work rolling a joint. After a few moments, he lit the joint, put it to his lips, and inhaled. He slowly exhaled and passed it to Peek, who did the same.

"You heard Mr. Towers was fuckin' students, right?" Ziggy said with a giggle.

"I'm sorry, what?" Rahman asked. Jordan's eyes got big.

"I mean, is that your friend-friend? Or like a coworker?"

"I met him at a workshop or two," Rahman said.

"Well first of all, he play for your team, if you ain't already know."

"I did not."

"Well, now ya know. And besides that, his security guard over to the school is his boyfriend. Remember a few years ago, when the school got took over and the old principal went missing or died or some shit? Well, I got there in the middle of all that. And the students was gossiping about him fuckin the students, but ain't nobody care because they said he looked good. Ain't that some shit? Only ugly people are predators. Anyway, Towers replaced the old dude, his mans got his GED and got a job as a security guard, and now they a happy family."

"You're certainly full of news," Rahman said.

"Yeah, but I still ain't no snitch," Ziggy said, taking another drag. Jordan stifled a laugh.

"How long y'all been together?" Peek asked.

"We've been friends for a long time. Married for a few years," Jordan said.

"Was it hard back then when y'all first met? Like before y'all getting married was legal?" Peek asked.

"It was the 90s when we first met," Jordan began. "It's funny. I think the 90s was a great decade. But looking back, it was also hard. A lot of things happened then that were firsts for us, but old for you guys. We had a March on Washington in '93—"

"You went to the March?" Rahman interrupted.

"Yeah—Sophomore or Junior Year, I think. Culturally, a lot of good was going on. Shit, RuPaul was new back then! But there was a lot of pushback, too. 'Don't ask, don't tell' policy in the military. Defense of Marriage Act in congress. And Matthew Shepard's murder in '98. So, it wasn't easy for us who were out."

"And you wasn't out, was you?" Peek asked Rahman pointedly. In the distance, a DJ played hip-hop from the top of Slope, and the beats cascaded down the hill while families sat on their porches, eating their meals and laughing. Children played touch football in the street.

"Nah. Jordan held it down much earlier and longer than I did."

"We got a trans girl around here. She ain't really from Slope, but she be with us. Netta. She cool as fuck," Peek said.

"We straight, though. The four of us," Ziggy said before he could stop himself.

"Four…" Jordan's echo was like a cool gust falling over Slope and breezing through the porch. Peek bit his bottom lip and looked away, over the street.

"Fuck!" Ziggy shouted and stomped his feet. He cried, instantly, a heaving sob that sounded like laughter to those who had never been in the middle of painful, primordial grief. Peek's eyes flooded and his teeth chattered trying to stifle his own cry. Their bodies pointed away from each other, too wrapped in their own grief to find solace in one another.

Jordan immediately sprang up and went to the boys, now brown puddles of tears and snot. He sat between them, put both arms around them, and drew them close. He did not have a bosom for them to bury their faces in—his slim chest and pointy collarbone would have to suffice. But he had arms and fingers and thighs and cologne and love, so much love and compassion and pity to give these boys, these sons of Slope who had seen it all and lost as much.

He said nothing. He didn't tell them it would be okay. He didn't know it would be okay at all. But he was all that he knew to be—present.

Rahman walked to the trio and stood over them.

"I'm sorry," he said. He dropped to his knees next to Peek and sat on the floor next to him. He hugged his waist and rubbed his thigh in the same circular motion he used when his own children were sickly or sad.

Pat. Pat. Pat.

Circle. Circle Circle.

They were out there in the world without a care for their father now, so his pats and circles could go elsewhere now. To his husband. To these young men he barely knew. To his students in DCPS, if he dared.

He looked at Jordan, whose eyes were closed. He held those boys tight, so tight as the tears flowed through them all. Rahman let himself cry, too. He missed his kids. He missed Gino, even though he could barely remember his face. He missed the good parts of his old life. And he felt guilty for missing his old life when all he ever wanted woke up next to him in bed every morning.

Nobody remembered how long they sat on the porch, but it was so long that the DJ's hip-hop set turned to reggae, and then go-go, and then the kids started lighting the fireworks.

Long live Gino!

Long live Gino!

Long live Gino!

Peek and Ziggy left the Gaffney-Bruces with not a tear left in their bodies. They walked up the hill a little closer than they ever had as adults, wanting to be hand-in-hand like they might have been in kindergarten, or before. But the few inches between them would have to be enough, because they were men now—men of Slope—and everybody wanted them to be strong.

But for one night, they weren't. They allowed themselves to be safe in someone else's arms for a change and they did just fine.

The Tragedy of King Gino: Thursday, August 4, 2022

The echoey *pap* of rototoms and the *clang* of the cowbell blared from his phone, plugged into his charger on the other side of the room. He always kept his phone as far away from his bed as possible to discourage himself from hitting the snooze button when his alarm went off. It was one of many habits he picked up from Mr. Towers, his favorite teacher at Alternative Futures.

"Little habits can change your life, if you let them," Towers admonished on a day he'd tired of Gino traipsing through the front doors after 10am for the umpteenth time.

"Man, an hour ain't gonna do nothing, Mr. Towers," Gino hissed.

"Ask somebody running a marathon how much can happen in an hour," he retorted.

He was always good for little quotes like that, followed up by real life skills. When he'd told Gino to stop scrolling through his phone all night and commit to getting rest on purpose, Gino gave it his best attempt. Eventually, it worked. Gino got his eight hours of sleep and woke up feeling rested. He didn't even miss his phone.

"Ugh, turn that thing off," Dana mumbled through her pillow. Gino opened his eyes and strained to see his girlfriend in the dark. All he could make out was the sheen of her bonnet.

He rose, went to his phone, and turned off the alarm. He sat on the bed and scrolled through social media, chuckling at Tik-Tok videos, silently judging photos from his contemporaries on Instagram, and catching up on the group chat between him, Peek, Ziggy, and Korey. They were the night owls of the group. The older Gino got, the less he liked being up late, much less out late.

Dana stirred under the cotton sheet. Gino became aroused by her shapely body's silhouette. He shook her ankle, then her calf, then her thigh. She was soft and warm.

"What?" she whined. Her eyes were closed as she tried to hold on to the final moments of sleep. Gino slowly pulled the cover up, revealing Dana's manicured feet. He leaned over and kissed them, first, with small pecks, then, with passionate, open-mouthed kisses, tasting her skin from her toes to her ankles.

Dana shifted her weight and rolled from her side to her back, ready for Gino's favorite extracurricular activity. He continued his kisses up her legs, alternating from her left side to her right side. As he kissed her inner thighs, he grabbed her panties. She closed her legs and assisted, finally pulling her underwear from her ankle and tossing them to the nightstand next to her. Gino smiled, spread Dana's legs, and devoured her until the sheets were damp.

Around 25 minutes later, Gino stood while Dana laid prone, exhausted.

"You have work soon," he announced.

"I know," Dana sighed.

"I'ma hop in the shower. You better be ready to hop in as soon as I get out. We getting better habits."

"I know. But…don't you want me to take care of you?" Dana purred.

"Later. You got frozen yogurt to make, and I need to see Mr. Towers." Gino took off his sleeveless t-shirt and his cotton boxer briefs and let them fall to the floor.

"And stop staring at me like I'm some kind of floozy," he joked.

"Boy, shut up!" Dana laughed. Gino smiled as his dark, toned body went down the basement hall to the bathroom.

He had lived in his aunt's finished basement since he came to Slope as a teenager. Like many of the houses on Slope, the basement was divided into three rooms: the first, smaller room where the bar was located; a second, larger room, which in this case was used as a bedroom, and then a final room, on the way to the back door, which had the washer, dryer, utilities, and a small bathroom with a shower. Although one went downstairs to the basement, the back door was flush with the ground. This is what happened when houses were built on hills.

Gino thought about all he had to do that day. Taking the Green line in to Columbia Heights with Dana had the dual effect of keeping his woman on time for work while giving him an excuse to pop in on his old teachers at Alternative Futures. Although they'd never tell him to his face, he knew he was their favorite former student, if for no other reason than he actually obtained his GED. Although the graduation rates were improving, the difficulty of the four-part test and the mountains of distractions the students faced meant only a few dozen a year completed the requirements in time for a June graduation.

He made it, though.

As Dana dozed off on Gino's shoulder while the train shuttled them further uptown, Gino practiced what he might say to Mr. Towers.

Mr. Towers, I wanna go to college.

Mr. Towers, can you help me get into college?

Mr. Towers, I'm trying to do right. What I gotta do to get into college?

The last time he'd talked to Mr. Towers in depth, they'd gotten into a terrible argument about Dana's pregnancy. Gino's voice, a trembling, nervous tenor, was like a child compared to Mr. Tower's booming, disappointed baritone. Gino had never felt so ashamed. He'd entered Mr. Towers' office with excitement and pride that he had successfully reproduced with a girl he loved. He exited the office knowing he'd let down the only man he'd ever aspired to impress.

"Your life has barely begun," Mr. Towers said, framing his Socratic inquiry: "How can you raise a child when you don't have a job or a home of your own? How do you expect a child to look up to you when you've barely accomplished anything besides finishing school? Do you think that's enough?"

Gino felt small, so small that when God took care of the pregnancy a few days later, he was relieved to get a second chance. He dared not share that relief with Dana, but he knew love wouldn't be enough to give a kid a life.

But he did know he loved Dana. When he looked at her cherubic brown face, he could see their entire future. He imagined them at a gala—him in a tuxedo, diamond studded earrings, and a Rolex; she in whatever couture gown she wanted as long as it was her favorite color: green. He imagined her dripping in emeralds as large as the ones he'd seen on display at the Natural History Museum on the Mall.

He imagined her giving birth to their children, then raising them together. He could see them dropping kids off at kindergarten and then cheering them on at their graduation from high school, then college.

He could see her as a middle-aged woman, with forty extra pounds, her upper arms jiggling as she fried chicken for the holidays. And he could see her as a little old lady, slowly climbing the hill toward Sunday worship on Slope, as he carefully followed behind her.

She was a Jones—Peek's cousin—and there was something different about that family. Almost like they knew they'd come to DC for a reason, and they were determined to make that dream of a better life come true, even if it came a few generations late. He could see them going out to the suburbs, like Qiang did, but coming back to Slope after they'd made their money. They'd buy up all the houses, fix them up, and bring everybody together who wanted to be there. If anybody could convince folks to come back to Slope, of all places, for a better life, he knew Dana could.

She was confident and sassy, usually the witty jokester out of all her girlfriends. But she was tough. She could fight more fiercely than some boys on the block and could outsell them if the game was cannabis. She had one more GED section to complete before she, too, would join Gino as a graduate of Alternative Futures.

Gino liked all sides of her. The first lady. The gangster. She was all his, despite their arguing about childish things. He knew they were each other's endgame, no matter what.

Their ride into Columbia Heights, their walk up the broken escalator at the station, and their stroll down 14th Street, past the empanada carts and incense men, was taken largely in silence. They walked closely, hands grazing one another every few steps. They'd walked this path hundreds of times, whether going to school around the corner, to work at FroZenYo, or to get groceries at Giant. Every time, Gino felt like he was in the greatest city in the world, despite having to watch for passed out immigrant men in the sidewalks and in the plaza.

Outside the FroZenYo, Dana hugged Gino and kissed him on the cheek.

"I close today, so I won't see you 'til late," she said.

"You want me to come get you?" he asked.

"Naw, I'll be fine. Kiki and I walk to the station together. Nobody bothers us."

"Shiiiit, I know they won't. You be getting these niggas with the hi-ya," he deadpanned.

"Boy, shut up," she laughed. "Where you gon' be?"

"Up Alternative to see Mr. Towers, then you know where I'ma be."

"At Newman Enterprises with the Board of Directors?"

"You always want me to be on a soap opera," he growled.

"That's how y'all act. You run shit, but it's always some drama."

"Nah, that's Korey and Ziggy ass. Peek the only one steady, for real."

"Be careful on the block, babe. Okay?"

"I'm always careful. Love you." Gino gave Dana a quick peck on the cheek and turned to cross the plaza. He looked back one time, but Dana was already in the FroZenYo clocking in.

Alternative Futures was two blocks from the plaza. To the right were apartment buildings Gino was sure he couldn't afford, even though he never checked. To the left were restaurants serving Ethiopian, Vietnamese, and Dominican fare; head shops; a tattoo shop; and discount stores with an occasional feline making a home in the window. Park Road was always busy, as it connected major streets and led to Mount Pleasant Street, another enclave of international restaurants, banks, and bakeries.

He made it across busy 16th Street as the traffic sped by. He galloped up the concrete stairs and rang the buzzer at the double doors. The receptionist let him in.

"Dang, you back again?" the shapely Latina receptionist teased.

"Stop, Miss Catalina," Gino begged.

"You know we not hiring, right?"

"I know."

"Let me guess, you're here to see Mr. Towers?"

"Of course. I need his guidance as a young, Black man tryna make it in the world," he sarcastically droned.

"Sign in for me. I'll see if he's available," she sighed.

"Mr. Towers, your son is here to see you. Yep, that one. Okay."

Catalina hung up her phone and told Gino to go upstairs to Mr. Towers' office.

Gino had come to Alternative Futures shortly after a series of terrible incidents at the school: a shooting on the grounds; the disappearance and presumed death of the principal; and an unexpected takeover of both AF and the school next door, Bayard Rustin. Despite all the turmoil, his school quickly became his safe place. Neither the building, nor its students or staff, looked like what they had been through, as the old gospel song said.

The school's head of security, Delonté Oakes, a dark and lanky young man, came out of Mr. Towers' office as Gino approached.

"Sup, fam?" Delonté greeted.

"Ain't shit," Gino replied, pulling Delonté's handshake into a hug.

"Aye, you trying to smoke this evening?"

"I gotta work," Gino said. Delonté sucked his teeth and side-eyed Gino.

"Work? Since when you got a job?"

"I make money," Gino smiled. Delonté was not impressed.

"Come on, man. We gotta get you something with a pay stub and benefits."

"Leave me alone, man. I'm already gonna get fussed at by your husband."

"You funny," Delonté said as he disappeared down the school staircase. Gino entered Mr. Towers' office.

"Now why would I be fussing at you, Mr. Powell?" Mr. Towers rose from his executive chair and gestured to an empty chair. Towers, quite literally, towered over most people at the school, and even had two inches on Delonté, who was one of the tallest people Gino knew. But unlike Delonté, Mr. Towers was as wide and muscular as a WWE wrestler. He was known for strong classroom management before his promotion to Head of School, but one couldn't quantify an imposing stature. Gino shook his hand and took a seat.

"I was just messin' with your boy."

"Mmm-hm. You're messing with my employee, but where are you working?"

"Don't worry about all that, man. I got something to tell you."

Mr. Towers exhaled and folded his hands together. His honey-colored, sun-bleached dreadlocks swept the tabletop.

"Well…spill it."

"I'm trying to go to college."

Mr. Towers raised an eyebrow.

"Trying?" he asked.

"Well, I want to. I wanna go to college. Take this thing to the next level, dig?"

"And what level is that?"

"You know. Everything you been talking to me about all along. I wanna make sure I got the right … foundation. You know? When I came to DC schools, they wouldn't accept all my credits. So, I had to start H.D. in tenth grade, even though I had already damn finished tenth grade. Then they put me out in the eleventh grade. Then I came here. Then I finally got my GED. I ain't make it quickly, but I made it, Mr. Towers. And I ain't go through all them lost years for nothing. They gotta mean something. Look, everybody say getting an education is the thing you gotta do if you want to have a chance. And I gotta take that chance, for my family."

Mr. Towers raised an eyebrow.

"And I don't mean she pregnant again, Towers. We are careful. More careful. But I know this girl is the one I wanna spend my life with, and I know *when* we start having babies, I don't want them to have the life I had. So…college it is. And I need your help, okay?"

"What do you need my help with?"

"I wanna start at UDC. Maybe even finish there. Stay for law school. I could be in a courtroom before I'm 30. Wouldn't that be a trip?"

"Yes. Yes, it would be." Mr. Towers smiled, grabbed his car keys, and put on his sunglasses.

"Where you going?" Gino asked.

"You said you wanna go to UDC? Well come on, friend. We're going to UDC."

"Oh. Well damn."

He followed Mr. Towers down the back stairwell to the small staff parking lot. He watched Mr. Towers text Delonté that he'd be back in about an hour, and to tell Catalina. Soon, they were pulling out of the alley and driving toward Rock Creek Park.

"You know somebody up UDC?" Gino asked.

"Nope. Not really. But why not see what happens when we go to the admissions office ourselves?"

"You think we can just walk up in there?"

"You walk up into Shoe City when you want some Dunks, right? Why not walk into the college when you want an education?"

"Yeah…you right." Gino watched the row houses in Mount Pleasant become trees in Rock Creek Park.

"Aye man, why you wanna be in schools? You used to grow up wanting to teach people?" Gino asked Mr. Towers.

"I dunno. I've always been a teacher some kind of way," Mr. Towers answered.

"Didn't you say you lived overseas?"

"Yep. I was in Greece before I came back over here."

"Greece. Damn."

"You'll go some day. If you want to."

"I want to, Mr. Towers. I want to see the whole world."

"What about your boys? You gonna take them with you?"

"My boys. Hmm. They gotta want it, too. I guess."

"You're a wise man, Mr. Powell. And a natural leader. You gotta lead your men to the promised land. Show them they can do it. And believe that they have it in them to follow the path."

"Can I say something terrible, Mr. Towers?"

"If it's factual and compassionate, can it really be terrible?"

"It might be."

"Well…tell me what's on your mind."

"I…don't know if they wanna be led."

"What makes you say that?"

Mr. Towers turned onto Connecticut Avenue and headed north toward UDC.

"Ziggy and Peek just be out here in the wind. And Korey unpredictable. And mean."

"They are kites, my friend."

"Whatchu mean?"

"When a kite catches a breeze, it wants to be free to follow that breeze. Even if it's too strong, or dangerous. It wants to go. But every kite needs a tether and an anchor—a line that connects them to what's important, and someone weighty enough keep them from flying away. That's how you can think of leadership. It doesn't have to be like being a CEO, or barking orders at people. It can be a soft touch that lets people soar."

Gino closed his eyes for a moment and smiled.

"You make me sick, Mr. Towers. Ain't no reason you should be this damn good at this," he laughed. Mr. Towers laughed along with him.

"I've lived long enough to master the art of the metaphor, my friend."

"You know…I ain't never been up here before," Gino said, still taking in his surroundings: stores, restaurants, and hotels he'd never seen before.

"Never?"

"Nope. I ain't never been further than the zoo, I guess."

"It's a big city, Gino. But small enough to own, if you want to own it."

Mr. Towers turned left, then right into UDC's parking garage.

"We here already?" Gino asked.

"Yup. We here."

Gino and Mr. Towers left the truck and within moments had emerged from the shadowy garage onto the bright, sandy colored pavement of UDC's main plaza. Even during the summer, the campus bustled with activity, from summer classes for undergraduates and grad students, to workshops and day camps for middle and high school students. UDC was alive.

They wasted no time finding the admissions office. Mr. Towers had a quick gait and long legs that Gino struggled to keep up with at times. He walked like this when they went on field trips to museums. Gino and Peek would be leisurely looking at paintings on display at the National Portrait Gallery, and before long, Mr. Towers would be at the end of the hallway, waiting for them to see the next wonder.

Behind that strong gait was a determination Mr. Towers usually reserved for trips to the GED office, to register a student who was ready—and likely—to pass the exam; or to court, when a student needed a compassionate voice to advocate for them during a sentencing hearing.

Gino watched in awe as, once again, Mr. Towers advocated for him to an admissions officer. He described a young man who conquered insurmountable odds to be the first in his peer group to pass the GED; a man who is full of love, humor, compassion, bravery, and leadership; a person who will not just enroll and be successful at UDC, but will graduate and keep pushing himself and everyone around him to greater heights.

At times, Gino wondered who Mr. Towers was talking about. But in those moments, in between the glowing words that Gino accepted were about him, he started to feel something change within him. He *is* full of love: for Dana, who filled something in him he never thought another person could fill; for his great aunt, who took him in to save him from his mother, who would have surely killed him if left to her own inclinations; and to his friends Korey, Peek, and Ziggy, who welcomed him to Slope as the older brother they never realized they wanted. He *is* full of humor, laughing at and with all the joyous things that happened to him and for him, the joy that existed in between and all around all the other terrible times. He *is* brave, happily being the first in his group to try something, to do something, to be something. And all those things made Gino the leader Mr. Tower said he was. He would do more. He would be more. And he would make this community something better, as Miss Sandra said he was destined to do, and drilled into him every Sunday at worship, and afterward at family dinner.

For the first time, Gino knew he could, so he must. Passing the GED was not a fluke. God was leading him someplace and he could finally see a real finish line, beyond passing a test.

Gino smiled and his eyes watered as he shook the admissions officer's hand. She welcomed him to UDC and gave him a packet of paperwork to complete and return to her as soon as possible. He beamed with pride and Mr. Towers took a photo of him with his admissions packet.

Mr. Towers walked with Gino around the campus—now *his* campus—and at times, placed his arm around his shoulders.

"I'm proud of you, man," Mr. Towers said.

"I don't know how I'm gonna pay for it, but I'ma be in this bitch," Gino laughed. Mr. Towers stopped walking.

"Gino, you're going to have to pay very little. You're a low-income, GED graduate…living in-state…with no family contribution. Financial aid is gonna have you covered as soon as you fill out the paperwork. The Foundation that runs Alternative Futures can help with the rest. You're covered, my man."

Gino beamed again. The men wandered through the student center, the crown jewel of the campus. Banners hung from the rafters, representing campus organizations, including the fraternities and sororities.

"I wanna join one of those after I get situated," Gino said aloud as members of a fraternity walked by, smiled, and nodded. He could not make out what the letters were, much less what they meant—but he knew they meant belonging to something.

"You can be anything you want," he said softly.

Their walk took them back outside the student center, to the top of a long staircase that could take them down to Connecticut Avenue. A Metro pylon representing the Van Ness-UDC train station stood in the distance. They paused and stared into the busy street below.

"I should get back home," Gino said.

"Or, you could come back with me. Hang out. Maybe have a celebratory smoke?" Mr. Towers asked hopefully.

"So it's true," Gino said. "You really do be smoking with your favorites."

Mr. Towers blushed a bit and looked down.

"I wouldn't say it's *only* my favorites…but yeah, I do like to unwind. Naturally."

"Naturally," Gino playfully mocked. "But nah, I gotta get out there and make this money."

The back of Mr. Towers' neck got prickly and his shoulders tensed.

"You don't have to go back out today. Let Peek handle things. Come. Smoke with us tonight."

"I…" Gino's thoughts trailed off as the busy traffic on Connecticut Avenue sped by.

"I can't. Not tonight. But maybe…"

"Another time…" Mr. Towers sighed.

"Yeah. Another time. I gotta make this money now. But I'll be back, Mr. Towers."

"I know, friend. I know."

"Thank you. For everything you've done for me. And for just being a good dude."

Gino shook his teacher's hand and then pulled him in for a hug. They embraced long and hard as a few people walked by them, going down the stairs. Gino could smell Mr. Towers' organic fragrances perfuming his hair and skin. He'd still smell him, even on his subway ride back to Northeast.

The men let go of one another.

"I'll see you later, friend," the teacher said. The student smiled, then walked to the stairs. He stopped short and spun back around.

"I'm proud of me, too," Gino said with an impish grin. Mr. Towers smiled back. Gino turned back around, held the railing, and carefully descended the stairs to the street below.

Mr. Towers never saw Gino again.

There was no way for Mr. Towers to know what was on Gino's mind as he took his last trip on the DC Metro, but he suspected that perhaps Gino was devising a plan to get Peek, Ziggy, and Korey focused better on their tasks, so they could join him at UDC someday. Perhaps he pondered whether he could quit the drug game cold turkey, or if he'd ease out of it slowly, so as not to disrupt the fragile economy among them. Perhaps he thought the best way out was to relocate entirely—to investigate how he could get affordable housing much closer to campus, and maybe pick up a part time job on that side of town.

Or maybe that dark cloud of depression fell over him, as though nothing this good could be true. Maybe he thought of his violent mother or absent father, cursing him for daring to be more than his zip code.

Mr. Towers never knew what those last hours were like inside Gino's mind. He only knew Gino was a person who had a future, and nothing Gino could have done warranted an instant death sentence.

During Gino's memorial, Mr. Towers instantly recognized it as a Quaker memorial, even though no one called it such, and he didn't otherwise know Gino to be a Quaker. He sat in silence waiting for whatever gods were out there to tell him something, anything to make sense of yet another senseless tragedy hitting his school family.

Near the hour's end, interrupted only by spirit-led ministry from Gino's loved ones, Mr. Towers' consciousness became filled with a warm light. In this silence, a message arose:

Every person is a song. Some are jingles or children's rhymes. Others are power ballads, hip-hop tracks, or a gospel hymn. Some people are complicated enough to be symphonies, requiring space, time, and expertise to be understood—and sometimes they are never understood. Gino was an experimental symphony, full of triumphant peaks, and moody valleys, ending with a victorious crescendo into abrupt silence. We may never know the meaning of Gino's death, but perhaps in the studying of his life, we can make meaning of it for ourselves, so that he may live on forever through us.

He did not break the silence to share that message, but he did later share what he'd heard with his friends and colleagues who had known Gino. They, too, agreed he had been a symphony that would ring in their ears for all the days of their lives.

The First Wife's Curse

Jordan Gaffney-Bruce liked old things, such as vintage leather jackets, the faint musty odor of well-read books, and objects that reminded him of his great aunt: faded blue lottery dream books, old Chryslers, and sturdy rocks glasses with semi-abstract designs on them, straight out of a mid-century modern dream.

The set of eight glasses he carried out to the buffet were a recent purchase from a vintage shop in Bethesda, Maryland. Visiting Montgomery County was a slog when one lived in Slope, but it was his escape when he wanted to disappear into a multicultural background.

Jordan walked around Bethesda Avenue and saw nice things: pastel paper at the stationary store, plants at a nursery, cookware in an array of colors. In the vintage shop, he noticed a collection of glasses that reminded him of his upbringing parked in front of a black and white console television while his great aunt cooked the meal for the evening, while his parents worked.

The orange, blue, and black geometric shapes etched across the glass had a rhyme and reason known only to the designer. Jordan imagined himself entertaining his and Rahman's friends with these quirky glasses. What would he serve from them? Bourbon? Gin? What would Isaiah have to say about them? Something complimentary, probably. He always recognized Jordan's taste. And what about Bryson? Getting a compliment from him was like pulling an unerupted wisdom tooth. But even he would get a kick out of drinking from something so fancy—with their own metal carrier, to boot.

Eight glasses for $150 seemed like a steal compared to the other stuff for sale, like bulky sofas and wardrobes easily going for over $1,000. They could afford it if they wanted it, but larger purchases needed consulting. A set of glasses for their upcoming get-together would be fine. Jordan purchased them and headed home.

"What did you buy this time?" Rahman asked once Jordan got back to the house. Jordan shrank and acted like it was nothing, just a little something nice for the party. Rahman palmed a glass in his massive hand and pretended it wasn't impressive.

"Do you like them?" Jordan asked, suddenly unsure of himself. Rahman rolled his eyes cartoonishly.

"They're…okay," he sighed.

"Whatever," Jordan whispered. Rahman, satisfied, eased up on his husband—literally and figuratively—and kissed his neck.

"You have exquisite taste…always," he said.

"You play too much," Jordan retorted, kissing him back. Their beards tickled.

"I only tease the ones I love."

Most Black students at Penn in the nineties couldn't tell you how they first met each other. You enrolled, sat with the other Black kids in the cafeteria, and knew you were home. Before Instagram, Twitter, or Facebook, you could spend an hour in the cafeteria being seen and gathering the news of the day.

Rahman was a Junior when he'd first laid eyes on Jordan in the cafeteria. Jordan had his card swiped at the door, then glided into the room, with nobody else at his side. That was unusual for freshmen, who usually traveled in packs. But Rahman knew this guy was a frosh. He had a wide-eyed look about him as though he was trying to commit every inch of the room to memory. His sandy face was crowned by a short, curly afro and framed by the most ambitious of ideas of a beard.

He was definitely "family." Rahman could tell by the stray glances of judgment that Jordan could barely contain, or the slight flick of his wrists when he spoke. He couldn't help his affect, Rahman thought. In this day and age, if you could hide it, you would, especially if you were Black at Penn—or in the world.

Rahman liked men who were a little soft, a little artsy, just a hair away from masculinity. But those kinds were dangerous to his lifestyle. He liked being unclockable. He could fall into the shadows as a football player, or fraternity man, and allow people to stereotype him. That was fine for him, at age twenty.

He barely listened to his teammates at his table, as he was keeping Jordan in his peripheral vision. He'd lock eyes with him, say hi, then ask if he was new. Then he'd quickly tell him to grab a seat and get to know the guys.

But Jordan walked a little too fast, a little too intently, and breezed past Rahman at a speed faster than his gumption. He sat by himself, in a picture window overlooking University Avenue.

Believe it or not, the next three semesters were like that. Near misses one day. A person or two too many on an elevator the next day. Too far away from each other at a party on another day.

Rahman was dating Lashonda by his senior year, anyway. If he was going to be too chicken shit to make his move on Jordan Bruce, art history major from Dorchester, Massachusetts, then he needed to at least lay a foundation for a life after Penn that would make him happy otherwise.

Lashonda was smart as hell—an engineering major and president of the city-wide chapter of her predominately Black sorority. She'd run for student body president and only lost by 10 votes. She was vivacious and carried the social load for the both of them. He could be in the background, looking good, minding his own business, and bothering nobody.

That's one of the reasons why Lashonda liked him. She carried a healthy amount of jealousy, but Rahman wasn't known to date anyone on campus, much less entertain their attention. Rahman was good for having a seat in between classes on wherever the "Black bench" was that year. He smiled, nodded, made small talk, but could never, ever be accused of being a flirt. That's how he liked it. That's how Lashonda liked it. He was the perfect trophy boyfriend.

But he *did* flirt. He happened to save it all for Jordan Bruce, one early February afternoon in between classes.

Rahman's line brother worked in the registrar's office and thought nothing of it when Jordan's name came up.

"He trying to get down?" Kenny asked, thinking Jordan might be interested in their fraternity.

"I dunno man," Rahman bullshitted. "He seem like our type, though. Right?"

"Eh, I don't know. The bruhs don't really do artsy like that."

"I bet his grades on point, though. Can't really flunk art, right? It's art!"

Kenny looked to the left and right, then punched a few keys on the computer.

"Yeah, grades on point. 3.8. And his schedule this semester seems like more of the same. English, African art, intermediate French…shit, he express interest yet?"

"Nah. I'ma see where his head at, though. Aye, where he at on Wednesday afternoons?"

Kenny peered at the screen.

"He got Buddhist Literature in Logan," Kenny reported.

"Bet. I'll see what he's talking about," Rahman said.

So Rahman skipped lunch, where he never saw Jordan anymore anyway, and sat under the tree opposite College Hall, in the park on the way to Logan. It was twenty minutes before class.

A minute went by. Rahman immediately regretted committing to this level of stalking. What business did he possibly have in front of College Hall that would sound plausible to Jordan?

Another minute went by. It wasn't too late to abort the mission. Rahman could head back across campus, or to the library, or to see Lashonda.

At the third minute, just as Rahman lost his nerve, Jordan walked toward him, engrossed in thigh-slapping banter with a middle-aged white lady he presumed to be his professor.

Good, Rahman thought. I can smile, nod, and get the fuck out of here while he's talking to this lady.

Jordan's face, now sharpened with the wisdom and misery of nearly two years at Penn, and a good shape-up from the Black barber that all the guys on campus patronized, looked down, then looked up, making eye contact with Rahman. He never broke from the story he was telling his professor, even though he looked away from Rahman briefly, then back at him, smiling slightly. His pace slowed. Rahman was frozen. Did he look guilty? Did Jordan know? Why couldn't he move?

"I'll see you in class," the lady said softly as she picked up her pace, waving at Jordan, then again at Rahman. Rahman waved back with three fingers.

"Hey, Rahman," Jordan said. He wore a New Jersey Nets hockey jersey and wide-legged, loose-fitting jeans. A red bandana held back his short dreadlocks, exposing his round face and uneven beard.

"Hi Jordan."

"I never see you anymore," Jordan said. He stuffed his hands in his pockets and his shoulders tightened a bit.

"Yeah, I guess I always saw you in the caf," Rahman reasoned. "I been off campus, so…less caf. Maybe."

"Maybe," Jordan said.

"Funny running into you here, though."

"Yeah! It is, right? I was just…getting some air. Before class."

"Is that right?" Jordan asked.

"Mmm-hm. Yup."

"So…wanna grab some air together?"

"You…what?"

"You're getting some air. I got 15 minutes. Can I join you, or is there a cover charge?"

Rahman pondered, then laughed. He never knew Jordan had a sense of humor like this. Sarcastic. Quick.

"Sure. I got time," Rahman said. He grabbed the straps on his leather bookbag and walked to the bench. Jordan followed. Denim hit faded, cracked paint on wood, and the men were buoying the bench.

"It's a nice day," Jordan said. Rahman agreed.

"Warm, for February," he said. Jordan nodded.

"Your last February on campus, huh?"

Rahman sighed and nodded.

"It goes by quick." Rahman thought about the moment he visited Penn as a high school senior, hoping he'd get in. Then he thought about the day he got the thick envelope with his acceptance. Then move-in day. Then the parties. Now today.

Eight semesters. Four before he laid eyes on Jordan. Three more before he found the courage to make this moment happen.

"We've never had a conversation before today, you know," Jordan mused.

"Then I guess we better make it count, right?" Rahman said, his charm finally breaking through this awkward armor he couldn't seem to shed.

"It's hard getting to know folks, sometimes," Jordan began. His cheeks began to get hot, and he fidgeted with the silver ring on his right ring finger. "At a school like this, you go from not knowing people one day, then knowing everybody the next day. Because you went to the same party, or event. I mean, I've always known who you are. But how do you go up to somebody and say 'Hey, we should be friends, right?'"

"You could have said that. You could have always said that," Rahman said.

"Yeah. I could have. But be for real, for a minute. You know me. How do you think it would turn out if I rolled up on any number of Black men on this campus and said we should be friends?"

"You think that wouldn't be received well?"

"I'm trying to live, Rahman."

"So, you buying into the narrative that Black men are dangerous, even though you Black, too?"

"I'm Black and queer, friend. I gotta be vigilant at all times."

"Don't say that."

"Say what?"

"That word. 'Queer.' Ain't nothing strange about you."

Jordan rolled his eyes.

"Is that what it's gonna be, Rahman? Our first conversation, and you really just wanna put me in a box?"

"Not at all, Jordan. Not at all. I'm just not used to no Black man calling himself that word. But if that's what you want, that's what I'll say."

"Oh. Well okay, then." Jordan smiled slightly and looked away.

"Is that why you never come to my bros parties?" Rahman inquired.

"You mean your little fraternity parties?"

"Oh, I see you got jokes. Yes, my *little* fraternity parties. I think you'd have a good time."

"Maybe I would. But I didn't want to cause any confusion by being there. I'm interested in another organization, so I don't want any drama when it's time to make it official."

"Oh. Don't tell me you're trying to be—"

"Discretion is key. I am not coming up off that information."

"Okay. Well played. And that's too bad."

"Why so?"

"I think you'd look good in my colors," Rahman teased.

"Oh yeah? I think I'd look good in any colors, actually," Jordan laughed. Rahman joined him.

"That's true. You would."

The men smiled, then got quiet. Something happened in the silence that made the hair on the necks of both men stand up straight. In Rahman's body, he got warm and felt more like himself than he'd felt in four years. In Jordan's body, he grew cold, and became aware of every skin cell, like he was now something new.

This was not the moment they met. This was the moment they saw each other, both overdue and premature, the right place and wrong, the moment they never expected and the moment they'd waited all their lives for. They were feet away from each other yet knew they ought to be holding hands. And though they could have sat there for years, it was Jordan who had the presence of mind to check his watch and bring them back to reality.

"It was nice sharing some air. For a little while," Jordan said.

"I'd share air with you any day," Rahman flirted.

"I'm here every Monday and Wednesday." Rahman, of course, already knew this, but at least had the presence of mind to pretend not to.

"Bet. Then, I'll see you next time." Rahman stretched his hand across the bench. Jordan paused, looked at Rahman's huge, brown hand, and shook it. His grip was tighter than Rahman expected and lingered longer than Jordan expected. He rose, walked into the building, and finally smiled so hard that his face hurt by the time he sat in class.

Rahman's face hurt, too.

2

Help me. Please. It feels like I went crazy and stayed there.

Adrift on U Street in Northwest DC, sometime after Barcelona but before his thirtieth birthday, Jordan had grown accustomed to taking a novel to the bar and reading a few chapters while sipping a cocktail. Usually, he wanted to be left alone while enjoying the white noise of the crowd. The bars he attended were straight, so he didn't worry about getting cruised. Sure, there was the occasional "down low" man as Oprah had recently introduced into the Black lexicon, but his novel was usually the best possible shield against unwelcome advances.

Jordan had forgotten that Kaffa House had open mic nights for poetry on Thursdays, and by the time he'd realized it, he was virtually trapped in the standing room only venue. His seat at the bar was perpendicular to the tiny stage, and the exit might as well have been a hundred yards away.

He closed his book and resigned himself to the show. On the inside, he laughed, as it was the kind of scene he and Rahman would have had inside jokes about for weeks to come. Quasi-militant dead prez wannabees hawking their incense, mixtapes, and chapbooks, while the well-oiled Erykah Badu clones snapped their fingers at the insipid poetry being recited. Their silver jewelry clanked every time they finished snapping and lowered their arms.

The audience looked young: fresh out of college—if not high school. That would explain the total awareness of their own drag personas. Still, the drinks hit the spot, and to Kaffa House's credit, despite everyone strictly adhering to the neo soul costuming, the people were attractive, friendly, and trying to be intelligent.

Jordan's own swag placed him in-line with the poetry set: a plain white, collared shirt; a corduroy blazer with suede patches at the elbows; baggy blue jeans; and an old pair of beige Asics. He didn't mind that people asked him if he was a professor. There were worse things he could be called.

The host, a tall, skinny guy with long dreadlocks, returned to the stage and took the mic.

"Coming to the stage, ladies and gentlemen, is a dear friend to Kaffa House. Outta Potomac University via NYC, and ready to set the world on fire…give it up for Savion Cortez!"

A slim Latino dude wearing black slacks, a black t-shirt, and a purple bandana climbed to the stage. His silky curls spilled out from under the purple cloth. His low beard barely concealed his youth.

He centered himself behind the microphone, inhaled slowly, then went to work.

Red is for the rage bubbling up through my chest
And orange is for the sun that sees you not doing your best

Yellow bile spewing forth when I take a hit
Green-eyed bandits thinking they the shit
Blue is how I'm feeling Pride after Pride
I wear purple on purple because these suckers lied
Where's the black for my people who did their best
It's Bayard and Marsha's names that should be on your chest
And where's the brown for the colonizer's taint
Creating something new to add to the paint
And I won't never wear the rainbow because… fuck the rain
And I won't never cry for you because… fuck the pain
I'm just me, just coolin', just living in sin
Queer, gay, bi, whatever nigga – I'm gonna win

"Well alright," Jordan thought as he clapped with the rest of the audience.

"This next one is called 'Psyche: I Hate You, Actually.' It does not rhyme," Savion announced.

All…of my love…my peace and happiness
Happiness.
All…of my love…my peace and happiness.
Happiness.
Happiness.
I hope it was worth it.
I hope it was worth the sleepless nights and tired days.
They filled something in your soul that I could never have
But you didn't ask me to.
And maybe I could have.
But that's on you.

I hope they don't squander all of your love
On frivolous things.
I hope they surprise you by spending your love on the deep things. The meaningful things. Things that you will remember and cherish after a lifetime.
You were my lifetime.
Maybe they can show you more than I could have.

I hope they give you the peace you never gave me.
With us, it was always love and war.
And at the end of the day, love couldn't win if both sides weren't fighting for it.
All of my love, my peace, my happiness: I gave it to you.
And now we're through.

"Thank you," Savion said with a smile. A few of his teeth were crooked, and Jordan thought he would have been totally insufferable had he been perfect.

The crowd clapped and cheered as Savion waved and took his seat again. Accidentally, Jordan locked eyes with Savion, who smiled, then looked away.

Oh God, Jordan screamed in his head. He was no good at flirting unless it was with Rahman. He had no clue what he was doing here. He wanted the performances to end and the crowd to thin out so he could slink away and do better things, like die of embarrassment.

Jordan felt a tap on his shoulder, and he looked up.

"Anybody sitting here?" Savion asked. Jordan's demeanor was cool, but his consciousness was in disbelief.

"Nah man, you can sit," Jordan said, moving his small bag to the other side of him. Savion glanced at Jordan's empty cocktail then gestured for the bartender, a shapely young lady wearing a black polo shirt. Her cornrows went straight back and ended in butterfly clips.

"Two of those, please," Savion said.

"Gotchu," she said before Jordan could refuse. Jordan thought all this was escalating quickly.

"I'm Savion Cortez," he said with a smile and an outstretched hand. Jordan couldn't believe how smooth Savion's hand was, except for a little hair at his knuckles.

"Jordan Bruce. Excellent poetry."

"Thank you, thank you. I try to do a little something every now and then."

"More than a little. That was powerful. And…unexpected," Jordan said, struggling to find the right words. Savion smiled.

"Never heard unambiguously queer poetry in mixed company before?" Savion teased.

"Actually? No. Not at all," Jordan said.

"Well…neither have most of these bozos," Savion quipped. Jordan laughed.

"I see you got your book with you," Savion continued. "You know what they say about men who bring a book to the bar."

"What?" Jordan asked.

"They get a free drink." Right on queue, the bartender produced two screwdrivers and placed them on napkins in front of the men.

"You really didn't have to do that," Jordan asked.

"But I did. Cheers," Savion said, lifting his glass. Jordan did the same. They clinked, let the glasses tap the bar, then sipped.

"Not bad," Savion said.

"Where are you from?" Jordan asked, making small talk, but the kind he liked.

"New York. Washington Heights. Back and forth between here and there since I graduated though."

"You went to school down here?"

"Potomac," Savion nodded.

"Good school," Jordan said.

"Yeah. It was something. How about you?"

"Oh, I went to Penn. A little while ago."

"How long?

"'96," Jordan said.

"Damn, pa, you look amazing," Savion said.

"We're only a few years apart," Jordan said.

"Yeah. I said you look amazing. That wasn't a statement about your age—just a statement of fact."

"Oh. Well. Thank you."

"You're welcome," Savion said. He coyly looked away while he took another sip.

"Your poetry. Was that…was that all based in real life?"

"Yeah. That's a real nigga," he chuckled.

"Seems like he lost one," Jordan said.

"Nothing wrong with being a free agent."

"Cheers to freedom," Jordan said, once again clinking glasses with Savion.

"Hey man…I'm not trying to be too forward… but crowded bars ain't really my scene. And it seems like it's not your scene either. You wanna continue this conversation someplace more quiet?"

"You know what? I thought you'd never ask."

The haste with which Savion and Jordan made it out of Kaffa House was like they had known each other for years.

They hailed a taxi and headed west to Jordan's place in Dupont Circle. They could have walked to Savion's apartment, but Jordan preferred to feel in control, especially if things went left. He was part of the generation where kids got snatched off the street by all sorts of people, so he remained vigilant, even when throwing caution to the wind.

They laughed on the entire ride over, up the stairs, and over a nightcap. As northeasterners, they had similar tastes in hip-hop, humor, and politics. Moreover, Savion was impressed by Jordan's varied tastes in fiction, from Paul Beatty to Robert Heinlein. Jordan appreciated Savion's ambition to be a recording artist and published author. Likewise, Savion was impressed to meet a Black art historian who had studied in Europe.

The glint of Jordan's fraternity paddle leaning in the corner caught Savion's eye. He scoffed.

"I didn't know you were in one of those. I might not have come over," Savion joked, with a slight hint of seriousness.

"I did it for the chicks," Jordan joked back.

"Oh please," Savion said.

Everything was clicking. Everything felt legitimately perfect. Yet, there were elephants in the room.

"You got somebody," Savion said, sensing the underlying tension.

"No. I'm single. Remember? Cheers to freedom?"

"It wasn't a question. I know you got somebody."

"How do you figure?"

"Your adrenaline is pumping. I see the vein in your neck pulsing. You feel like you're doing something you shouldn't be. And don't no grown man feel like that unless he's cheating. Who is he?"

"He's not…I'm not with him. At all."

"Ah…unrequited love. I know it well."

"You're killing the vibe, man."

"Not at all. Just setting a reasonable expectation. Surely, a man of your talents and stature can appreciate knowing who's who and what's what."

"And what's that?"

"That another day, another time, we might be good for each other. But tonight? Tonight we're each other's escape from whoever is haunting us. Me? I understand exactly what you're feeling. I'm not with my dude, either."

"Why not?"

"He's a good dude. Just…immature. He'll make a good man someday."

"And in the meantime, there's me?"

Savion laughed.

"They say the best way to get over someone is to get under someone else."

"I think you might be onto something," Jordan said with a smile. He looked at Savion's lips, leaned, and kissed him. Savion opened his mouth and touched tongues with Jordan, who quickly palmed Savion's fuzzy beard.

"You know I have a few years on you, right?" Jordan said in between kisses.

"Then teach me something," Savion defied.

In the morning, Savion woke up first. He scribbled something on a sheet of paper, caressed Jordan's cheek, and then hurried out. An hour later, Jordan woke up and found the note, along with a phone number.

Making rainbows
With the man in the corduroy blazer
His smile: unforgettable
His pain: palpable
May he find the joy he deserves
May he always be my friend

That night in Barcelona turned me upside-down. We never spoke about it, but we should have. Instead, I let that moment, that one little moment, lead me into years and years of ~~chaos~~ uncertainty.

Brother Willis was always one of the last people to leave the chapter house after monthly business meetings on Thursday nights. He held not a single office in the alumni chapter, but everyone knew who he was and understood his clout. Made at Morehouse in the early 90s, he was a rare undergraduate chosen to represent his region on the national board of directors. After law school, he moved to DC, moved up the ranks at Latham & Watkins, and maintained his fraternity membership.

He met Jordan at a happy hour on Capitol Hill, right before the fraternity's centennial year.

Jordan sat at the far side of the bar, nursing a dry martini, and pondering his life choices. He'd left his book at home in an effort to follow his therapist's advice.

"Enjoying yourself?" the handsome, bald stranger with the full beard said. His look and deep baritone reminded Jordan of a sexier Isaac Hayes.

Jordan looked up and nodded.

"Yeah. I am. I know it doesn't look like it. As it turns out, I might be an introvert," Jordan said.

"So, the small talk of forty Brothers at one time is slowly killing you?" he asked.

"Oh, I died 45 minutes ago," Jordan said. The man laughed.

"I'm Brother Willis. But I go by Spike," he said, stretching his hand out. Jordan offered him the fraternity grip, obscuring it from the public with their shoulders.

"Jordan Bruce," he said, mumbling his crossing information over the din. Spike returned the signature, not that either would remember it.

"Are you active?" Spike asked.

"No, I'm not," Jordan sighed.

"No judgment," Spike said, putting out both hands. "If it's meant to be, you'll come back to the house. We ain't going nowhere."

Jordan immediately loosened up. He loathed reclamation. Brothers always tried to brow-beat each other into coming back to "The House" yet they never asked why Brothers went inactive. But Spike decidedly not recruiting him into an alumni chapter put him at ease.

Spike slid onto a barstool close to Jordan.

"Did you enjoy Penn?"

"It was okay. Made some friends. Got the right start professionally. Couldn't ask for much more."

"What do you do?"

"I'm a curator at the Smithsonian."

"For real!? Which museum?"

"Sackler Gallery, currently, but I've worked at a few. Trying to get into the African American History Museum if it ever opens."

"What kind of major did you have to have to get into the Smithsonian?"

"I was an art history major, but they take all kinds over there, truly. Lots of different jobs to be done, just like any other government agency. Hey, what kind of work do you do?"

"I'm an attorney at a boring firm downtown."

"So…Morehouse undergrad…let me guess…Georgetown Law?"

"Close! George Washington."

"Not bad at all," Jordan said with a slight smile. And so began the five-year courtship of Jordan and Spike.

Spike was very much like Rahman in ambition and wit and was a dramatic improvement in many other ways.

He was decisive: "It's been six weeks since we started seeing each other. I'm certain that I'd like to focus all of my energy on you exclusively. Would you like that, too?"

He was polite: "I'd like to meet your parents, if you think that's appropriate and they would like that."

He was clear about his future: "I do not have children and I do not want any."

Jordan had no complaints, and to his credit, he did everything right, as well. Therapy had done him good.

Jordan was clear: "I'm not really interested in fraternity life outside of the chapter, but I have no problem with you being a convention-goer."

He was fair: "If I'm going to be at your house part of the time, I should pay part of the bills. And if you're going to be over here, you can help with groceries sometimes."

He was adventurous: "I'm not really into hiking, but I'll try it to see if I hate it."

They were an amazing couple, and everyone knew it. Especially Rahman, who slowly but surely withdrew from Jordan during this time. Jordan didn't hear about Lashonda's fertility struggles, and Rahman was tight-lipped about any of their family drama.

Jordan didn't like that. He missed his best friend and didn't know how to get him back.

After the chapter meeting, Jordan cursed the dress shoes pinching his feet, and he walked gingerly to Spike's BMW. As Spike gripped the last Brother on the premises, he unlocked the car. Jordan climbed in.

"Hey man, something's been on my mind," Spike said.

"What's up?" Jordan asked.

"Do you wanna get married or what?"

"Married?" Jordan laughed.

"Yeah…married," Spike repeated.

"You play too much," Jordan said.

"Wow," Spike said. His shoulders tensed and he started the car. He sped away from the chapter house and headed north to Michigan Avenue.

"Spike…are you okay?" Jordan asked when Spike got to the intersection.

"Yeah, I'm cool," Spike sighed.

"You were really serious about getting married, huh?" Jordan asked.

"I wanted to know what you felt. That's all."

"I just…I don't know, I didn't mean to laugh."

"That's how you feel. It's cool."

"It's just a surprise."

"Why would it be a surprise? We talk about the future all the time."

"Yeah. But…you never talked about an actual wedding before. Like…a wedding? Two grooms? Who is supposed to propose? Are you proposing?"

"Never mind, Jordan, damn."

"Why are you getting all sensitive about it? We talk about anything else directly."

"I asked if you wanted to get married and you laughed."

"It's not like that, Spike,"

"Why are you getting a tone with me like I did something wrong?"

"I don't have a tone. This is what I sound like when I'm confused."

"Are you dating your boy?"

"Am I dating…what? Who are you talking about?"

"Rahman. Your boy from college."

"Spike, you trippin'. I am not dating Rahman. He has a wife and two kids. Jesus."

"But you'd be with him if you could," Spike concluded.

"Don't be ridiculous. Let's go home, have a drink, and relax. You're worked up and I can't figure out why."

"Stop manipulating me, Jordan."

"Again, what are you talking about? I am only dating you. Not Rahman, not the dude down the block—you."

"Then why does it feel like I can't get any deeper with you than what we have right now?"

"You think what we have is superficial?"

"Yeah, I do.

"Actually?"

"Actually."

"Wow. Surprising."

"Stop that."

"What is it *now*?"

"You turn into a damn Vulcan. Condescending. Like all this isn't about you."

"You are making it about me but you're the one who has the problem! You're jealous of Rahman and for what? He don't want me! I don't want him!"

"Okay, Slim Goodbody."

"I'm sorry, what?"

"Don't act like that ain't what he calls you."

"And why would you know what he calls me unless you've been through my phone?"

"I sure did go through it. And you know what I found? Just enough. This man is begging for your attention, and you give it to him easy."

"He's one of my oldest friends. It doesn't surprise me that you wouldn't understand how we operate."

"What is there to understand about the pet names he calls you? Slim Goodbody. Handsome. Superstar."

"I'm sorry you don't have friends who hype you up."

"Hype, huh? What about all the selfies? How about *you* asking him for selfies at odd times of the day and night? As if all the gym photos he sends you aren't enough."

"We just have an odd relationship. It doesn't mean what you think it does."

"You think I'm an idiot."

"I don't think that at all. I think you're one of the smartest people I know."

"And you're too smart for your own good. If you don't know that man is in love with you, you a fool. But I know you ain't. So, what does that really make you?"

Jordan clenched his jaw. Not only was the betrayal of someone going through his phone finally hitting him, but so was the critique of his friendship with Rahman. What he had with Rahman was theirs, not Spike's.

"Not too much to say for yourself now, huh?"

"You don't have to be an asshole, Spike. You really don't."

"And you don't have to be a bitch, do you?"

Jordan's eyes grew big and he looked Spike squarely in the face.

"Let me out the car," Jordan demanded.

"We're a few blocks from your apartment."

"Let me out of the car. Now."

"Don't be a drama queen."

"Let me out the fucking car right now!" Jordan shouted at the top of his lungs. Spike pumped his brakes and Jordan was out in seconds. As Jordan walked furiously past the brownstones of T Street, Spike slowed the car and rolled down the passenger window.

"You don't have to do this," Spike called out. Jordan ignored him. Cars began honking behind Spike.

"Jordan, come on, be for fucking real."

After one more honk, Spike sped away. Jordan ignored Spike's calls for the rest of the evening and through the weekend. On Monday morning, Jordan boxed Spike's few personal effects and sent them to him via FedEx.

Spike waited until the next chapter meeting to transfer the duffel bag full of Jordan's stuff back to him. Based on their icy glances and smug stares, Jordan could tell that the old queens in the chapter already knew Spike's side of the story. Since Jordan had no other close friends in the chapter, he knew immediately his own alumni chapter was no longer a safe space for him. He took his duffel bag and left the chapter meeting immediately after singing the hymn. For the first time in months, he drove himself home.

I won't send this to him, and I'm not writing it for myself, since I know it all already. I guess I'm writing it to God.

Jordan never wanted for dates. His work, his travel, and his alumni connections somehow always landed him in the crosshairs of a new man, inexplicably more handsome and wealthy than the last. Through work, he'd met a MacArthur Genius—an award-winning photographer who'd traveled the world by the time they'd met. He had his own issues, but they'd enjoyed a summer together before he went overseas again.

He'd seen Savion a few more times over the years, and they were always passionate, nostalgic romps, even after Savion had finally gotten married. Jordan wasn't normally one for threesomes, but Savion and Gavin made an irresistible pair. On a triple date night with them, he'd met a guard for the New Jersey Nets. Their first night was hot and heavy, and ShaQuan begged Jordan for more incessantly for months. Turns out he'd fallen in love, and Jordan wasn't down for that at all.

Then there was the Grammy-award winning R&B singer who was reminiscent of Jean-Michel Basquiat. He, too, wanted more of Jordan, but Jordan didn't want to be wanted in that way.

Rahman knew all these headlines. The more important the man, the bigger his depression grew. Some days, he feigned busyness so he wouldn't have to hear more than he had to from Jordan. Other days, the gym photos came in more furiously, escalating from a bicep flex to a risqué photo of him in the teeniest of white towels.

In therapy, over the years, Jordan would bring up Savion. Why didn't he ever try to be serious with him? He was beautiful, talented, ambitious, and clearly heading to so much more in his life. He was envious that Savion had found Gavin—someone who loved him exactly the way he needed.

"I can't tell you exactly why things didn't work out," his current therapist told him during one session. "You seem to always go back to Savion, but that was such a fleeting moment in time, nearly twenty years ago now."

"I think I keep going back to that moment in time because my life would have been much different if either of us had been serious about the other."

"Hmm. Would you consider another theory?"

"Sure."

"What if your brain was transferring your 'what ifs' to the most convenient person from your past, instead of the person you really want?"

"And who would that be?"

"You tell me. You've been on this journey with me for a year and a half now. And you're making outstanding progress on the goals you've set for yourself. More responsibility at work. Finding meaning in activities with your fraternity brothers from Penn. Taking time for self-care. But every so often, you'll talk about *him*. And your eyes light up a little. And you smile a little. Every other man you've ever spoken about—Savion included—you've talked about them matter-of-factly. But this one? Oh, you love him."

"Rahman," Jordan admitted.

"Rahman," the therapist affirmed. "Is he your best friend? Sure. Is he married? Yup. Is he straight? That's for him to tell you. But at the end of the day, Jordan, he comes up for you, often. You are intertwined with him. And you've got to get free so you can live—for real."

Jordan's eyes watered.

"I hate his wife," Jordan sniffled. "I've known her since college, and I've hated her since then."

"Hate is a strong emotion, but it seems like you mean it. Why does it make you so upset?"

"Because I feel terrible that I hate this woman who has done nothing to me. Rahman is like my best friend, and he tells me when they're having problems. He stopped, though. I told him a few years ago 'If you ain't gonna leave her, don't tell me anything else about her.' And he stopped talking to me about her. But I resented her even more."

"Why don't you resent him?"

"Honestly? I think I do. But how can I resent the only man I ever really loved?"

My therapist has suggested that if I am ever going to get through this, I need to write it all out. Putting it in a letter feels stupid, as I am never going to give it to the person who needs to read it. Rahman, Rahman, Rahman. The love of my life. My headache. My archnemesis. My hero.

I knew he was never going to leave Lashonda. But he was never happy. All I'd have to do is search for 'Fraushonda' in our text messages. Thirty-seven times he's called her that.

Rahman and I have never even had an argument. We laugh through every disagreement. I've traveled with him, slept in the same bed with him. I could see doing that with him forever.

He is my favorite person. I told him that once. It was a big deal. And you know what he said? He said "You're my favorite person, too." And I felt so relieved to hear that. And flattered. And vindicated.

But nothing else ever changed. He stayed married. He never told me he was in love with me.

Remember how, in high school, people would say "What is understood doesn't need to be said?" That's what this feels like. Like the code is Omerta. Like if one of us says something, everything is ruined.

But I have to say something. I can't keep living like this. God can't want this for me.

A few months after writing those words, something, finally, was said. Rahman had finally finished his doctorate in education, and he'd invited Jordan to come to New York for a celebration of the milestone. Everyone would be there, from family to Penn friends to a sea of Rahman's own fraternity brothers. And of course, Rahman's children and his wife.

On a Monday night, Jordan called Rahman.

"I need to talk to you," Jordan said.

"Oh, okay. Cool. What's up?" Rahman asked.

"I'm not coming to Brooklyn for your get-together."

"Ah man, you're missing the graduation party of the year! Why?"

Jordan breathed in and breathed out, trying to recall the exact wording he had practiced. It was now or never. Everything was going to change.

"I don't want to be…in the same room…with the wife of the man I love."

"Oh. Okay."

Silence followed, then Jordan spoke.

"You understand why, right?"

"Well, yeah. I've confided in you a lot about my relationship over the years. And I remember when you told me before 'If you're not going to do anything about it, I don't wanna hear about it.' I heard you, and I understood. But I guess…I didn't take into consideration that I can't un-ring a bell. If I told you I was miserable, I should have also told you when things got better."

"So, things are better?" Jordan asked.

"Better than they were, yeah."

"I just…I just…I can't do this," Jordan said, exasperated.

"What do you mean?"

"Even now, you still don't get it. We've been…we've been…circling each other like sharks for years. For years and years. And I just told you the hardest thing I've ever had to say in my whole life, but you still don't get it. I can't be in the same room with your wife because I'm in love with *her* man. Okay?"

"Oh…that's what you mean?"

Jordan paced his living room, as he did when he was on the phone generally, but especially when Rahman stressed him out.

"Yes. That's what I mean. I'm not going to be watching you hugged up on her, being this happy family I know you're not."

"I—"

"So, I gotta do what's best for me, okay? This way we are with each other? It stops. Because Rahman, the thing is this: you don't treat me like your friend."

"Are you kidding me? Of course I do! We are friends. You're my best friend!"

"Bullshit. You treat me like you want me. And you know it. Everybody knows it."

"Everybody? Who is everybody?"

"Rahman. I love you. I have loved you since Penn."

"I love you, too, Jordan! I really, really do! But…"

"But what?"

"I'm not attracted to men."

Jordan caught a glimpse of himself in his hallway mirror as Rahman uttered those words. Disbelief, sadness, anger, and disappointment in himself—every emotion flashed across his face.

Yet, Jordan didn't fight. He knew after all these years of wanting Rahman, and sometimes actually needing him, that he was playing a dangerous game. There would always be the chance Jordan could have been mistaken, or that Rahman could lie to him to get out of it. It was a chance Jordan was willing to take until he got closure—or until a way opened for something bigger between them.

"Hello?" Rahman said.

"I heard you. You're not attracted to men. Got it."

"Jordan, you do so much for me. Materially. Spiritually. It's me and you. But I just don't…"

"You don't have to say anything else, Rahman. I've said my part. You've made your point."

"I don't want to hurt you."

"Okay."

"I just…the way we are is enough for me."

"I think the way we are is too much. It would be too much for anybody, and I think if you really looked at how we are, you'd know that to be true."

A knot grew in Jordan's stomach. This was it. This was the big goodbye.

"Rahman, the way you talk to me…a reasonable person—"

"Here comes the art historian invoking the reasonable person doctrine," Rahman laughed.

"It's not funny, Rahman. I have to think in these terms because the way you treat me is not normal between platonic friends. And it's not me—it's you. Every now and then, I share our texts or recount a conversation between us. You know what my friends say? They say 'Whoa.' They say 'He loves you, chile.' They say 'Y'all go together real bad.' You call me handsome, beautiful, wonderful. You send me heart eyes emojis. You make inappropriate sexual jokes."

"You never once told me to stop! I thought that's just how we joke around!"

"I didn't tell you to stop because it seemed like you were flirting with me, and people who don't know you think the same thing."

"Well, they don't know me. You know me. And maybe…maybe I do flirt with you. I just like to see you smile. You deserve it."

"See what you're doing right there?"

"What?"

"That's called 'breadcrumbing.' And you're doing it. You just give me a little breadcrumb and expect me to keep following you."

"I'm not asking you to follow me, Jordan."

"No…I guess you're not…but you're expecting it."

Rahman kept quiet. The silence threw kerosene on the fire.

"You think I forgot about Barcelona, don't you?" Jordan asked.

"Barcelona was twenty years ago. I don't even remember it anymore."

"God, Rahman, you make me sick. You're trying to make it seem like I'm just this old has-been forty-year-old who can't resist you. Like I'm making things up. But I'm not making things up. Maybe when we first met, I had a crush on you. Maybe, in our early twenties, I could have chalked it up to me wanting somebody who was unavailable. But we were in our late twenties in Barcelona."

"What do you think happened in Barcelona, for God's sake?"

"Our last night there. We went to a club. But we didn't know it was a gay club. Or really, gay night at a regular club. And I was stiff and uncomfortable. But you…you were the one who said we should stay and have a good time. And we drank. And we partied. And you took me by the hand when 'Been Around the World' came on. Remember that? Puff had just dropped it, and we hadn't even heard it in the states yet."

"Yes. I remember that."

"And it was slow but it had a beat. And you danced with me. *You* danced with *me*."

"I know. I wanted you to be comfortable."

"I was. And so were you. We got in a cab to go back to the hotel. And I laid on you. And you put your arm around me. And you thought I fell asleep."

"I…thought?"

"You held me. When you thought I was asleep, you held me. You stroked my temples…and my beard. And you kissed the top of my head."

Silence.

"And that one kiss lasted me twenty years. It sustained me through all your little breadcrumbs, here and there. Your touch sustained me through your marriage. Through your children. For so long I thought I was imagining things, but I wasn't, Rahman."

"I…I didn't know you…were awake."

"I was awake enough. And I always thought…no matter what you had going on personally, that we still had something. That somehow, we were the endgame. I know that's stupid. And I feel like a jerk for holding on this long. So, my friend, this is it. I decided a while ago that I was gonna return your little flirts. Your little jokes. That I would keep pushing, keep pushing, keep pushing until you finally said how you felt. That we'd stop staring at each other from across the room and finally dance again."

Silence.

"But I was wrong. Because you're not attracted to men."

"I…I'm sorry, Jordan."

"It's all good," Jordan said tearfully. "Hey, enjoy your graduation party. You worked hard for your doctorate, so I hope you party hard, too."

"Please come, Jordan."

"What? No. That would be crazy. I'm going now, Rahman. Goodbye."

"Jordan, please—"

Jordan hung up his phone and turned it off. He poured himself a shot of Ciroc, neat, from his bar. He downed it, then poured another. He laughed to himself. Puffy's liquor was right on brand for this stupid moment in his pathetic life.

Jordan had found his apartment in Dupont Circle fresh out of grad school, a two bedroom above a bakery, near Lambda Rising bookstore. It was expensive but doable on his government salary at the Smithsonian. The landlords were a kind, aging gay couple that wanted to keep the neighborhood gay for as long as possible. They were delighted to rent to a young, Black queer man, and hoped he'd get many years of use out of the place.

It was convenient to everything he'd wanted out of DC, including restaurants, a park, and easy access in and out of town through the Metro, plenty of buses, and taxis if need be.

Rahman had spent many a night in this place as well, whether he needed a place to crash during the Kappa Konclave or was at a conference for work.

Jordan woke up the next morning after his argument feeling gross, like everything about his apartment reeked of Rahman. He put on his slate gray suit, tied his dreadlocks back, and went to work. He wore Nike Air Max 97s when on public transportation and changed into his dress shoes in his office.

His homegirls at work noticed a difference in his demeanor, but they knew not to prod too much. He ate in his office with the door closed and clocked out a little after five in the evening.

He walked home, still sad, still not having vented anything that had transpired with Rahman. He felt so simple. So stupid. So…old and useless.

Jordan had dated. He'd even had boyfriends over the past twenty years. Serious ones. But they weren't his best friend. They weren't his favorite person. It was going to take him a long time to get over this.

It was around six thirty before Jordan got to his block north of Dupont Circle. He noticed in the distance, at the bench in front of the bakery and entrance to his stairwell, that there was an obnoxious balloon bouquet, slowly swaying back and forth. They were in black and old gold, his fraternity colors. He wondered briefly if someone had just crossed, but the timing wasn't right for that. DC chapters were already done with their spring lines.

Behind the balloons were a pair of legs wearing charcoal gray slacks with light pinstripes, navy blue socks, and brown leather dress shoes.

The wind moved the balloons. It was Rahman, wearing his finest suit, a straw fedora, and round sunglasses, looking like a neo soul singer dressed for an awards ceremony.

"Rahman? What are you doing here?"

"Jordan! Hi!" he quickly stood.

"Hi…what are you…"

"These are for you, obviously." He gestured at the balloons with his free hand. "And so are these."

He shoved a bouquet of at least fifty red carnations into Jordan's arms.

"Carnations?" Jordan asked.

"So…I know I fucked up. Like big time. Like, life could change for the absolute worst—forever—if I don't fix this. And Jordan, I know your love language. You like receiving gifts. I know this. I been known this. It's one of the things I do to keep you happy. You got me. And I'm sorry I led you on like that for so long. But since I know that's your love language, and I been doing it all along, I know I gotta come even harder if I'm gonna fix this," he babbled.

"So, I didn't know if it was better to give you something that reminded you of your fraternity or if I was supposed to give you something that reminded you of mine? I don't know how this works. So…I got both."

"Wow."

Rahman's jaw quivered with nervousness as he continued.

"I also got a platter of paella from this spot in town. I don't know if it's any good. But I figured since Barcelona is where things went left…maybe we could use some Spanish food to get back to where things were."

Rahman gestured toward the bench, where a foil-covered container of paella sat.

"You were a little late coming home from work, so it's cold now. But we can warm it up."

"Yeah…I walked home today."

"I figured. You walk when you're stressed out."

"Rahman, why are you here?"

"Because…I love you, man."

"I love you, too. But you shouldn't have come here."

"Give me ten minutes. Let me bring the balloons and the paella upstairs and just give me ten minutes. After that, I'll leave you alone for the rest of your life if that's what you want. But please, man. You gotta let me say my piece, okay?"

Jordan turned around, punched his security code in the front door of his walk-up, and opened it. Rahman followed him upstairs.

Once the paella was settled on the stove, the balloons were in a corner, and the carnations were placed in a vase, Rahman wasted no time with his opening arguments.

"I barely slept last night, for two reasons. The first reason was because everything you said to me was correct. I have been breadcrumbing you. I've been flirting with you for a long time with no promise of reward. You were absolutely right to call me out about that. I should not have been doing that to you, at all. As a man. As a married man. But most importantly, as your friend. A friend should not be treating you the way I did, for so long. I'm sorry for that. I hope you will forgive me some day."

Jordan nodded, acknowledging the gesture, but not yet accepting the apology or giving forgiveness.

"What was the second reason you couldn't sleep?" he asked. Rahman crossed his arms and rubbed his elbows slowly.

"I slept on the couch."

"And why'd you do that?"

"Shonda…she…kicked me out the bedroom."

"Why?"

"I told her about our fight. I told her you called me out for how I'd been treating you. And that you were right."

"Great. So, you told her I was in love with you. Now I gotta deal with that."

"No, Jordan. I told her that I was in love with you. And that she and I had been over for quite a while."

"What?!" Jordan panicked. The world around him seemed to suddenly be fake, like he woke up from a dream and realized he was someplace that he couldn't remember getting to. He became aware of the weight of his tongue in his mouth, the tickle of his locs on his ear, and the tension in his knuckles. He stretched and flexed his fingers as his lungs expanded and contracted.

Rahman walked to Jordan and held his hands. Jordan relaxed but pulled away all the same.

"Jordan, you know just about everything there is to know about me. Something I said to you last night…I believed it. I do believe it, but it's not complete. I said that I'm not attracted to men. That's true. I'm not attracted to men as a species. I think we're dumb, and gross, and ridiculous, and the cause of most of the problems in the world. And I think being a man who is attracted to men is probably the dumbest thing I could do, given the state of the world…and homophobia…and violence. We came up in a time where we could be killed just for being different. And I was scared for me. But more than that, I was scared for you. How you were carefree, living your life, dating men, not giving a shit. I envied that about you because I knew that's somebody I could never be. So, when I held you in Barcelona and kissed you on your head—when I thought you were asleep—I was saying goodbye. That was my coda. I knew I could never have you. That the world was meant for you, not for cowards like me. That if anybody could change how things were meant to be, it would be led by you. Not me.

"I thought I was leaving things in Barcelona and mentally setting you free. But I never stopped loving you. And over these past few years, we've gotten closer and closer. Jordan, you *are* my favorite person. You don't deserve second place. You don't deserve being in the shadows. You deserve to be loved out loud.

"I have done a really shitty thing by not being honest with you about my feelings. And I hope you understand I thought I was doing the right thing for you. But I should have been a man about it. I wasn't. But I'm trying now."

"But…Shonda…" Jordan muttered.

"The mother of my children and my soon-to-be ex-wife."

Jordan blinked.

"I'm filing for divorce. Called my lawyer on the way down here."

"Oh my God. You're getting a divorce," Jordan echoed. He placed his hand on his chest and sat.

"It's happening," Rahman said. He sat next to Jordan on his sofa and their knees touched. "No matter what happens with us today. My kids deserve two happy parents, even if they are happier apart."

"They're gonna be so hurt," Jordan said. Rahman grabbed Jordan's hand.

"People get divorced every day. But this? This doesn't happen every day. The chance to make things right."

"We wasted so much time, Rahman."

"No. I wasted time. You were nothing but my friend."

"But I loved you. This whole time. I loved you."

"I know you did, babe."

Jordan recoiled.

"'Babe.' Is that what you call me now?" he asked. Rahman palmed his forehead and sighed.

"It's better than Slim Goodbody, ain't it?" he laughed.

"I kind of like it," Jordan admitted. Rahman leaned over and kissed Jordan's bicep. He shivered.

"How are you sure? How can you be certain it's…me? How do you know—how do I know—it won't be somebody else next year? Or in five years?"

Rahman whispered in Jordan's ear.

"It has been you since your first day at Penn. Since the first day I had a conversation with you. Since Barcelona. Since before they killed Matthew Shepard. Since before gay marriage was legal. It was you when I broke down on my wedding day because I knew the mistake I was making. It was you when you called me out last night. And it's you now. I will spend the rest of my life proving to you that it's you."

He kissed Jordan's shoulder. More shivers.

"Have you…have you ever even been with a man?" Jordan asked.

"Never."

"I can't…teach you anything. I'm not a teacher, Rahman."

"I don't need you to teach me anything."

"I don't have a lot of patience."

"I don't need your patience. I am team Jordan, all day."

A tear formed in Jordan's eye and rolled down his face into his beard. Rahman kissed Jordan's cheek and wiped the tear away.

"I bet you don't even know how to kiss good," Jordan quipped.

Rahman caressed Jordan's neck and turned his head toward him. They closed their eyes and kissed softly on the lips for the first time in their lives. It was as tender and loving and rugged and passionate as each of them had hoped.

It felt like home.

"Needs work," Jordan joked. Rahman smiled and tried again and again. His hands found the buttons on Jordan's shirt, exposing his chest. It was the first time he'd seen Jordan's body in person since the beach in Barcelona.

"I'm still working out," he said proudly.

"I see, Goodbody," Rahman said. He dove his face into Jordan's chest and kissed him everywhere that he saw skin.

Jordan finally couldn't take it anymore. He peeled himself away from Rahman and stood up, pulling his partner up with him. He turned around and went to the kitchen with Rahman shuffling behind him, grabbing his waist the whole way. Jordan put the pan of paella into the refrigerator.

"Good thinking," Rahman said.

"Mmm-hm," Jordan replied. He took Rahman by the hand and led him to his bedroom, where they continued getting acquainted with one another, as though this moment hadn't been in the making for decades.

Jordan woke up exactly where he wanted to be—entangled in Rahman's limbs, stuck to him, and stuck on him.

3

The next few months were a whirlwind. Rahman and Lashonda were like two permanent powers of the United Nations Security Council threatening all-out war, but never really wanting to make the first move. Shonda was an investment banker and the thought of having to pay a man alimony after a divorce made her sick to her stomach. Rahman, in turn, didn't want to lose custody of the children.

Their mutual friends took sides. Most of their fellow Penn alums, her Sorors, and their whole church clique were firmly on Lashonda's side.

Rahman was a selfish son of a bitch who deserved nothing better than banishment to a Siberian penal colony. But Rahman's colleagues at work, his Harvard cohort, and most of his fraternity brothers had his back firmly, if quietly.

Everyone knew life would change for the whole intertwined friend groups, especially if the divorce was messy.

In the end, though, only two conversations mattered: Rahman's talk with his children and the initial talk with Shonda.

Rahman's elder child, Ramon, and his younger child, Melody, were typical teenagers of the Jack & Jill ilk. They were smart, well-spoken, and absolutely scandalized that their father was gay. They were not homophobic, and were not raised to be, but blamed their father for hurting their mother in such an unforgivable way—with a family friend, regardless of their gender. They made it clear they wanted nothing to do with "Uncle" Jordan and to not ask them to be around him.

With their words, they stated that they loved him, but they would need time to navigate this. Their actions, though, were cold. One-word texts. Forgotten Father's Day and birthday cards. No more invitations to school plays and track meets.

When he and Shonda finally sat down to talk about the terms of their divorce, he decided not to fight her on custody. She wanted the kids all the time, but Rahman was entitled to see them with notice. He knew that although Shonda was the mouthpiece of this decision, it was the children themselves who wanted the distance. They were close enough to being adults to make their own decisions.

Shonda would keep the house. Rahman would not seek spousal support. All he wanted was freedom. He needed it because he knew who he wanted.

Rahman knew he was a son-of-a-bitch and had nary a leg to stand on, either with his soon-to-be ex-wife or the love of his life. He knew if he wanted any future happiness, he would be a "yes, dear" to Jordan for all his days. He owed it to him, and he was more than happy to give it to him, not just because he was in love, but because Jordan's love freed him from the million decisions he had to make in a day. All he needed was to see Jordan smile and he'd be content with whatever he told him to do.

The day finally came when Rahman left Brooklyn. The children had gone on a ski trip with the teen group while Shonda stayed behind to make sure Rahman didn't fuck up her house or steal anything. Rahman did everything possible to avoid a conflict between his ex-wife and his love, so Jordan stayed at 42 Hotel on 5th Street in Williamsburg. It was a nice, cozy place for a working vacation.

Jordan took his laptop to the hotel lounge and checked his emails. It was early afternoon—late enough for a fancy cocktail in his estimation. He slowly sipped his cranberry-apple margarita. He shifted in his barstool as the alcohol loosened him up, and he daydreamed about the next phase in his life.

"I'll have what he's having," a woman's voice said as she slid into the seat next to him. He couldn't forget a voice—it was the sultry alto of Lashonda. She wasn't at home guarding the house after all.

"Lashonda," Jordan said, wide-eyed and caught off guard.

"Good afternoon, Mr. Bruce," Lashonda said with a smile.

"What are you…what are you doing here?" he asked.

"About to enjoy a cocktail with a family friend," she said unironically. Jordan didn't like the game she was playing.

"I don't want any problems," he said.

"Oh, we're about 16 years past 'problems,'" she chuckled. It was not the cold cackle of a witch with a final trick up her sleeve, but the warm laugh of an auntie holding a bad bid whist hand. Jordan was temporarily disarmed.

"I'm sorry about all this," he said.

"You're not. But…I appreciate you saying so." Her matching margarita arrived and she took a sip. It was delightful.

"Does Rahman know you're here?" Jordan asked.

"He doesn't clock my movements."

"I see."

"You know what I never liked about you, Jordan?" she asked after a few moments.

"I'm sure there's a lot about me you wouldn't like now," he replied.

"Cute. Aside from the rather obvious pining for my husband every day of your adult life—which I found adorable, if not pathetic. I never liked that you were never a straight shooter. Indirect at best. An outright liar at worst."

"I never lied to you, Lashonda."

"You lied to me every day you stood in my house and said happy birthday or merry Christmas. You are not sorry at all about what's going on here. This is, in fact, among the best possible case scenarios for you."

"I didn't take him from you, Lashonda. I always wished the best for your marriage."

"Cut the shit, Jordan. You think I'm here because I want some confrontation with you. I'm not gonna scratch your eyes out because you took my man. And make no mistake—you definitely took him. There is no other narrative now or in the future. No matter how much you love him, or he you, the fact will always remain that he was married. To me. It won't matter if you never touched him. Our children will know their father left their mother for you. That's not my burden."

"It's not."

"So what's next for you? And him?"

"I don't think—"

"You ready to play stepdaddy to these kids?"

"It's my understanding that they have no desire to see me that way."

"You understand correctly," she barbed. She gulped her margarita.

"You know what I wish for you, Jordan? I wish for you everything you wanted. Everything you prayed for. I hope you have a marriage just like mine was, with the man of your dreams. It's him, isn't it? It's Rahman. No matter what extraordinary, high-fallutin' men you might have dated, it's always been Rahman. And I want you to have him—I *want* you to have him. I want you to have the same sense of security I did. I want you to make all the sacrifices I made for him. For us. For whatever we were building. I want you to have all that. I want you to know—just how I knew—that I could only satisfy him 80 percent of the time. I want you to know what that feels like, Jordan. To love and marry someone who you know will always be looking someplace else to be complete. Enjoy that, Jordan. Enjoy the life you waited for. All the nice men you ignored, the relationships you undermined because they weren't Rahman. It all comes down to this. I hope you get what you prayed for."

Jordan's heart raced. He wanted to scream and swear and share all the mean things Rahman had said about his wife to him over the years. How she emasculated him in public and in private. How she hadn't had a shred of maternal instinct for their children or nurturing for her own marriage. He wanted to go deeper to the things he should have never known, such as the status of the moisture of her lady parts, or how her teeth got in the way when she tried to please Rahman. How Rahman hadn't touched her in six years. How Rahman's mother had hated her until the day she died.

He said nothing. It wasn't his moment. It was hers. Jordan's friends had convinced him that he'd gotten Rahman fair and square. That his patience and compassion for Rahman's situation had finally paid off. That he'd won—outright won Rahman away from Lashonda, just by being himself, and by playing the right card at the right time.

When he'd told Rahman he wouldn't be in the same house with the wife of the man that he loved, he never assumed that the best-case scenario could have played out. In fact, he'd expected everything to end then and there. Those words could have ended the breadcrumbing and 20 plus year courtship. But it didn't. It stoked a fire that had been burning for years and got the molasses out of Rahman's ass.

He became the man he was supposed to become because of Jordan. He stepped up for Jordan. He changed his life for Jordan. Jordan won.

And yet, the first wife's curse loomed over him like a dark cloud over Slope, insistent and insidious, forcing him to remember each word she'd said every day of their marriage, chipping away at who he was, and reminding him that no matter how much he loved Rahman, there was a reason his children were not interested in knowing the man he was now, or the man he loved. They were strangers to them.

Peek With the Good Hair: Friday, August 19, 2022

Peek placed a nickel-sized dollop of coconut oil into his palm, rubbed his hands together, and moisturized his scalp and hair. He cared about his appearance and always smelled good. He never dressed up and didn't care much about name brands, but he did want to look presentable and be memorable in a good way. He brushed his fine, curly hair down against his scalp and then wrapped it in a black du-rag.

He had performed this ritual countless times in his bedroom, where his old mahogany dresser had a huge mirror attached. When his mother watched him preen, she sucked her teeth and wondered from where he'd picked up his vanity. When Korey slept over, he would roll his eyes and accuse Peek of thinking he was cute.

"I don't think I'm cute. You think I'm cute. And that's your problem," Peek would say matter-of-factly.

Korey would then roll his eyes, curse, and change the subject—usually devolving into a terse game of the dozens, clowning Peek's shoes, off-brand fashions, and "Puerto Rican" hair.

Audree, Peek's sometime cuddle-buddy, called it "good hair" one night.

"What makes it good?" Peek asked her. She was taken aback. Nobody could question like Peek could.

"You know. It's soft. Pretty. Not beady-beads. Maybe even too soft to be dreadlocks."

Peek nodded.

"It's just hair. Like Pops' hair. Like most people in my family."

Audree smiled.

"All y'all got good hair."

Peek deflated. He was never going to get through to her.

"Yeah. We got good hair."

Now protected by the du-rag, Peek's hair would magically become wavy as physics and chemistry worked together to stretch his curls out against his scalp. He wanted his cousins to know he was somebody who cared about himself.

Dear Peek,

I am so sorry about the loss of your friend Gino. Thank you for telling me about him. He seems like he was an amazing friend to you.

Would you like to visit Howgill? We don't have as much to do here as there is in DC, but there is a spare bedroom in the family house, and we could surely feed you. Maybe you'd like to get away from all the excitement and just relax for a while.

I can't say this often enough: you are family and DNA proves it. As long as you are family, you will have a home in Westhampton County.

Love,
Cousin Kathy Stubbs

Korey, Gino, and Ziggy had all said Peek was crazy for doing a DNA test at all, much less for some private company collecting all sorts of data. They said he was even crazier for replying to the message from the crazy white lady claiming to be Peek's second cousin, once removed—whatever that meant. But Peek always knew his friends would never understand why.

Peek had been hearing he was the negative image of his great-grandfather all his life. Once he learned the common definition of negative, his feelings were hurt. Why would everybody say he was the bad version of someone else?

"Who said you were bad?" his grandmother asked him on the day he'd found the bravery to ask someone.

"My teacher. Sometimes. But everybody else say it all the time. 'He the negative version of Pops' is what y'all say all the time."

"Let me show you something, Peculiar," she said. She slid open a door in her buffet and grabbed a handful of small, blue envelopes with the word "Peoples Drug" printed on the outside. She opened the envelope and showed Peek the photographs inside.

"You see these pictures?" she asked. Peek nodded. "That's the final product. But back in the old days, pictures were taken with film. You put the film in a camera and then took the picture. The film gets exposed to light in a special way. You could only fit like 20 or 24 exposures from one roll of film. Then you took the film to be developed. When you develop the film, you get a negative. Look in that little pocket on the side."

Peek peered deep into the envelope and saw a short stack of brown pieces of plastic. His little fingers carefully removed them.

"That's the negative, Peek. The negative then gets projected, inverted, and printed. We get the prints. But we can't get the prints without the negative. Hold it up to the light. What do you see?"

"It looks like a picture, but it looks funny. All the dark people look light. But the sky looks dark."

"And that's why they say you're my daddy's negative. Not because you're bad. But because you look just alike, except he's light and you're dark."

"Oh," Peek said. He shrank with embarrassment.

"Now you know! And there's nothing wrong with not knowing something, unless you're determined to keep not knowing."

Young Peek hugged his grandmother and then ran outside to play. Grown Peek had no more time to play.

"I'm going down to Westhampton," Peek announced as his mom and great-grandfather ate their lunch on the porch. A breeze blew through the neighborhood,

His mother immediately stopped eating her sandwich. Pops continued without meeting Peek's gaze.

"What you wanna go down there for? You ain't never been before." She was a big woman with a round face and round eyes—showing very little common DNA with either Peek or Pops and their hard, angular features. She took after her own father in that way.

"That's exactly why I'm going. I got questions about where I come from."

"You come from Slope. We all come from Slope. This just sound stupid, Peek—going someplace you ain't never been to get answers you ain't even entitled to. You wanna know something, ask Pops."

"Pops knows I gotta do this. Don't you, Pops?"

Pops finished chewing a bite of his sandwich.

"Ain't nothing in Westhampton County but cotton fields, pitiful corn, and white trash. But you wanna go? Go. You'll see for yourself why I left and never came back."

"All you gotta do is tell me why I got white cousins, Pops."

"I don't have to do shit but stay Black and die!" Pops shouted. Shocked, Peek lowered his chin, blinked slowly, and curled his mouth.

"Aight. Bet." Peek stormed into the house and stomped up the stairs to his room.

"Peek! Peek, come back here!" his mother called. He ignored her as he began putting underwear, socks, and joggers into his bookbag. In no time, his mother arrived at his open door.

"Ain't nobody finna bass on me like that, not even Pops," he said.

"Peek, he just scared for you. He don't want you to get hurt."

"Then he need to say that. I'm tired of people talking at me, barking at me like I'm not a person. I'm a person, Ma. I walk down East Cap and niggas on the block look at me like a target. I walk down Wisconsin Ave and I look like a threat to them white people. I walk down Park Road in my school shirt and everybody act like I'm in the way, and the teachers think I'm dumb. I am a person, Ma. I shouldn't have to come home and be treated like I don't belong here, either."

"I understand that, Peek. But do you think it's gonna be better down in the country?"

"I gotta see it for myself. I wanna know the things Pops won't tell us. I'm old enough. I'm smart enough. And I'm not gonna let nothing bad happen to me, at least nothing that could be worse if I stayed."

"Don't go by yourself, then."

"You coming on the bus with me?"

"Hell no. Get Ziggy to go with you."

"Ziggy gotta work."

"Then wait."

"I'm not waiting."

"Please. Find somebody to go with you."

"Ma. I'll be fine."

With tears threatening to fall from her eyes, Peek's mother left the room.

The next morning, he left the house before everybody rose. Though he was still angry at everyone, he left them a note with Cousin Kathy's address. He was out of the house by seven.

At Slope's intersection, he could walk straight and make it to the Capitol Heights Metro station in about ten minutes, but he caught a glimpse of the Gaffney-Bruce porch down the hill. He didn't feel right leaving the neighborhood without letting them know.

Jordan wasn't sitting on the porch yet, although Peek knew that's where he liked to start his day. He also noticed that Rahman's car wasn't in their driveway, but Jordan's was. He walked the short path to their door and knocked. Jordan's footsteps tapped their way to the door. It swung open.

"Peek?" Jordan stood in bare feet, gray sweatpants, and a black sleeveless t-shirt. His hair was all over his head, like he didn't sleep in a du-rag or bonnet or anything.

"Good morning, Mr. Gaffney-Bruce," Peek said.

"What's wrong?"

"Nothing's wrong. I'm going out of town for a little while and I thought telling you would be a good thing."

"Where are you going?"

"North Carolina."

"To do what?"

"It's a long story."

"Well…come inside. Have some breakfast before you go. And you can tell me the long story."

Peek stepped inside, placed his bookbag on the floor, and stepped into the Gaffney-Bruce living room. As Jordan cracked eggs and fried bacon, Peek explained how he took an interest in genealogy during a school project. How he started working on his family tree, first for credit, then for fun. How he saved up for a DNA test. How he uploaded his results and got contacted by a white lady in Westhampton County, who had also done a test, and it proved they were related. How everybody in the family had kept their mouths shut when he shared these developments. And how now, more than ever, he had to get some answers.

"I told Pops. I told my mother. Now I'm telling you where I'ma be," Peek concluded. He took a sip of organic orange juice.

"Oh. Why me, though?" Jordan asked.

"You seem like the type dude know what to do if something happen to me."

"Peek, what do you think is gonna happen to you?"

Peek shrugged.

"So, you're just gonna go all the way to God-knows-where North Carolina, to visit some white chick that says she's related to you, and then what? Stay?"

Peek shrugged again.

"Boy! This is not a plan!"

"I ain't say I had a plan. I said I had to go."

"Listen. I appreciate that you came to me before you left. That's very responsible of you. And I am very grateful that you told me your story. It seems like you trust me."

"I do."

"I hope that you hear me when I say this next thing to you. I respect you immensely, and this whole community loves you. I do not think it's wise for you to go visit someone you do not know. You don't know this woman. You've only communicated with her through the DNA app, right?"

"Yeah. And text."

"Have you even heard her voice? What if the person on the other end of the texts isn't even her?"

"But it's her DNA."

"Maybe it's Kathy's DNA. But what if it was another family member who did the test? Or a friend? What if the person you've been talking to isn't connected to the results? They could be setting you and Kathy Stubbs up."

"Why would anybody do that?"

"Why does anybody do what they do? People are crazy. Look, why don't you at least call this lady and hear her voice?"

"Right now?"

"Yeah. Right now. Put her on speaker phone."

"Okay." Peek started dialing Kathy's number and put on speaker phone so Jordan could hear.

"Hey Peek!" a soft drawl said.

"Hey Kathy. I'm about to leave DC in a little bit to come down there."

"Oh, wonderful! The spare bedroom is ready for you."

"Hi Kathy, this is Jordan Gaffney-Bruce. I'm a friend of the Jones family. How are you?" Peek had never heard Jordan's professional phone voice before, and it made him giggle. Jordan rolled his eyes.

"Well, hello Jordan!"

"Yes, I'm sure you can understand that nobody's excited to send their child to another state to meet family members they've never heard of before." Jordan had a knack for getting to the point.

"I can imagine. Some of my family members feel the same way about discovering a new cousin and having them in my house. I'm glad we're getting this out in the open."

"So, will Peek be safe there? Let's get real for a second, okay? Do they fly confederate flags down there?"

"There are no confederate flags on my property, but I can't promise he won't see any elsewhere. But by and large, this is the kind of community that doesn't really wear our politics on our sleeves. We've got Black folks and white folks in this community. Very little crime. We mind our business and keep it moving."

"And does the bus stop in town?"

"No. I imagine I'd pick up Peek from Ahoskie. I'm about 45 minutes from there."

"Can you hold on for a second?"

"Sure!"

"Put her on hold," Jordan whispered. Peek's finger pushed the hold button.

"Ahoskie! How long is this bus ride?"

"Like six, seven hours. Transferring in Richmond."

"How long would it take if you drove?"

"You know I don't drive, Mr. Gaffney-Bruce. Ain't got no car anyway."

Jordan Googled the answer on his phone while Peek spoke.

"Four and a half hours. Not bad. Take her off speaker." Peek complied.

"Hi Kathy, Jordan Gaffney-Bruce again. Listen, I'm going to accompany Peek on this little odyssey. I presume there are hotels in Ahoskie?" Peek's eyes widened.

"Yes, there are a few places in Ahoskie. I'm looking forward to meeting you both."

"We'll call when we're settled in. See you then."

Jordan pushed the phone to Peek, who hung up.

"You really gon' take me to North Carolina?" he asked.

"Yeah. I guess I am," Jordan said with a slight grin.

"Your husband gon' be okay with that?"

Jordan's smile disappeared.

"Let's get one thing straight, young sir. My husband doesn't own me or control me. He a grown ass man and I'm a grown ass man. If I wanna take a weekend trip to see…I don't know, farms and cows? Then that's what I'm gonna do and letting him know about it is a courtesy."

"Oh. Y'all having a fight."

"Never mind that. I'm gonna shower and get ready. And hey, put your mama's number in my phone. I'm gonna call her to let her know I got this covered."

"Thank you, Mr. Gaffney-Bruce. I really appreciate this."

"Somehow, I feel like if the shoe was on the other foot, maybe you'd do the same thing for me if I wasn't thinking straight."

"I'm thinking straight, man. Trust me."

Jordan nodded and walked to his bedroom, peeling off his t-shirt along the way. Peek put his mother's name and number in Jordan's phone and added the landline for good measure. Before he put Jordan's phone back down, he noticed the wallpaper: Jordan and Rahman's wedding day, both wearing black tuxedoes.

He put the phone on the coffee table and walked to the sofa, noticing a carry-on suitcase already packed.

The other one went somewhere without him, he mused. He made a note to ask Jordan about it later. Not now, though. He needed them to get on the highway before Jordan changed his mind.

2

"I've never seen you smile this much, young sir."

"Wouldn't you be happy to be leaving DC, too?"

"Maybe so, if I went through as much as you have."

Peek nodded.

"So…you wanna tell me why you beefing with the other Mister?"

"We're not beefing. We were supposed to be going to New York this weekend to visit Rahman's kids. But…they decided they only wanted to see him."

"But you they step-daddy. They can't uninvite you."

"I'm not their stepfather. I'm Jordan to them. And that's fine."

"They wack as fuck."

"I don't think they're wack. They just expected things to be a certain way. Then everything changed."

"They still don't need to be blocking you from traveling with your man."

"I could have gone. But what's the point, you know? I'm getting too old to have conflict in my house."

"How old are you?"

"47."

"Damn! How old is your mister?"

"49."

"Got damn! Why y'all look so young?"

"Gay Black don't crack," Jordan quipped. Peek's mouth opened wide and he wheezed.

"Yeah, I guess not having no woman and no kids keeps you young."

"Maybe so," Jordan sighed. "How old are your parents?"

"My mother 41. My father dead."

"What happened to him?"

"Standing on the wrong corner. He got shot down 34th. I was real little, two or three. I don't remember him."

"That's too bad, Peek."

"It is what it is. Life gotta go on."

"What about Ziggy? His father dead, too?"

"Naw. I mean, I don't know. Ziggy don't know who his father is. He used to say David Bowie was his father, but he stopped saying that when he died. Korey father around, though."

"I still haven't really met Korey."

"You ain't missing nothing," Peek said curtly as he looked out the passenger seat window.

"It's a lot of trees and shit out here," he mused.

"You ever been camping?"

"Hell no. Fuck I look like camping? What I need to sleep outside for when I got a bed indoors?"

"It's not so bad."

"You be camping?"

"Every now and then. It's fun when you're with people you know. I went one summer as a kid, too. Camp Catoctin, out Maryland. That was okay. Stressful as a child, though."

"Lotta white people?"

"Yeah, it was. But it was cool. It wasn't no racism or anything like that."

"Still. Leave me home. I gotta put my head down on a mattress and a pillow."

Jordan nodded. The ride was full of spurts in which Peek revealed more and more of himself, and long stretches of silence.

I could have done this, Jordan thought to himself. He never thought of himself as a parent, and besides a brief spell when he was 26, he never had the urge to be a father. But riding with Peek felt easy to him. Maybe it was because he knew he would take Peek back to his parents, or because he felt more like a consultant than a manager, but he felt like Peek was listening to him and might be all the better for the conversations.

Or maybe he was a bit sad that he couldn't have this with his stepchildren. Ramon and Melody were spoiled children, and he knew it— as "Uncle Jordan" he was one of many who supplied the children with endless gifts and visits to museums and plays. It was hard to forget they were once very special to him, just because they were Rahman's.

But the moment they were old enough to realize Uncle Jordan meant so much more to their dad, they rightfully assessed Jordan as an interloper. And perhaps Jordan and Rahman married far too quickly after Rahman's divorce, but this is what they'd wanted: to prioritize their own lives and their own wishes for once.

That came with consequences. That meant sometimes, Jordan would be at home waiting for his husband to return from uncomfortable visits to New York. That meant Jordan would be left feeling like the other woman after all, despite finally getting the ring.

"We're not far from Howgill now," Jordan told Peek. The woods gave way to rolling fields of green cotton plants and short cornstalks.

"I'm getting a little nervous in my stomach," Peek confided.

"Nah playa, don't get nervous now! You wanted this. You wanted to meet your DNA test cousins."

"I know, I know. I can still be nervous about doing the right thing, though."

"Yeah. You're right. But I support you, okay? However this turns out, I got your back."

"I appreciate that, Mr. Gaffney-Bruce."

The Charles Mingus track "Goodbye Pork Pie Hat" interrupted their moment. Rahman was calling—finally—and Jordan wasn't looking forward to it.

"Hey," Jordan said through speakerphone.

"Where are you?"

"On 258 about to cross the North Carolina line."

"Are you serious right now?"

"Yes. Didn't you get my voicemail and my texts?"

"Yeah, when I got to Brooklyn. I'm trying to figure out how you think it's a good idea to take a neighborhood kid to meet a stranger from the internet."

"First of all, you're on speakerphone—"

"Hi, Mr. Gaffney-Bruce!" Peek said cheerily.

"—and second of all, we know Peek and we know his family. I had nothing to do this weekend, for reasons well-known to you, and I thought it would be cool to make sure he got to his destination safely while taking in some sights."

"Sights of country-ass North Carolina?"

"I could have been in Brooklyn, couldn't I have?"

Rahman was silent for a few tense moments.

"Take me off speaker," he demanded. Jordan picked up the phone and put it to his ear. Peek could hear half of the conversation.

"You're off speaker...yup...yeah. Of course. That's not my fault, is it? My bag was by the door and you—uh-huh. Yeah, whatever. There's nothing else to say. Excuse me? *Excuse me?!* It's not like that at all. You think so little of me? Of us? Listen...You wanna talk to him? Because you know he'd tell you the truth...no? Yeah, I thought not. I'll let you know when we get there, okay? Enjoy New York."

Jordan clicked off the phone and put it back in the holster. He noticed a sign reading "Virginia is for Lovers" and sighed.

"You good?" Peek asked.

"Yeah. I'm good."

3

It was a miracle anyone had thought to put a motel anywhere near Howgill, North Carolina. The Sunshine Motel wasn't in Ahoskie proper, as Cousin Kathy had said, but was a few miles outside of town, facing an expanse of land that headed to Howgill via Highway 35. Next door, about a hundred feet, was a Dollar General. On the other side, a vape shop.

"That vape shit weird," Peek announced.

Peek didn't know how funny he really was, Jordan thought. His quips always caught Jordan off-guard, but he wasn't sure if he should laugh or not. One thing he did know about the young people of the day is that they were sensitive and liable to fly off the handle at any perceived slight.

That's what must have happened to Gino, he surmised. Another life lost for no reason at all, taken by God-knows-who. They'd probably never find out who did it. Even if Peek and Ziggy knew—which Jordan doubted—they'd never snitch anyway.

Jordan booked two adjoining king rooms and deposited Peek in his own. Immediately, Peek went to the door that connected the rooms and opened his.

"Hurry up and open the other side," Peek said with a laugh.

"Okay, okay. Jeez," Jordan said. He opened his own door, a few feet away, wheeled his bag inside, and opened the door in between the rooms.

"Now it's like we got one big ass room," Peek announced.

"Call your mom to let her know we got here safely," Jordan said. Peek complied, while Jordan started unpacking.

The Ritz-Carlton, it was not, but a few nights here wouldn't kill him, Jordan thought. He smiled a little to see Peek light up when talking to his mother about the hotel room.

"Ayo…" Peek called out.

"What's up?" Jordan asked.

"Kathy said we could meet her for dinner at this pizza joint nearby."

A few hours later, after a nap, Jordan pulled up to Tony's Pizza in Howgill. As he and Peek got out of the car, Jordan asked him if he was still nervous.

"Yeah. But I'ma be aight." He pushed open the tinted glass door. Everyone in the restaurant was white—something that had never happened to either of them before, at least not in America, in Jordan's case. Most of the folks sitting at the tables were older, perhaps in their 60s, but there were also a few families with small children in booster seats.

A middle-aged woman wearing a white tank top waved her hand high in the air.

"Hey, y'all!" she called. "It's Kathy!"

Peek smiled and laughed nervously as the woman rose from her chair and raised her arms out. Peek hugged her and she gripped him tightly.

"I'm Peek," he said.

"I know. I'm Cousin Kathy," she replied, choked up. As she let him go, Jordan extended his hand.

"Jordan Gaffney-Bruce." Kathy's grip was as tight as her hug.

"I'm so glad you're here. Please, have a seat," she said. The server quickly came by with menus and took their drink orders.

"How was your trip?" she asked.

"It was good," Peek said softly. "Saw a lot of crops and cows and whatnot."

"Well, I just bet you did," she teased. "It's about all there is to see down here!"

"How do the folks down here spend their free time?" Jordan asked.

"Some folks are really into hunting. The kids get into sports and 4-H. A lady has been trying to get an arts program running for the kids, too. But the grown-ups mainly mind their business and work. Might see some old men in the lodge. Oh, and some ladies do things with the firefighter's auxiliary."

"So…big fun, huh?" Peek asked. Kathy laughed.

"You are so sarcastic, I love it. And what about y'all? I bet there's plenty fun to do in DC."

"I just be chillin'," Peek said.

"Peek's got a tight little friend group," Jordan offered. "There's a small circle of guys, but there's also a group of girls that hang out with them, too. All good kids."

"I bet they are," Kathy said. "If Peek's any indication. Now what do the adults do for fun?"

"I guess we mind our business, same as you all. Me and my husband like traveling. And concerts. And throwing small house parties, when we can."

"Oh y'all seem *fun*," Kathy said.

"Yeah. I guess we are fun."

The server, a brunette girl of about 17, came back and took their orders. She wondered what sort of thing Kathy had going on now.

"Cousin Kathy, I appreciate you taking time to meet me, especially on short notice. But with everything going on, I needed to get away from home for a little bit. I got questions about…about who I am. And I gotta know…how are we related?"

"Peek…I just don't know. The website said we could be anywhere from second to fifth cousins. We don't have the same last name. There are no interracial marriages in my family. And my family…well, let's just say I'm the outsider."

Jordan sipped his Sprite slowly.

"I've always been the curious one. The one who travels—when I can—to other places. I voted for Hillary while they all voted for Trump. I help that lady with the art program, when I can. And they all look at me like I've got three heads. But I just try to do what's right. It's all we really have, isn't it? The freedom to choose right or wrong."

"So, when you told the family you found a distant, Black cousin…" Jordan began.

"They laughed it off. Didn't believe me."

"Judging by these glances I keep noticing from everyone else in the restaurant, seems like the whole town will believe you, now."

"Howgill is a sad place, really," Kathy said. "The owners of this restaurant don't have a racist bone in their body. But because it's on the so-called 'white' side of town, the Black folks don't even bother coming over here. Just like the white folks never go support Trina's Diner. It's not hate…it's culture. And nobody challenges it."

"Because they just be minding their business," Peek concluded.

"Exactly."

Their extra-large supreme pizza arrived, and they picked at it somberly for a few minutes. Peek, especially, was lost in thought.

"Why didn't you ever leave Westhampton County?" Jordan asked.

"Oh, I did. I went to East Carolina University. Got my master's in counseling up at Montclair State, and stayed in New Jersey for a few years. But when my mother got sick, I came back. She died right after I turned 30."

"I'm sorry to hear that," Jordan said.

"That was many years ago, now. I'll be 'bout ready to retire in a few more years."

Peek nodded.

"Peek…we're gonna make this thing right. I'm guessing my uncle Jed is going to be about the only person alive who can answer your questions."

"Uncle Jed?"

"He's 82. My mother's oldest brother."

"Pops is 90. You think they knew each other?"

"I don't know, Peek. If you think Howgill is segregated now, I'm sure it was decades ago."

"Well, I guess it's only one way to find out."

"I'll take you to the family house tomorrow. We have brunch there most Saturdays. You and Jordan can come."

"That's gonna be awkward," Peek said.

"And I think necessary," Jordan said.

Back at the motel, Peek remained quiet.

"Are you okay?" Jordan asked. Peek nodded. "You don't look okay."

"Something tell me I ain't gon' get no answers down here."

Jordan sighed.

"That's a possibility. But how does your life change if you don't get any answers? The easy parts of life will still be easy. The hard parts will still be hard. And you will still be you."

Peek nodded.

"You want kids?" he asked.

"I'm child-free," Jordan said.

"Yeah, but did you ever *want* kids?"

"Not really…" Jordan said. Peek nodded.

"I want kids…someday," Peek said. "But I don't…like…wanna raise 'em the way I was raised. I know my family loves me. But they love got rough edges. Like the military. I know everything they did, they did because they love me. But I ain't always need strict. Sometimes I needed soft. I don't wanna have to raise my kids like they gotta be ready for war."

"I hear you."

"You seem like you get it. You know, you not having kids is your business. Not wanting them. Okay. But I know you know you be good at it."

"Thanks, Peek." Jordan smiled, never knowing how to take an authentic compliment.

Like clockwork, Jordan got up at three am to go pee, as he had since the day he'd turned forty-two. Enough neon light peeked through the curtains to illuminate his path to the bathroom. He sighed silently, relieved himself, and flushed, forgetting for a moment that Peek was in the adjoining room and had left the doors between them open.

He washed his hands, patted them dry, and walked silently back to his bed. He stopped at the open door. Peek's light snoring broke the silence. Slope was the kind of neighborhood where even though there wasn't much violence or disturbance, there was still always something going on, somebody moving, somebody coming in late from work. As Peek's chest rose and fell, Jordan was grateful that out here in Westhampton County, Peek could get the good night's sleep he deserved.

4: Saturday, August 20, 2022

White Corelle bowls with etched blue designs contained mountains of grits with melted butter. Matching platters of bacon, country sausage, and buttermilk biscuits contrasted glass pitchers of orange juice and lemonade. Freshly scrambled eggs emanated steam next to slices of white toast, while sticks of butter finally warmed enough to be sliced into small pats.

The Saturday brunch spread at the Stubbs house, the stateliest manor in all of Howgill, was legendary.

Kathy grew up attending those brunches, and she hated them. The food was amazing, of course, but the conversation was as stifling as the dresses she had to wear. As a nearly retired adult, she attended them more often now than when she was raising her own children her own way. Now, she knew any of these Saturdays could be the last time she saw some of her elders, and she'd hate losing them. But in the eighties, when her grandmother had slapped her across the face for speaking ill of President Reagan, she knew these meals were her family's way of maintaining the status quo in Westhampton County.

Her sons lived in Denver and Houston, respectively. Dan was gay and married to a nice young man he'd met in graduate school, and they owned a coffee shop together. Richie, on the other hand, had married a Black woman with three children of her own already. It didn't matter to the rest of the family that the children had been born in wedlock and their father had died in the line of duty in Afghanistan, or that she made her own money as a successful realtor. She might as well have been the type of "welfare queen" her grandfather had spoken about while he was alive.

Kathy's ex-husband lived near Dan in Colorado and had found work as a housepainter. It was the same work he'd done in the county, but he was happy to follow his son as far away from Howgill as possible. He still loved Kathy, but didn't love how she couldn't seem to escape from her family's influence. She was a masochist that way.

Peek had never seen a house as big as the Stubbs family manse, although he'd heard Qiang's house in Prince George's County was big. Nor did he expect to see so many acres of lawn surrounding the house, with fields of soy plants surrounding the yard lawn. Far in the distance were trees. What was beyond those trees was outside of Peek's imagination.

Old Mr. Stubbs stood at the top of the porch. Peek was startled by him—he was tall and lean, with a sullen face full of liver spots. But beneath the irregular patches of flesh and wispy white hairs spotting his skull was a man who looked like a sickly version of Pops.

He leaned on his cane. Two strapping boys who appeared to be Peek's age flanked him. Jordan noticed the porch's white paint flaking off, exposing drab gray wood underneath.

"Hi Uncle Jed," Kathy cheerfully greeted. "Bud, Tommy. I'd like you to meet the cousin I've been talking about, Peek Jones. And his friend, Mr. Gaffney-Bruce."

"Cousin…" Uncle Jed repeated with a groan. Bud and Tommy sized up the men, then extended their hands.

"Hey," Peek said. Silently, they shook hands. Peek then turned his hand to Jed. Jed turned around and entered the house.

"Paw don't really shake hands," Tommy said with a shrug. Jordan clenched his teeth. The old wooden porch sagged under his weight as they all entered the home.

To Peek, the house immediately seemed smaller on the inside. It smelled of humid wood and dusty furniture. To the right was a sitting room with about a hundred tiny ceramic objects decorating every flat surface. To the left was a much larger living area with a big screen television mounted to the far wall. Beyond the living room, behind sliding wooden doors, was the dining room, where all the food was on display. The greasy pork smell finally overpowered the smell of old house, right before Peek thought he would sneeze.

A few old ladies and one other old man were already seated. Kathy's female cousins worked away in the adjoining kitchen, while some of the male cousins walked up behind Jordan and Peek.

"Hello," they grunted.

"Hi everyone," Peek said. The vibe was already off. He wanted to go home right away. Yet he pushed through his anxiousness and took a seat.

"You got this," Jordan whispered.

"Say grace, Maggie," Uncle Jed barked at his niece who had placed a pitcher of sweet tea on the table. She flinched a bit, then complied.

"Gracious Father, thank you for this food we are about to receive for the nourishment and strength of our bodies. Bless the hands that prepared it and bless those at this table, including our guests. In Jesus' name we pray, amen," she prayed.

"Amen," the table said in unison.

Kathy tried hard to carry the mealtime conversation. She loudly asked Peek flattering questions about himself, like what subjects he liked in school (Social Studies), what his plans were after getting his GED (Not sure, but he'd like to get some computer certifications), whether he was dating anyone (yes), and whether it was serious (no). She asked him what his favorite part about DC was (the people), and if he could travel anywhere in the world, where would he go (Nigeria, since that's where Ancestry said he was from).

The only question anybody else asked him was from a lady who had been cooking.

"Your name…Peek…it's got to be short for something. Is it?"

Peek blushed under his dark skin. Nobody had asked him his real name since he had enrolled at Alternative Futures.

"Peculiar, actually."

The woman's eyebrows furrowed.

"Who looks at their baby and decides to name them Peculiar? That's like calling them strange," she said softly.

"My mother did. She looked at me and decided I was special, and there would only ever be one of me. 'Strange' ain't even the first meaning of peculiar in the dictionary. But, whatever, I guess."

The woman shrugged, glanced at Uncle Jed, and resumed eating.

Jordan was proud of how Peek had handled that interaction. Further, Jordan noticed the rest of the family ate quietly and kept looking to Uncle Jed for their cues, like this woman had. Like Peek, Jordan didn't have a good feeling about the guy, but his resemblance to old Mr. Jones seemed obvious to him. They were certainly related.

After a while, forks clinked on empty plates and Stubbs family members cleared their throats. Peek's heart raced. He looked at Jordan, who nodded.

"Mister Jed—" Peek began.

"Mister Stubbs will do," the old man warbled.

"Mister Stubbs…thank you for having me and Mr. Gaffney-Bruce in your home for brunch. We really appreciate it."

"Thank my niece. She invited you here."

"I was hoping you could help fill in some gaps for me. Our DNA test said we're cousins."

"I can't vouch for what the Mormons and their data collection says about your DNA."

"Well, the science—"

"Science can certainly be manipulated. Forged even."

"That's not—"

"Besides, I can't vouch for Kathy's parentage anyway. Who knows who her Momma was laying down with."

"Uncle Jed! How dare you?" Kathy said.

"How dare I? No, how dare you? Bringing strangers into my house, eating my food. Can't even pull their pants up to their waist good."

"My pants ain't got nothing to do with why I'm here, sir. Respectfully." Peeks fists clenched in his lap. "You look like my grandfather, Mister Stubbs. I ain't wanna see it. But I do. You could be siblings."

"I have seven brothers and two sisters, and I can assure you, none of them look like you."

"But he looks like you. See?"

Peek held up his phone and showed the table a photo of Pops, complete with his slicked down hair and sharp nose. Uncle Jed turned his face away.

"I reckon it's about time for you to go," Jed said. Tommy and Bud stood, as did Jordan and Peek, with a rumble as the wooden chairs slid across the hardwood floors.

"Uncle Jed, be reasonable," Kathy pleaded.

"Shut up, Kathy," a man said.

"Let's go, Peek," Jordan said.

"I'm going," Peek announced, pushing past Bud.

"Thanks for…well…whatever this was," Jordan said, nodding to everyone at the table before he made his own exit. Kathy tearfully reached out to Jordan.

"I don't know what you're crying for," Jordan spat. "You knew your family wasn't ready to be related to Black folk. And you're just here eating all this up on the sidelines."

Kathy covered her mouth with her hands and turned away. Jordan hurried out. Peek was already standing beside Jordan's car.

"Man, fuck this place!" he shouted.

"I know. Let's just go," Jordan said calmly.

"Peculiar. Wait one second." Uncle Jed stood at the top of his porch, leaning once again on his cane. Peek and Jordan walked on the gravel driveway and stopped.

"My family has always been good to the people of Howgill. Always. We were one of the first families to renounce slavery. Look it up. It's right there in the county history books. Don't leave Westhampton County thinking the Stubbs family is like everybody else down here. We're not."

"With all due respect, Mr. Stubbs, who can tell the difference?" Jordan asked earnestly. Jed scoffed.

"You don't know the whole story, Mr. Gaffney-Bruce. This is a sensitive matter. My father was accused of a vicious, terrible crime in the early 1930s. He was sixteen years old. A boy. For my daddy to be accused of what that woman accused him of…it's simply unconscionable."

"Who? What did she accuse him of?" Peek asked.

"Dorothy Anne Jones. A name I could never forget—the woman that almost took down my family. Miss Dorothy pops up with a little beige baby and accuses my daddy of being the father."

Peek's eyebrows rose.

"My daddy was a boy. She was a greedy Jezebel who wanted to steal everything my family had worked for in Howgill."

"How you know that?" Peek asked.

"Everybody knew it, boy. What would my daddy have wanted with a Black woman?"

"Be cool, Peek," Jordan said. Peek nodded.

"Ten years go by, and despite this woman going around trying to ruin my daddy's reputation, he marries my mother, a good Methodist woman from the next county over. She gets pregnant with my sister Mary, who's born first. And that's when the shit hits the fan."

"How so?" Jordan asks.

"She could never prove rape. And she got around—anybody could have fathered the mongrel. She couldn't get anything from the civil courts, either. So, she goes to his Sunday morning meeting with her story, and you know what these people did? They believed her—and forced him to acknowledge the child as his own. They did this in an open meeting, and then made him draw up a will that legitimized the bastard as one of his heirs."

"He admitted…?" Jordan asked.

"Under the coercion of a religious cult, he changed his will to acknowledge the half-breed. Can you believe that? In these United States of America, a religious group guilted a man into acknowledging a child that wasn't even his."

"What happened to the woman and her baby?" Peek asked.

"His mother died. Poor thing walked off into the night soon after this meeting. Must have gotten confused and fell into the river. Body washed up the next day. The boy got raised by his grandparents. When he came of age, he went up north as a young man, never to be heard from again."

"He never came back to reclaim his legacy?"

"He had no legacy here. His parentage was a lie."

"Seems to me, Mr. Stubbs, that the lie is what you were told. The truth is in the will, and those meeting minutes. The truth is in my blood. Seems like I'm the descendant of the baby that came up north."

"Descendant? Boy, you ain't worth the spit it would take to cuss you out."

Peek squinted his eyes and laughed at Mr. Stubbs. It was not the cackle of a supervillain or the chuckle of arrogance. It was a good old sudden guffaw. The south sure had a lot of colorful phrases and even more colorful people, Peek thought, but this guy took the cake.

"Whatchu laughing at, boy?" Stubbs huffed.

"I'm laughin' at you, man!" Peek howled.

"Peek, let's go," Jordan whispered.

"Yeah, get outta here, man," Bud hissed.

"This man said I ain't worth the spit it would take to cuss me out," Peek repeated. "That sound like some shit somebody would say on Netflix. The fuck?" Peek laughed some more, doubling over. Stubbs began to turn around and climb the steps up his front porch.

"I am worth it, you know," Peek continued, now deadly serious. Stubbs turned back around and rested his hand on the wooden post at the top of the stairs. He stared.

"I am worth all the spit it would take to cuss me out, sir. I'm worth the gas it took to drive here. I'm worth the risk cousin Kathy took when she reached out to me on Ancestry. And if I don't know nothing else, I'm worth the years of secrets your family was depending on to keep me and mine away from here. Seem to me like all this land you standing on? I'm worth it."

"Gon' and get outta here now," Tommy barked.

"I am, Cousin Tommy," Peek teased. "I know y'all just afraid."

"The hell we got to be 'fraid of?" Bud demanded.

"You see me and think about everything you could lose, because you got it the wrong way. This house. This land. Everything you think special about Howgill. But what you got here that you think I would want? A run-down house? Overgrown fields? God don't even know you here, why would I wanna be here with you?" Peek demanded.

"Get off my granddaddy's land, ni—" Tommy shouted. In the milliseconds before the "gger" could spew from Tommy's lips, Peek's long legs carried him and his black fist to Tommy's jaw.

And that's how the fight started.

Peek and Jordan had two different recollections of that afternoon. If you believed Peek, a dozen white supremacists with 'roid rage emerged from the house like the Crazy 88s did in *Kill Bill*, and he took them out, one by one, with help from Jordan. That he stood over their broken bodies and swore he'd reclaim his land. That Jordan drove them off into the sunset with tears in his eyes.

If you believed Jordan, who'd never been in a fight in his adult life, you might be closer to the truth: that the fists flew suddenly, that he put himself between Peek and the redneck cousins, that he caught a few blows to the body and one to the face, and that seeing his cut cheek sent Peek into a rage the likes of which he'd never seen before.

In any case, by the time they sped off the premises, Bud and Tommy lay prone on the ground, Kathy was in hysterics, and Uncle Jed was throwing rocks at the car as they left. It wasn't until they got to Roanoke Rapids that Peek even realized that his left shoe was somewhere still on the ground at the Stubbs property.

Peek remembered that fight for the rest of his life—not just because it was epic, but because, for the first time, he knew what it meant for someone to really take a hit for you. Mr. Gaffney-Bruce was his main man fifty-grand from that moment onward.

The Party

Through dumb luck and a distracted afternoon surfing eBay, Jordan found a vintage ice bucket that matched the tumbler set he'd purchased in Bethesda. He placed it on the mahogany buffet that served as the centerpiece of the Gaffney-Bruce living room and arranged the tumblers on either side.

He sniffed something foul.

I know he didn't...

Jordan stomped to the kitchen. Two bags of trash taunted him at the back door.

"Rahman!" he shouted upstairs.

"Yeah?" his husband called back.

"Can you please take out the trash like I asked you to three times since yesterday?"

"Damn, I forgot! My bad!" Rahman bounded down the stairs in his sleeveless t-shirt, gray sweatpants, and crocs. Within two minutes, the trash had been taken out.

"All done!" Rahman triumphantly announced. Jordan rolled his eyes.

"What?"

"I make 20 million decisions a day at work and in support of this household. I'm handling every single aspect of this party and all you have to do is show up. The very least you could do to help would be to be mindful of the trash. Now the kitchen stinks."

"My bad, babe." He went to the first-floor bathroom and got some air freshener. He started spraying the whole kitchen.

"Can you please stop that? Now the whole house smells like rancid oranges. And who brought Glade in the house, of all things?"

"Well how am I supposed to make the smell go away?"

"Just light a damn candle. We get all these overpriced white woman candles every year for a reason."

"Oh," Rahman said. He fanned away the Glade scent and lit a candle.

"Can you please shower and get changed?" Jordan asked Rahman.

"Are we okay, Slim Goodbody?" Rahman asked. Jordan's face turned red every time he heard Rahman's nickname for him.

"I'm fine."

"You're not. Seems like you're picking a fight with me before this party. You were one of them kids who got your ass beat on your birthday for acting up, didn't you?" he laughed. Jordan looked away.

"I just want…more help," Jordan said.

"Then we hire some housekeepers. Or something. All this doesn't have to fall on you."

"But it does. It always does."

"You don't have to be perfect, my love."

"I've gotta come pretty damn close, don't I?"

"No, actually. You don't."

Jordan sighed, looked away, and saw a dust rag. He picked it up and wiped down the coffee table for the third time. Rahman walked up behind him and hugged his waist.

"Put that down." He grabbed the rag from Jordan's hands and tossed it to the floor.

"This…always feels like it's one bad day from all going away," Jordan whispered.

"This again?"

"Yes, this. Again."

"What can I say to make you not have to feel this way?"

"There's nothing you can say. I'm just not used to it. Still."

"Jordan, you gotta stop. We good. We solid."

"We weren't always, though. Right? This morning, in the shower, I thought about that day."

"The day? Oh, the day. The day you announced to me, and I quote 'I don't want to be in the same room with the wife of the man that I love.'"

"Do you have to make my voice sound so high?"

"No matter the pitch, tone, or timbre, I heard you loud and clear. And I thank the Lord Jesus Christ himself that I finally heard you. Ain't you thankful, too?"

"Yes. I'm grateful."

"You my man—my husband. You deserve everything. None of this is going away. Ever."

Jordan nodded.

"I'ma stop worrying, one day," Jordan said.

"But not today?" Rahman laughed. Jordan shook his head.

"Nah…not today."

When the Gaffney-Bruces raised their blinds, the whole neighborhood could peer into their showplace home, immaculate and well-appointed. Ziggy and Peek sat on Miss Sandra's porch, watching the various luxury cars pull up to find parking. Their job was to keep an eye on the cars, though they felt like they were also at the party. Every time Jordan made eye contact with them through the window, they raised their pinkies and took a sip from their imaginary champagne flutes.

Jordan served light appetizers while the party goers arrived between 6:45pm and 7:15pm. They were greeted with a signature cocktail—Jordan's orange sangria, a recipe that he picked up after a trip to Portugal.

The guests were:

Kyle Bowery, who was used to being the only white guy in the group. He was a year ahead of Jordan at Penn, and a year behind Rahman.

The widowed Isaiah Aiken, a retired NBA star, best known for being among the first openly gay professional male athletes.

Darryl King, Rahman's Harvard Graduate School of Education classmate, and a principal in Prince George's County, Maryland. Nearly as tall as Isaiah, he once had professional football aspirations.

Caresha King, Darryl's wife, an accountant.

Jean Wright, a fellow curator at the Smithsonian. She was in her late fifties.

Her husband, Alan, about ten years older than her.

Miss Sandra, the matriarch of Slope.

Bryson Nichols, Jordan's line brother, also from Penn. He was the ace of their line, and his height and attitude matched his position.

Representative Melissa Breckenridge, a white woman representing Massachusetts in Congress. She was an old friend of Jordan's from his hometown.

Zachary Hull, Rahman's fraternity brother that he met after relocating to Washington.

"Would you like to say grace?" Jordan suggested. Rahman bowed his head.

"Father God, we thank you for the safe journeys of all those assembled here today. May this food and the hands that prepared it be blessed this evening and for the rest of our lives. For the nourishment and strength of our bodies, in Jesus' name we pray. Amen."

"Amen," echoed the party.

"My, my, what a spread!" Jean exclaimed as Alan salivated.

"Oh, Jordan can cook," Melissa said. "He stayed in the Home Ec. department for a whole year."

"You was cookin' like that, frat?" Bryson asked.

"Once we found out he could, the girls wouldn't let him leave!" Melissa laughed.

"I might have made more friends, but y'all had me on lockdown! 'Make us this, Jordan. Make us that, Jordan.' *Pft.*"

"Listen, my mother couldn't cook to save her life. Everything I learned about a kitchen, I learned from Jordan," Melissa said.

"You got a real one, Rahman," Zachary said.

"I know it," he beamed.

"Before we begin, I'd like to toast the happy couple," Kyle announced. "Please, raise your glasses."

Everyone around the table raised their wine glasses.

"To the best men I know, Jordan and Rahman. May their legacy be as solid as their relationship. May they continue to be an example to us all. Cheers."

"Cheers!" the room repeated. Jordan blushed a little as Rahman kissed him on the cheek.

Garlic hummus, chicken pitas, Balkan salad, and strawberry cake were on the menu, along with an Aperol spritz, the second signature cocktail of the evening. Jordan loved doing the unexpected for his dinner events, and his guests were not disappointed. Hearty laughs and often-told stories served as the soundtrack for the evening.

"I still can't get over your haircut," Bryson said to Jordan.

"Yeah, I liked the dreads, too," Kyle chimed in.

"Oh, please," Jordan said. "That was two years ago."

"I can't believe you cut them right before your wedding," Kyle said.

"It was time for a change. Fresh start. Anyway, it's just hair," Jordan said, waving off the interrogation.

"So, you ever gonna tell us how your trip to North Carolina was?" Miss Sandra asked.

"Oh, it was fine," Jordan demurred. Rahman, ever so slightly, rolled his eyes and tensed up.

"So fine you got a little scar on your cheek," Miss Sandra sassed.

"You getting in barroom brawls now?" Bryson teased.

"It was a time. But I think I'd rather hear about Principal King's transformation of Largo High," Jordan steered the conversation to a safer topic.

"Oh, it's going great. Got a good staff that's getting better every day," Darryl said.

"We need good schools in this entire region," Alan said. Caresha placed her hand on Darryl's.

"We sure do. And we're so lucky to have a colleague so close by," she said.

"We just need to figure out how to play each other in football one good time so we can prove who really got it goin' on," Rahman said to Darryl.

"You think Eastern can beat Largo? Eastern?" Darryl snickered.

"Just you wait," Rahman laughed.

"You know, I gotta say, the best dressed men in Washington aren't on Capitol Hill. They are in the schools. I have never met a poorly dressed high school principal. And look at you both. What is this, Brooks Brothers?" Alan asked.

"He's a Nupe," Zachary interjected. "Of course he can dress."

"I don't know," Rahman said sheepishly.

"I mean, part of it is authority, right? Being a principal used to mean something in our community. Doctors, lawyers, educators, you know. Give something the kids can aspire to," Darryl said.

"He's got a closet full of suits for every occasion," Jordan added.

"Dressing up makes me feel…more like a person. I can be casual. But I've always liked being…noticed. I don't need the attention, but I like for people to notice me and say 'there's that guy. The one that be dressing.'"

"Vanity," Kyle coughed.

"No, I get it," Melissa added. "There's a certain something about a man who can wear a suit well."

"But when the suit comes off and I get to dress down, my students don't even recognize me. The last Field Day I went to, I had on a t-shirt and skinny jeans and the kids kept asking me where Mr. Gaffney-Bruce was."

"The years just fell off like autumn leaves," Bryson said.

"And yet time keeps marching on, no matter how young we look," Alan said with a hint of melancholy.

Isaiah smiled and sipped his cocktail. He'd hardly uttered a word all night. Jean picked up on this and decided to break the ice.

"How did you meet Rahman?" Jean asked him.

"Through my family foundation. We do some mentoring with inner-city athletes, and he was the Assistant Principal at a school we partnered with."

"I didn't know your foundation did that kind of work," Alan interjected.

"We prefer to work quietly," Isaiah continued. "Those first few years after I came out were rough on all of us. We took the family foundation website down to avoid the hate mail. We serve in stealth, usually."

"That's terrible. I'm sorry you experienced that," Jean said.

"Thank you. It didn't stop the work, though. And now that I'm retired from the league, I can focus on it full time."

"How's your son?" Rahman asked.

"He's okay." Isaiah smiled and nodded. He looked into Rahman's eyes and his jaw clenched, then quivered. His eyes watered in the silence.

"He's a grown man now, of course…but he misses his Papa." He reached for the cloth napkin in his lap and raised it to his eyes.

"Goddammit I said I wasn't gonna cry today," Isaiah laughed through sniffles. Rahman held Isaiah's free hand while he wiped his face.

"It's only been a year, friend. It's okay to cry."

"One year, three months, and 27 days," Isaiah said. "But who's counting, right?"

"He was a great man, Isaiah. I know there's nothing more I can say that would be a comfort. But he was great. Truly the best of us in every way," Jordan stated softly. Isaiah nodded.

"He sacrificed so much of his life for me and for Zion. He was a brilliant leader."

"Is there anything we can do for you? For the family?" Rahman asked.

"No, it's okay. Adrian is…passed away," Isaiah said. "But he's not gone. He's just as present now as he was before he left. I'll never remarry."

"Never say never," Kyle quipped.

"I will never remarry," Isaiah repeated. "Should you ever be so lucky as to have a love like ours, you'll understand."

"Life is so short. Lord knows," Miss Sandra said.

"It is. You know what really comforts me? Adrian knew God. He regularly attended Quaker meetings wherever we traveled. His devotion is what brought me back to church myself."

"Quaker? Adrian was a Quaker?" Rahman asked.

"Yup. For the last ten years of his life."

"He didn't dress like a Quaker," Jordan mused.

"You're thinking of the Amish, I think," Isaiah laughed. Jordan was embarrassed.

"I'm sorry," he said.

"Quakers are the ones who have church in silence and don't have clergy."

"That sounds like Sunday service, don't it Miss Sandra?" Jordan asked.

"I guess. I don't know nothing 'bout no Quakers, though. Ain't no Quakers in Slope. Any church is alright with me as long as they are all about love."

Isaiah sighed and smiled.

"How long have you lived here?" Isaiah asked Miss Sandra.

"All my life."

"A real Washingtonian!" Kyle remarked. "They don't make too many of you anymore."

Miss Sandra stared at Kyle for a few moments, making it as awkward as she could without being impolite.

"And where are you from, Mister Kyle?"

"Bucks County, Pennsylvania," he said.

"And do they make any more like you up there?"

"I'd like to think I'm one of a kind!"

"Mm-hm," Miss Sandra mumbled. "Me too."

Rahman touched Jordan's knee under the table. Jordan stifled a laugh.

"Who wants more dessert?" he joyfully announced.

The evening continued with great conversation, reconnections, and new friendships. Melissa and Isaiah promised to do community work together. Zachary and Bryson put their colors down and got to know one another, despite being in rival fraternities. Miss Sandra enjoyed getting to know the Wrights, and vice versa. And the Kings and the Gaffney-Bruces made plans for a double date.

At the end of the evening, the attendees slowly trickled out, finally leaving Kyle and Isaiah.

"I guess I should head on back up the road, too," Isaiah announced. He stood, stretched, and walked to Jordan, who he hugged and kissed on the temple.

"Love you, bro," he said.

"Love you, too," Jordan said. Kyle sneered as he nursed his brandy.

"I'll walk you to your car," Rahman said. The men pushed through the wrought iron storm door and walked down the concrete stairs. Peek and Ziggy had long since retired for the evening, leaving Isaiah and Kyle's cars to fend for themselves. The August air was still thick after a day of oppressive heat. They sauntered down the hill toward Isaiah's 2022 Mercedes-Benz G-Class.

"You got a good thing going, man," Isaiah said. Rahman smiled.

"Yeah. I know."

"Remember how you almost messed it up?"

"Stop."

"No. I want you to remember where you were before the house. Before the husband. That man in there is your wildest dreams come to life. Ain't this what you prayed for?"

Rahman choked up. He nodded.

"When I got to know you in Brooklyn, I could tell something was up with you…"

"You read me for filth, real quick," Rahman added.

"You were so pitiful. So sad. If I seen it once, I seen it a million times. Athletes. Military men. Politicians. You know how many men be in my DMs asking me how I do it? Where I find the courage? I could turn Washington, Wall Street, and Hollywood upside down with everything I know."

"You was everybody's best case scenario, man. Everybody's hope. First active NBA star to come out the closet. You were destined to be everybody's guru."

"And never asked for it, not once," Isaiah said. He leaned against his truck and sighed.

"But I really appreciate you, man. That advice you gave me back then stuck with me in every aspect of my life. You remember what you said to me?"

"Of course I do. Because Adrian taught me that lesson, too."

"Never be ashamed," Rahman said.

"And how long did it take you to stop being ashamed of who you really was?"

"A while. But now that I'm here…and got who I want and what I want…I ain't never going back."

"My man," Isaiah said, slapping Rahman's hands and pulling him into a hug.

"I really miss Adrian, man," Rahman whispered as tears welled up in his eyes.

"I do, too. We all do."

"My man, please, if you need us…"

"I do need you. I'll always need you. And thank you for always being there for me and my family."

"Always, man. Just a phone call away."

Rahman stood on the sidewalk as Isaiah drove away. Peek and Ziggy came up the hill, smelling faintly of weed.

"Yo man, I know you better watch your social distancing," Ziggy said.

"What?" Rahman asked.

"You was too close to ole boy back there," Peek said.

"Yup. We peeped. You know we slice tendons around here for disloyalty," Ziggy said with a scowl.

"Hey man, I don't want no smoke," Rahman laughed.

"He he, hell," Peek said.

"We got our eye on you," Ziggy said with a knuckle in Rahman's chest. Rahman laughed and tousled their hair.

"You know we just fuckin' with you, man," Peek said.

"Yeah, tell Isaiah Aiken we need some new housing out here. Fix up some of these houses," Ziggy proposed.

"And some Amazon gift cards," Peek added.

"Or…maybe I can help with your resumes and see if Mr. Aiken got any internships at his foundation. Maybe make your own money rather than asking a celebrity to take care of you."

"Shit, can't we get both?" Ziggy quipped.

"And goodnight, gentlemen," Rahman said with a shake of his head.

"Goodnight, Mr. Gaffney-Bruce," Peek said.

"Tell your huzzbind we see him tomorrow," Ziggy added.

Rahman reentered his house, empty save for Kyle seated on the sofa on one end and Jordan in the love seat next to him.

"Ziggy and Peek said they'll get with you tomorrow," Rahman said.

"They definitely aren't going to forget to pick up their stipend for the parking services," Jordan chuckled.

"They called you my 'huzzbind,'" Rahman laughed.

"Why they gotta drag out every syllable like that?! They're so silly."

Kyle's eyes ping-ponged between the couple.

"Who knew, all these years later, that you two would be each other's endgame?"

"I think it's as big a surprise to us as it is everyone looking from the outside," Jordan said.

"You think so?" Rahman asked.

"I mean, we come from a different era. We didn't have any gay role models, *per se*. Gay marriage wasn't even legal. Hell, the kids say 'husband' like it's taboo."

"Yeah but fuck all that—I mean us. As endgame. I think I knew all along."

"Even if you did…took us long enough to get here," Jordan said.

"I love you guys together. A real storybook ending, I think," Kyle interjected.

"Happily ever after," Jordan chuckled.

"Are you guys adventurous?" Kyle asked. Rahman immediately got tense.

"I mean, we like to travel," Jordan responded.

"Yeah…but I mean like…*adventurous*."

"I don't follow."

"He wants to know if we're swingers," Rahman grumbled.

"Swingers!" Jordan gasped, then laughed.

"What's so funny?" Kyle asked.

"Me and Rahman? Swinging? Nah, that's not us at all."

"You sure?" Kyle asked. "You know, Rahman used to be pretty wild back in his undergrad days. He ever tell you about the time…"

"Kyle, shut up with your stories. That's not us."

Kyle laughed.

"Maybe it's time you went home," Rahman said.

"Oh, I'm too tipsy to drive, thanks to your cocktails. And I thank you for it. Maybe I could just crash on your couch?"

"Fine. I'll get a blanket and a pillow," Rahman said as he headed to the linen closet.

Kyle laid his hand on Jordan's.

"I appreciate your hospitality. And I love how you're so good to Rahman. I hope you're together forever."

"Thanks," Jordan said coldly. He removed his hand from Kyle's clammy grasp. Rahman entered with the pillow and blanket, tossed them to Kyle, and said goodnight. He reached his hand out to his husband.

Jordan stood, took Rahman's hand, and retired to their bedroom.

Jordan hadn't been sleeping well since North Carolina. His dreams had turned a lot more vivid as he confronted random collections of aggressive men, fighting—again—in some cases, evading in other cases. He wasn't used to combat in his dreams, but he certainly was seeing action in them.

As he woke from yet another iteration of his nocturnal battles, his eyes fluttered open. Rahman snored soundly next to him.

To Jordan's surprise, Rahman wasn't angry at him for the sudden trip to Howgill, especially when he realized he would have done the same thing for one of his students. He wasn't in love with the idea of his husband fist-fighting racists, but the idea of a version of Jordan with raw aggression rather than cool intellect really turned him on.

From the corner of his eye, Jordan saw that their bedroom door was ajar. Rahman always closed it—he'd seen a movie in the eighties about a house fire that informed his habits for the rest of his life.

Kyle stood in the doorway, shirtless, with his hand in his boxer shorts, pleasuring himself. They locked eyes. Kyle removed his hand and scurried away.

Appalled, Jordan froze for a few moments. He considered waking up Rahman, but he knew his husband would have thrown Kyle through the window. Instead, he got up, closed the bedroom door, and locked it.

Jordan woke up again a little after 8am, still unsettled. Rahman snored mightily next to him. Rather than ask if he would be coming to worship, he let his husband sleep.

After showering, Jordan went to the kitchen to boil some water for a cup of tea. He almost forgot Kyle was still in the house.

Creep, he thought. He had never truly liked Kyle and the older he got, the less patience he had for his obnoxious shenanigans. Still, he never wanted to be so controlling that Rahman couldn't maintain his own friend group. But would Rahman consider someone so reckless to be a real friend?

He pondered the question on the way out the door and on his brief walk up the hill to where Miss Sandra was already seated in silence. He met Peek at the intersection and helped him drag a traffic barrier to its regular spot, deterring any vehicles from entering the sacred temporary space.

Ziggy jogged to the circle, almost missing Peek's customary opening speech. He sat near Jordan, making the group assembled an even dozen.

Jordan's eyes fluttered closed and he slowed his breathing, inhaling for a count of four, holding for a count of four, and exhaling for a count of six.

When he opened his eyes, Kyle was walking up the hill toward the group.

Please God don't let him sit with us, don't let him sit with us, just let him go away.

Kyle got into his BMW, parked at the top of the hill. He idled for a moment, then sped off.

Thank you, God.

Jordan settled into silence and waited for God to speak to him. After about ten minutes, Rahman joined him.

At the end of the hour, after everyone had shaken hands, Jordan turned to his husband.

"I really love you," he said.

"I love you, too, babe."

Royce and the Deplorable Word

Every now and then, Qiang visited his mother in Slope on a weekday. Sometimes he had business in the city that gave him a reason to be in Northeast, but most times he simply wanted a midday sit on the porch with his mom.

He parked down the hill and walked up toward his childhood home. His mom's eyes were closed, and her hands were at her sides.

"Wake up, lady," Qiang said.

"Ain't nobody sleep," she replied.

"Why you out here with your eyes closed? Talking to God again?"

"You know it." Her eyes fluttered open and she smiled at her youngest child.

"Hey Ma," he said.

"Hey boy," she responded, opening her arms for Qiang's strong hug.

"You want anything to drink?" she asked.

"Nah, I'm good. You know Quiana be sitting in the back yard with her eyes closed and palms out, just like you."

"Good. You teaching my grandbaby how to pray."

"I ain't do it. She saw you doing it and now she sit quietly and pray just like you."

"Aww…well that's nice!" Miss Sandra smiled.

Qiang was exceptionally handsome, especially to the girls in the neighborhood that were enthralled by his biracial heritage. He had his mother's full lips and a muscular body built through years of football and healthy eating. From his father, he'd received high cheekbones, almond-shaped eyes, and a shrewd business sense. His hair was thick and wavy. Usually in cornrows, today it was in a ponytail.

"Ma."

"What, Qiang?"

"When you gon' let me move you outta here?"

"Boy, stop. This my home."

"It's a house in my neighborhood on sale. You could be right around the corner from me. Nice big back yard."

"Now what I'ma do in a big backyard? Play football? I'm 70, Qiang."

"You would see some green for a change."

"Only green I need to see is right there by the sidewalk and the little bit out back. And my plants."

"The house would be big enough for all your kids at one time. And their kids."

"Uh-uh! That's too much house! I don't even wanna think about the gas bill!"

"Ma, it's all electric out there."

"Electric? Nah, that's gon' mess my cakes up. Better stay here. I don't wanna get used to no new kitchen."

"Ma, just say what the problem is. Let's put the shit on out there."

"Ain't no problem. I'm just not trying to move."

"So it ain't about how I make my money?"

"Boy, please. I ain't studdin' you or your bank account."

Qiang rolled his eyes.

"You like when I be riding around the neighborhood throwing twenties to the rugrats, or paying for funerals for another knucklehead who ain't have the sense to finish high school. But you won't let me make sure you have a comfortable retirement. It don't make no damn sense."

"I am quite content in my retirement, thank you very much, and I am not trying to move out someplace new."

"I think, deep down in your heart, you ashamed of your drug-dealing son."

"Hush, now. You talkin' crazy."

"I'm talking facts."

"I don't love you no less than any of your brothers and sisters. All of you chose your own path. All I did was insist that you went to college. Whatever else you did was on y'all. I ain't no more shamed or no more proud of any of you."

"But Ma, I got the most money. And I can do the most good. It ain't about cars and houses for me. It's about making sure the lady that got me off on the right foot gets what she deserves. And you deserve more than this tiny house in the hood."

"You got love in this house. You got fed in this house. You grew up in this house. It was never too small for all that, and it ain't too small for me. Now, whatever you got going in your head about whether I'm proud of you or ashamed of you, you can get that out your head right now. You don't owe me nothing. You don't owe me being a law-abiding citizen. I ain't no fool, I know what you do. You just like my first two husbands. The irony is that your daddy was the square and you became a gangster anyway. But the point is this: do you. I'ma love you no matter how you decide to do you. And if I'ma let you do you, then let me do me. Understand?"

"I got you, Ma. I got you."

"Now can you please hush? Here come Royce. I don't want no mess with her."

The friendly neighborhood police officer drove slowly up the hill with her windows down. She honked her horn.

"Hey y'all!" she called.

"Good afternoon, Detective Johnson," Qiang said with a nod.

Royce Johnson was a daughter of Slope. She could trace her lineage back to Sergeant Preston Johnson, her grandfather, who had retired from the Marines and enjoyed a second career driving the paddy wagon for the Metropolitan Police Department. His claim to fame was that he was in the building when Marion Barry got shot by terrorists in the early 1980s—a fact that many people forgot since most only knew Barry by his drug addiction and womanizing.

Royce remembered and loved her grandfather, despite his raising a ne'er-do-well in her own father. Royce knew from an early age that she wanted to help people and was never one to sing along to "Fuck da police."

She graduated from Coppin State with a degree in government at 22 and immediately went to the DC Police Academy. She worked foot patrol Uptown out of the Fourth District for four years, then transferred to an investigative unit in the First District. Although she was a young Detective by rank, she had truly been an investigator all her life. In another time, she might have been a prosecutor, what with her love of people and deep knowledge of the Constitution. But it was police work for her.

Her peers at H.D. Woodson remembered her as super smart, super poised, and down-to-earth. She had been both a cheerleader and a runner. She knew H.D. was a tough school, but she never saw it as a bad school, even if her peers seemed to fear the kids who came from Slope to H.D.

Royce knew she was a lesbian by her sophomore year of college. She'd tried to make relationships with boys work, yet she simply thought they were gross. Sexually? Yuck. Intellectually? Ick. The phrase "Females be like…" was an instant turn-off that told her everything she needed to know about a man.

At Coppin, she spent time with Tatiana, a young lady who was a member of a sorority. They'd met through class—sociology—and had been forced to do joint projects together. They hit it off, and soon spent more time together outside of class. Tatiana was a girly girl, and Royce viewed herself as just regular. She thought for a long time that Tatiana's interest in her was mostly friendship, and perhaps Tatiana had wanted her to join her sorority. But when Tatiana finally took a chance and kissed her, Royce was relieved. She didn't want to have to tell Tatiana she hated her sorority's color combination and could never see herself flipping her hair and being all *chi-chi* to be part of it.

Although Royce and Tatiana's love affair was deep, it was brief. Tatiana was now married to some Baltimore Alpha while disavowing her previous predilection for vagina. And Royce was entertaining Denise, a criminal defense attorney six years her senior.

Royce wasn't assigned to the Gino Powell case. She was too close to it. Still, she was determined to solve it. Everyone had a deep suspicion of who had taken Gino's life, but there was no concrete evidence, and the crackers assigned to the case weren't exactly deep enough in the community to convince anyone to talk.

Even as a kid, Royce knew that Slope didn't snitch. That was not because Slope was a bunch of criminals, but because Slope had peculiar practices the outside world would never understand. Rather than fix up the burned-out church on the corner, folks sat in the intersection and prayed. Royce joined them faithfully every Sunday, as she had as a child.

She thought, sometimes, that the reason there were no murders in Slope proper was because of that prayer. Black folk had assembled in that one space for so long, interrupting traffic patterns, if need be, that the place was blessed. Hallowed ground. Like God himself had said "Not here."

That didn't mean people from Slope never died. They died all the time—just never from violence in this four-block radius.

Royce knew Gino had died clutching at the air. She saw the crime scene photos for herself and wondered if Gino had been reaching back to Slope, like if he could have crawled back home, he could have lived.

She knew it was a ridiculous thought. Gino couldn't have even known which way was north or south. But maybe he, like so many of them, felt like the ground under Slope was holy and healing.

She missed that boy. She knew he was a knucklehead, like the other boys on Slope had been for decades, but she loved him. Every chance she got, she poured into him, in case nobody had told him he was smart, or special, or loved. And he received that love and spread it around as best he could.

Now Peek was a different animal altogether. He was less talkative, less charismatic. But for some reason, Miss Sandra had deemed him next in line. Royce respected the hierarchy but didn't understand it. Who had made Miss Sandra the one who deems others worthy? Why Gino? Why Peek, who by most accounts, struggled in school just as bad as Korey and Ziggy did? Why not a girl? Why not Royce?

She felt ashamed for being jealous of the boys, when she was a decade older and had so much else going for her. Still, this was her community, too, and she didn't like being overlooked.

Royce pulled her Acura into the spot in front of her house, handed down from her grandfather and vacated by her father. Peek walked slowly by, like an italicized capital I, sauntering down the street.

"Peek," she called. He rolled his eyes and tried to ignore her.

"I know you hear me, 'Dark and Lovely.' Come here, boy," she said, calling him by his least favorite nickname. Peek blushed and she laughed. He walked to her car.

"How you been?" she asked.

"Fine," he said. "You?"

"I'm aight. Busy. Heard you took a trip."

"Yeah. I did."

"How was it?"

"It was…crazy. But it was cool," Peek said, holding back his still-unprocessed emotions about that weekend.

"You know my people been investigating this thing with Gino, right?"

Peek nodded.

"We gotta bring this thing to some conclusion, Peek."

Peek lowered his eyes and clenched his jaw.

"What that gotta do with me, Royce?"

"You on camera. You was at the corner, looking at Gino, and whoever shot him. You saw it, then you ran toward Ziggy. Ziggy ain't see shit. He was around the corner, walking to you."

"I told y'all, I ain't see shit."

"But you did. You saw the whole thing. You can put an end to all this, friend."

Peek's tongue throbbed, and he chewed it softly, first one side, then the other. He looked up to the sky and his eyes watered.

"I know you think you can't say it. But I need you to say it. Just one word. One name. Confirm what we already know so we can get some closure."

"I can't say it," Peek shook his head.

"You got to, Peek."

"Everything will change."

"Everything already changed. It changed when that jealous coward put a bullet in your friend. It changed when we poured his ashes over the bridge, like so many before him. Only thing, Peek, we ain't never buried one of our own *because* of our own. It's Slope against the world, like it always is. Slope don't hurt Slope. We family."

"We ain't family. Not for real. We niggas on a block in the hood. I been out there, Royce. I seen where we really from. Ain't nothing out there. Ain't nothing in here. We just killing each other in here slower than they could kill us out there. But we gon' die for sure either way."

"Aw, Peek."

"Ain't no 'aw, Peek.' This real shit, Royce. This shit you want me to say is the worst shit I could say. If I say what I saw, it ends us all. Let it die with Gino. Okay?"

Royce sighed.

"Okay Peek."

She got out of her car and headed toward her stoop. She stopped, inhaled, and called down the way to Peek.

"I'll be here if you change your mind."

Royce's section of Slope was a line of row houses that were taller and narrower than the rest of the single-family homes. However, for the extra height, the homes sacrificed front porches, instead having small stoops. She and Denise still sat on the steps, though, when the weather was breezy.

Denise called it "community policing" since everyone knew Royce was the cops.

Royce immediately took off her shoes and slid on some Adidas slides. She hated the out-of-date dress code for detectives. She felt like she was always going to funerals in her dark suits rather than focusing on actual police work. She'd much rather be wearing a sweatsuit to work and envied those who got to work from home after COVID hit.

Denise, although she was always on the go, at least got to have virtual court most of the time now. A blouse up top and boy shorts down bottom sufficed for the work she had to do.

"Hey babe," Royce greeted as she entered.

"Hey! How was your day?" Denise asked.

"Ugh. We saw the footage, finally."

"Gino?"

"Yeah. Hella grainy. Still can't tell who did it. But Peek has to know. They showed him reacting."

"And y'all are sure it definitely wasn't him?"

"For sure. It wasn't. Denise, it was so sad watching them kneel over Gino."

"Damn."

"And you know he's never gonna say who it was. It would take an act of God for that to happen."

"Ain't nobody snitched in this neighborhood since slavery days, I'm sure," Denise joked.

"And even then, probably not." Royce stretched her back and unleashed her dreadlocks from their tight bun.

Despite both being involved in the law, Royce and Denise had not met on the job. They met at Lace, a lesbian bar on Rhode Island Avenue, on the way to Mount Rainier, Maryland. That block, anchored by a Rita's Italian Ice on one end and a nonprofit called Magdalene House on the other end, tried so hard to be gentrified. At the time, Lace was a new addition. The owner wanted so hard to bring a Black business back to the community, but it seemed like nothing could outpace the developers erecting flimsy apartments over Trader Joe's in places like Union Market and 14th Street.

But if Lace was only open for a brief period, it served its purpose by introducing the defense attorney to the detective. Almost immediately, over Long Island iced teas, they debated the decriminalization of marijuana in the city. Royce had let Denise's soft, feminine looks fool her: she was relentless in proving her points. Royce liked being right, liked sparring even better, but most of all, liked not having to guess about what was on a woman's mind. Denise was clear, direct, and honest always.

In typical DC lesbian fashion, they began dating immediately and moved in together shortly afterward. They'd be married already if Denise believed in it.

"Did you notice that black BMW as you came in?" Denise asked.

Royce looked out the window.

"Yeah, but I assumed it was some social workers or something."

"They circled the block like three times before parking. They've been out there like twenty minutes."

Inside the car, the twenty-something-year-old Michael asked Kyle "Why are we all the way over here in the ghetto?"

"It's not the ghetto. Some of the houses here are bigger than the houses in Georgetown," Kyle said, already exasperated with his part-time lover.

"It's so run-down…" Michael whined.

"Look around," Kyle continued. "Sit in the silence for a second."

Michael folded his arms and listened.

"I don't hear anything," he said.

"Exactly. This neighborhood is perfect. I looked up the crime rates here. Not an arson. Not an assault. Not a murder here since they started collecting that data. You, sir, are sitting in one of the safest neighborhoods in DC."

"It's so far from…everything."

Kyle was getting annoyed with the boy, who was showing enough privilege to make him reconsider whether bringing him to Slope was a good idea, much less dating him in the first place.

"Listen…I told you, the night after the party—"

"Which you didn't invite me to."

"In which I wasn't given a plus one," Kyle lied.

"Yeah, yeah. You said you saw my weed man in a Quaker meeting. Well first, that's racist that you think all young Black dudes look alike. And second, there are no Quaker meetings out here."

"That lady said they didn't use the word Quaker. But I'm telling you Michael, there was nothing different from what I saw there and what I saw when I visited Tenley Friends Meeting with you. The silence. The testimony. The shaking hands at the end. It was the same. And I was sitting right across the way from the guy that you told me was your weed man. I am sure it was him."

Michael sighed and looked at his phone.

"Can we go get Chinese after this?"

"Sure."

"Yelp is saying this place called Blaq Dragon has the best chicken. They call it 'General Moe's Chicken.' O.M.G. I'm dead."

"Is that supposed to be funny?"

"Ugh, gosh, you don't think anything is funny. General Moe's. Get it? Like General Tso's?"

"Who is Moe?"

"Never mind, ugh."

"There he is!" Kyle said, gesturing toward Ziggy, who was walking down the street.

"Wow, that's definitely Zig. You were right. That's crazy." Michael rolled down his window and waved.

"Aye yo, what up, Zig?"

Ziggy stopped and squinted. His jaw fell open in shock, then he smiled.

"What up, big Mike?" He balled up his fist and reached out to give Michael dap.

"Me and my friend was just out for a ride. He said he thought he saw you around here before, and I didn't believe him."

"Oh…" Ziggy peered into the car and Kyle waved.

"Yeah, I seen you before," he said with a slight frown.

"I'm Kyle! I was at your meeting the other day."

"Meeting? You mean Sunday service?"

"Sure, if that's what you call it."

"So…you came out here because your buddy recognized me?"

"I mean basically, yeah."

"And you ain't got no other business out here?"

Michael shook his head and shrugged.

"Yeah…y'all gotta go." Ziggy stepped back from the car and looked off into the distance.

"Why?"

"This ain't your neighborhood, fam," Ziggy said.

"But we're friends, Zig," Michael said. Ziggy laughed.

"We do business. Don't make me tell you again to keep it moving."

Michael scrunched up his freckled face.

"What's the problem, Zig?" Royce said as she came out the house, still in her pantsuit from work.

"Nothing. These dudes were just moving along."

"Actually, we weren't," Kyle interjected. "We were exercising our constitutional right to assemble, and *this* punk told us to move along."

"And why didn't you?" Royce asked.

"Why didn't we *move?*" Kyle asked, flabbergasted.

"I don't believe I stuttered, sir," Royce snapped.

"Let's just go," Michael said, sliding down in his seat. Denise came to the stoop to observe.

"Now wait a minute. I was just in this neighborhood last week for a dinner party, and then Sunday morning for your little meeting for worship. But you're saying I can't just be here to be here? Maybe I want to move here."

"Sir, I suggest you keep moving toward your destination. I'm sure you'll fit in better where you're going than where you are."

"Are you suggesting I can't be here because I'm white?" Kyle asked incredulously.

"I didn't say that. You said that. I'm saying you look suspicious. Now if you trying to score, we don't have nothing for you here. Go down East Cap for that."

"Drugs?!" Kyle's voice raised.

"Sir, listen here…" Royce opened her suit jacket to reveal the MPD badge attached to her belt. Kyle deflated.

"I'm not telling you to go, but I am telling you what I know. It's time to move along."

"Officer—"

"That's Detective," Royce said.

"Detective. I don't want any problems. There's something unusual about this neighborhood. Have you ever heard of SPICES? It's what

Quakers believe. 'S' stands for simplicity…and…and I'm telling you, it's Quakers here. Black Quakers. Hand to God. And they're meeting right here in the intersection on Sundays."

"Even if that's true, sir—which it ain't—what difference does it make what these people are doing on their Sunday morning? Move along. Now."

His foot heavy with embarrassment, Kyle sped off.

"Watch who you do business with," Royce said to Ziggy.

"I ain't never told that dude where I live. Never," he said.

Royce sucked her teeth.

"Spices. Huh. Like white folks ever gon' really know about *spices*."

The Church That Burned

2022

Peek gingerly walked around the house, from his bedroom to the living room and back, nursing his wounds. He was still sore from the pummeling he got from the redneck twins, but he was satisfied that he gave it to them as good as he got it.

As he paced, he built up the courage to close the chapter on his odyssey. He loved Pops with all his heart, but Pops owed him.

On Monday, when his mother had departed for her job as a cashier at the Dollar Tree, and his grandmother had gone out grocery shopping, he would say what he needed to say to Pops. He knocked lightly on his door.

"Come in," Pops said, his voice especially gravelly.

Peek turned the glass doorknob and pushed the door open. His great-grandfather's room was still, save for the small television on his tall dresser. It was turned to channel four all day long, as it had been from the time Jim Vance had first debuted as the evening news anchor.

Pops had an impeccable sense of order. If Peek had opened the closets, he would have seen perfectly hung slacks, from slate gray to black, and button-down shirts, from white, through the colors of the spectrum in order from red to violet. His collection of hats was neatly stacked at the top of the closet, and his shoes were on metal holders at the bottom.

Pops sat up in his bed. Today, he hadn't felt like moving around a lot. His body swam in a Georgetown hoodie. Despite the heat outside, the house was chilly, as Pops liked it.

"You gon' let me talk to you now?" Peek asked.

"You can always talk to me, boy. The real question is whether I'ma talk back."

"Are we gon' have a conversation?"

"Yes. We are." Pops sighed and told his story.

1952

Tyrone had a knack for measurements. There was enough soap in his bucket of water to make the diner counters clean, and enough drops of bleach to give it an extra boost.

Florida Avenue Grill had a mad rush of student customers right after school let out. It was particularly chaotic on Fridays, as the students grabbed a bite to eat before the evening's basketball games or hot dates.

A lady who reminded him of his grammar teacher back at Westhampton County Training School came through the door at 4:01pm on the nose. He could set his pocket watch to her weekly return. He knew what she'd be ordering, too.

Her quiet power filled the diner like high tide. Without prompting, her students lowered their voices, quickly finished their drinks, and settled their bills. The students were not exactly *afraid* of Miss Mustapha. They just didn't want to have to speak proper English and fix their posture when they didn't have to. The world was hard enough for Negro kids, and they wanted to be regular for a moment—away from Miss Mustapha's watchful eye.

"The usual, ma'am?" Tyrone asked. Miss Mustapha raised an eyebrow.

"And just what do you think my usual is?" she asked. Tyrone grinned, grateful that he had prepared for the moment.

"A club sandwich; French fries with pepper, no salt; and an iced tea with extra lemon on the side."

"Is that so?" Miss Mustapha laughed.

"Yes, ma'am. And you eat nice and slow while you read your *Redbook* or *Woman's Home Companion*. The kids trickle out while you're eating and the old-timers come in for early supper. I like when you come. It's less busy."

"It's too bad Mr. J. Edgar Hoover doesn't hire Negroes. Seems like you have skills that would rival the best FBI agents."

"Nah, I'm just somebody who enjoys my job, ma'am."

"Well, you certainly do an outstanding job at it. And yes, I will have the usual."

Tyrone smiled and got to work. Miss Mustapha didn't recognize the lean, pale young man. His clipped, tangy dialect suggested he might be from North Carolina, or further south. As he fried her strips of bacon, she thought about what his hopes and dreams might be for himself. Was he happy in Washington? Was waiting on colored people at a nondescript grill all he wanted? How bad was wherever he came from that this corner of DC would be enough?

Her food came out before she knew it.

"Your usual, ma'am," Tyrone announced.

"Thank you so much, young man. Tell me, please, what is your name?"

"Tyrone Jones."

"I am *Miss* Jennie Mustapha. I work up the hill, at Cardozo. You're not from here, are you?"

"No ma'am. I'm from Westhampton County, North Carolina. A tiny little town named Howgill."

"I've never heard of it. What is it near?"

"Nothing you've ever heard of, I'm sure. About an hour from Emporia, Virginia. Near the border."

"I suppose I wouldn't have heard of it. I'm a Yankee. Born in Connecticut. Came to DC to go to Howard. I've lived other places in the world, but Washington is home now."

"Traveling the world, huh? Guess there's a lot out there to see," Tyrone mused as he wiped the counters clean.

"There is, if you want to see it," she said.

"Sure. If you want to," he replied.

She began her ritual exactly as Tyrone had described it. She took a bite of her sandwich, ate one French fry, and took a sip of her iced tea. She squeezed one lemon wedge into her cup, then another, letting her already full cup reach the brim. She stirred it slowly, letting the tart lemon juice marry the savory tea. She opened her *Woman's Home Companion* and began to read.

She was his teacher. She was his aunt. She was his mother. She was everything he left behind in Howgill that was maternal, and strict, and kind. He didn't know her, but he knew her, from her silk-swaddled bosom in her modest blouse to her short haircut with graying temples. He looked forward to her presence because he could rely on it. Maybe they could be friends.

He was her student—all of them, from Dunbar to Cardozo, from Camden to Columbus. His skin and soft hair told the story without saying a word. He wasn't just migrating—he was running from violence into the unknown. DC would be safer than anything he'd known, and he was grateful to be there. She'd seen this countless times and known it intimately.

"So, what are you doing after this, Miss Mustapha?"

"I'm going to a musical at St. Luke's."

"All by yourself?"

"I'm sure there will be other people there."

"Is it the kind of thing you think a young lady would like?"

"Old ladies were young ladies once…so, perhaps."

"See, I'm trying to get to know a young lady in my neighborhood better, and I'd like to take her places. You know, something I can afford. And I'm still new here. I don't know what all is out there."

"And I suppose most of your waking hours are here at the grill."

"You know it."

"Let me give you some free advice, friend. Don't worry about spending money on a gal when you're trying to get established yourself. What's your living situation?"

"I live in my cousin's attic over by East Capitol Street. The map calls it Grant Park, but all the colored folk call it Slope."

"You're living with family. That's fine. But be smart. A young lady will be most impressed with a man that's got his own. You don't have to have it all—but be on your way. In the meantime, take her for long walks by the Tidal Basin. And picnics. Go to an art gallery. But for God's sake, let a church musical be your absolute last resort."

She chuckled and took another sip of her tea.

"You got it, Miss Mustapha. Say, what do you teach up at that school?"

"I'm an Assistant Principal. I do more outside the classroom than inside."

"I see. Well, I'm glad to get to know you a little better."

"The feeling is mutual."

Miss Mustapha bid Tyrone farewell at 4:46 on the dot. She decided to tip him a little more than she usually would, and she'd repeat the gesture every Friday for as long as she walked down the hill to the Florida Avenue Grill after work.

1956

By 1956, Tyrone had married Wilma Ellen Lassiter, a young woman from Nat Turner country who had followed her sister to DC. Tyrone had never seen a gal so beautiful. She was almost as tall as him, dark as mahogany, and shapely. Her eyes disappeared when she smiled, which was often, but when she was serious, her irises appeared to be the unrelentingly black color of night.

Tyrone knew she was the one. In no time, he quit his job at the grill and got a job as a custodian at the Federal Courthouse on Constitution Avenue. Soon after, he and Wilma married at the small church in Slope. Earnestine came along in '54. She wasn't as dark as her mother, but was not nearly as light as her father, a fact Tyrone praised God for every day in her infancy. He wanted children the color of Africa, not a child so light that people would mistake his wife for their mammy.

Miss Jennie, now 58, had developed quite a friendship with Tyrone, and it had grown well beyond the confines of the grill. When Tyrone had finally saved enough to buy a house in Slope, Miss Jennie showed up with a truck full of used furniture, courtesy of her generous and enterprising sorority sisters. Tyrone didn't know much about college or college organizations, but he knew that *triangle-funny E-funny O* symbol meant "service" and he would be forever grateful to them.

Yet, he knew Miss Jennie didn't consider him a charity case—just a friend. He was there for her when she got ill, bringing her Wilma's chicken stew, casseroles, and sandwiches directly to her house uptown. He would drive by that same house to check on it when Miss Jennie traveled—sometimes out of the country. And she'd always bring the family a small trinket of her journeys, like a seashell from the Mediterranean.

Despite their close friendship, Tyrone still, at times, found Miss Jennie to be a mystery. Although she found great satisfaction in her friendships, Tyrone wondered why she never had children and never really mentioned family much at all. She was always present, in the moment of today, whatever the day was, and inquisitive about Tyrone's own development as a man.

She discussed work often, as most of her days were, indeed, spent in service to the youth taking up the business course at Cardozo. She sighed when discussing boy-crazy Susan, who was the best typist she'd ever known. She laughed when bringing up flamboyant Cecil, whose fashion designs would certainly take him far, if only he could focus. And when she leaned in to discuss one of the teachers she supervised, she lowered her voice an octave and spoke as though she was in danger of being caught.

But she was a lady. She never gossiped maliciously, and always delivered the news of the day to Tyrone instructively, asking him what he might have done if he was in her shoes.

Miss Jennie had begun attending church in Dupont Circle at that time, at a place Tyrone could never recall the name of. When Tyrone learned she had been worshipping in a predominately white community, he was surprised. Knowing her upbringing and travels, he could picture Miss Jennie being comfortable in a mostly white environment, but DC was still very southern and still had a segregated social and spiritual life. So, the white parishioners welcoming her came as a shock to him. As for Tyrone, Wilma, and Earnestine, they continued to attend Pleasant Stream Baptist Church, a two-minute walk from their porch. At Pleasant Stream, all the attendees were Black, but the Pastor was white. It, too, was an uncommon arrangement, but his preaching was good, and it was nice to have a kindly white man around to be an example of Christian love, rather than the scorn or disdain they were used to elsewhere.

Since Miss Jennie and Tyrone were no longer working near each other, they decided to start a new tradition. Wilma would cook dinner on Sundays and Miss Jennie would drive down to visit them, with dessert in hand. Of course, her health and her travels sometimes interrupted their schedule, but Tyrone never went anywhere. Slope was his home and that was good enough.

He read the newspapers religiously, and he knew how bad things were everywhere. It wasn't just the South, where up was down, down was up, and the Democrats and Republicans seemed one in the same. He was constantly reading about war and upheaval all over the world.

He was on a post-dinner diatribe about the latest conflict, when Miss Jennie touched his hand, smiled, and said "Everything is going to be alright, by and by." Wind blew softly through the porch. Wilma and Earnestine were inside.

"How can you still smile and tell me everything gon' be alright, by and by?"

"Why, everything will be alright. It just is. Don't you think so, too? Don't things usually turn out okay?"

"Naw…Miss Jennie, I don't think so. Sometimes it feel like we in hell. Came out of Westhampton County thinking life be better for me here. Now I got a family I can't half afford to take care of. And my kids don't even have fresh air. I got a mind to take everybody back down south, but I know things don't be no better there. We just sitting and waiting to die, I guess."

"Now, Tyrone. Come on. Things can't be that bad."

"They is, Miss Jennie."

"Do you believe in God?"

"Yeah. I do. But do God believe in me?"

Miss Jennie smiled.

"I think God does believe in you. But He's so big and so old that what feels like a papercut to Him feels like a stab wound to you. He still feels your pain. But it's different."

"I don't know about that, Miss Jennie."

"But I do know. Just as sure as pollen makes me sneeze, or that the sun is going to shine tomorrow, God is inside it all. Including you and me. That's why everything you and I do has to be in his honor. That's why you opening up your home to me every week for Sunday dinner is so special to me. The Bible says open up your home to strangers."

"But you ain't no stranger. You practically family."

"But I was a stranger when you met me. You are bravely forging a new way for your family, something you couldn't have done in Westhampton County. Right?"

"I guess things could be worse for us. But…it ain't enough."

"The Bible says 'be content with such things as ye have.'"

"Sound like a white man wrote that part."

Miss Jennie laughed.

"You should always want the best for your family. But don't fall in love with what others have. What is for you and yours will be for you and yours. Don't worry about what the white man has on Nebraska Avenue.

Plan and build right here on 57th street. That, my friend, is how you bless the Lord with your bounty."

Tyrone smiled.

"You sure do be preaching, Miss Jennie."

"And you preach to me too, friend."

"You really like that church, huh?"

"It speaks to who I am right now. Yes, I like it."

"I don't know if I could be around all them white people. Seem like I oughta have one day off from 'em."

"We're all the same, basically."

"I know God say we are. Just wish everybody else would catch up."

"Want me to show you what I learned how to do at my church?"

"Sure."

"I learned how to listen to God. It starts with silence. Here. Close your eyes and listen."

Miss Jennie folded her hands and closed her eyes. Tyrone sighed and did the same.

"Breathe," Miss Jennie commanded. Tyrone inhaled slowly, then exhaled. He became more aware of his position on his porch. He shifted in his chair and heard the wood creak beneath him. The birds chirped in the trees around them. A car drove by.

"Wait for God," she said.

Tyrone heard Earnestine's footsteps as she toddled around the house. Wilma giggled. It reminded Tyrone of what he could remember from his own mother's voice. He had not heard her since he was ten years old in Howgill, the night before she disappeared. Tyrone fell asleep one night, and the next morning, she was gone.

It was always just him and her, until it wasn't.

His mother's face emerged from a warm, white light. She smiled.

He missed her.

"Think of God as being all around you. A warm light holding you, but also coming from inside you. Not a faraway person in the sky, but a warmth all around," Miss Jennie said.

Tyrone was already there in the light. That's how he knew Miss Jennie was onto something. His mother continued smiling directly at him.

Tyrone's grandparents loved him, but it wasn't like his mother's love. It was a sad love—a pity. They gave him what they could, but they missed their daughter immensely. Burying her was the hardest thing they'd ever done. Living among the people they knew, but couldn't prove, had taken her life was the second hardest thing.

His mother's face disappeared and the warm light dissipated. He opened his eyes. Miss Jennie's eyes were also open.

"How did it feel?" she asked. Tyrone's eyes watered, but he fought back the tears.

"It felt good, Miss Jennie. I ain't never thought of God like that, before."

"It's different when there's nothing standing in between you and Him," she mused.

Tyrone thought she was right. This new, unmediated version of prayer felt different, and fuller than anything he'd ever done before.

1968

"Tyrone, no. Please," Miss Jennie pleaded. She was 69 years old now. Retired from her life as an educator. Spent some time teaching English in Turkey. Entrenched in an active volunteer life. 69 years old, but still strong enough to be the only person standing up to a crowd for what was right.

"Please, nothing, Miss Jennie! That church on that corner been a boot on my neck for damn near twenty years. The Bible that white man been teaching us about ain't done nothing but be his mask. He want peace. He want order. He want control. He don't teach us the good parts, how Jesus be flippin' tables. How Jesus be with the least of us. How Jesus be mad— righteous and mad!"

It was April 5th. Dr. King had been dead for 24 hours already. Night was falling over DC and the city was burning. Sections of Northwest looked like something out of a war zone, and the violence was spreading.

"That's right, Miss Jennie. Rev. Mather gotta pay for what he did to our daughters," Wilma Jones said.

"You cannot kill him, Tyrone." A cold sweat broke out all over Miss Jennie's body and her hands quivered. Her mouth dried out.

"Go back uptown, Miss Jennie. You don't need to be here for what's next." Tyrone pushed past her and down the three steps to the sidewalk. He stormed toward the church, flanked by men holding two-by-fours, crowbars, and bricks—the tools of the only trades they had been allowed while it seemed the rest of Black Washington flourished from mailrooms to senate offices.

Miss Jennie knew she had little room to debate Tyrone's ultimate goal, but she also knew he would regret this decision. His daughter stood shoulder to shoulder with Sandra, tears streaming down their faces. Miss Jennie hustled herself off the porch and jogged to the throng of men, pushing through them to get to the front.

"Tyrone. Tyrone, don't. Stop for a minute."

"Stay out the way, Miss Jennie. Ain't nobody trying to hear about peace now. What did it get Dr. King, huh? How many assassinations I gotta live through? Peace." Tyrone spit on the ground.

"Ain't nothing peaceful about this world, Miss Jennie," Scott Lassiter said. He was a seventeen-year-old, at least five inches taller than Tyrone, but looked like a man. He was Sandra's brother—and both were Wilma's cousins.

"Scotty, you can be the peace. Sometimes we sit out on the porches, hearing nothing but the birds and the wind blowing through the trees. We have that peace when we want it. Despite all the other noise happening in this city. It can start with you."

"Doctor King is dead, Miss Jennie!" Scotty screamed. "And this man been touching our girls! This man we trusted. Bringing us the word every Sunday. Whole time he touching our girls and making us be grateful to have a place to live that ain't the south. Where he from, huh? Where he come from? North Carolina, just like all us. And he brought his evil up here like a hurricane. I'm tired, you hear me? I'm tired of running and not having no safety nowhere."

Miss Jennie tried with all her might to swallow, but her throat was too dry. The boy wasn't wrong. Rev. Mather stood defiantly at the top of the steps of Pleasant Stream Baptist Church. He smirked at the throng approaching him.

"Hello, friends," he said sternly.

"You been touching my daughter?" Tyrone demanded.

"And my sister?" Scotty demanded.

"Ah, friends, remember what the Bible says about Jezebel. You must be wary of the girls in our community, for even—"

Scotty threw a brick that grazed the Reverend's ear and crashed through the glass door behind him. Mather winced in pain.

"You bastard!"

"It's over, Rev.," Scotty said. "That brick was a warning. The rest gon' be your tomb."

"Miss Mustapha, call off these men," Rev. Mather pleaded as he held his bleeding ear. "They'll listen to you. You're not from here, but I see how they follow your lead. Please."

For years, Miss Jennie had listened to the voices of those with whom she worshipped every Sunday morning in Dupont Circle as they wrung their hands and cried out for change in the world, in the name of peace. She, too, wanted peace.

Yet, she was still a Black woman in DC—in America—in a turbulent time. And all the times were turbulent. She remembered the Spanish flu epidemic. She'd seen girls struggling, from DC, to Ohio, to New Jersey, and somehow remaining joyful anyway. She had seen the world. And though her Sunday morning friends wanted peace, she had not seen all of them working for it. Risking their lives for it.

Some did. But not most. Not even many.

And here were her Sunday afternoon friends, crying out for justice, doing their best to make sure their girls knew they mattered. That they would no longer let this preacher—a grifter, in fact—any longer take advantage of the peace they had built for themselves.

So many on Slope had run from the South. So many had sought a better life and better opportunity, built on the hope that evil was behind them.

But evil had followed them. And they were going to exorcize it.

Miss Jennie stepped in front of the men ready to take Rev. Mather out. Her short heels clicked and dragged against the ground.

"I am willing, Reverend Mather, to put my own faith to the side. I am willing to walk away…turn my back…and let the justice that these men have deemed necessary prevail. And I will ask God for His forgiveness every day, just as I will pray for his mercy on your detestable soul."

The Reverend clenched his teeth and breathed in, then out, then in again. Blood trickled from the cut on his ear down the side of his neck.

"And I am also willing to be the voice in this gathering that beseeches those assembled to destroy not the man…but the house that protects him and his hateful theology. I ask you, my brothers, won't you instead leave the final justice to God?"

Tyrone closed his eyes.

"Daddy, please," Earnestine called out from their porch.

"Come back home, Scotty. He isn't worth it," Sandra begged. Scotty balled his fist.

"Miss Jennie…" Tyrone growled.

"Destroy the edifice. Not the life," Miss Jennie begged. From the back of the crowd, someone passed a bottle of vodka with a soaked rag coming out of the neck. Scotty took it, palming it in one hand. He closed his eyes, as if waiting for a heavenly sign.

"I think you better run, Reverend," Tyrone said. He opened his eyes and took a matchbook from his pocket. He took a match out and lit it.

Miss Jennie snatched the bottle from Scotty's hand before the flame lit the rag. She walked to Tyrone.

"Not him. You light it," she instructed. Tyrone nodded. Scotty gave him his matchbook. For a moment, Tyrone, too, closed his eyes. But he was not waiting for a sign.

He was the sign.

He lit the rag and cocked his arm back.

Suddenly, Miss Jennie took the bottle from Tyrone's hand. The flame nicked her knuckles. She hurled the bottle at the church with an *oomph*. Her throwing arm still had some strength some fifty years after playing softball at Howard.

The Reverend had already made it halfway down the block and to his Buick by the time the bottle crashed against the doors of the church. The sounds of the shards of glass were absorbed by the liquid, and the flames spread silently across the carpeted vestibule. Tyrone had a mind to run to the Buick, pull the good Reverend out, and cast him into the flames—yet he didn't. The car sped out of Slope while Miss Jennie and the men stood, transfixed by the blaze.

Tyrone put his arm around Miss Jennie's shoulder.

"Let's go, Miss Jennie," he said. She turned around as the flames licked the church, reaching to the night sky. The crowd parted as they walked toward the intersection.

Miss Jennie noticed that the ladies who had been standing back from the action had assembled lawn chairs and milk crates in a wide circle in the middle of the intersection. They sat there, silently, with eyes open and tears streaming, as the church burned. There was space enough for everyone who wanted to join the circle.

Scotty took Miss Jennie's hand and led her to the empty seat next to Sandra. He sat behind them. Tyrone joined his family at the opposite end. The flames continued crackling behind him. He lowered his head, waited for God to speak to him, and once again saw his mother in the Light.

Thursday, August 26, 2022

"Why you tell me this, Pops? Why you wanna relive all this bad shit?" Peek asked.

"Ain't reliving it," Pops declared. "But the silence has a way of keeping things alive. When I tell you, I release it. Exorcise the demons. You needed to know the whole story. When you don't know the whole story, the mind makes up things that make sense. But it don't always be true."

"Did the firemen ever come that night?"

"Not for a long time. The building was sturdy. But everything not made of brick disintegrated. And by some miracle, nothing else in this neighborhood burned but the church. We stayed in worship until the firetrucks came. Then we watched them put the fire out."

"Fifty years later…nobody rebuilt. That's crazy."

"The real church never went away. We the church. We stayed."

Pops sighed.

"What's wrong, Pops?"

"I should have never let you go to Westhampton without the whole story. I failed you, but I ain't gonna fail you no more. I don't have much time left, but I gotta start treating you like the heir that you are. I didn't have the courage to go back to Howgill. To avenge my mother. To claim what's mine. I was too scared. But you have more courage in your pinky toe than I have in 90 years of life."

"It wasn't courage, Pops. Just…a emptiness. Something inside me needed to know. And now I know."

Pops nodded.

"You proved yourself down there. Everything Sandra been saying is true. Slope wants you. They need you."

"I'm not ready, Pops. I can't do this."

"Ready is a lie. You think Miss Jennie was ready when God first talked to her? Hell no. She was already an old lady. But God talked to her. Convinced her. And for all the time she spent with them crackers uptown, she spent just as much time with us."

"I wish I knew her, Pops."

"You know me? You know yourself? You know her."

"But what would she do, Pops?"

"You already know what she would do."

Tears streamed down Peek's face. His heart was ready to explode.

"Korey did it. Korey killed Gino. I saw him."

"Mmm-hm," Pops nodded.

"I gotta tell Royce, huh?"

"You know in your heart what you have to do. And I think you knew all along. You just wanted a sign. You're the sign, boy. You're the one you've been waiting for."

Peek nodded.

"I love you, Pops." Peek stood up and walked to his great-grandfather. He leaned down, held his hand on his shoulder, and kissed him on the temple. He never kissed Pops before, as an adult. He didn't know why he'd done it but it made sense to him at the time.

Golgotha

1

Korey, Ziggy, Gino, and Peek met at 57th and Burr every morning. Peek, still in middle school, wore the navy-blue polo shirt of DC Scholars Public Charter School. The others wore the white shirts of Howard Dilworth Woodson Senior High School—or just H.D. for short.

It was 2017. Korey and Ziggy were fifteen. Gino was sixteen. Peek was thirteen, but tall enough to constantly be mistaken for an older boy.

"Don't make no sense. Peek might as well be going to H.D. with his tall ass," Korey said. Peek looked at his shoelaces.

"Like shit," Gino said. "He can keep up, too. Got us reading this bullshit ass Julius Caesar. Bet Peek already done read that shit."

"You staying out of trouble, Peek?" Ziggy asked. Peek shrugged.

"Might as well call you 'Peep,' nigga. As in you don't even make a peep when it's time to talk," Korey teased. Peek shrugged again.

"I talk," he said. The boys leaned in and waited for a beat.

"What?" Peek said.

"Seem like there was gonna be more behind that sentence," Gino laughed.

"Oh, nah," Peek said matter-of-factly. At the top of the hill, the boys parted ways.

"Aight, Peek," Gino led the receiving line of dap and shoulder hugs as Peek went off to his school while the boys proceeded toward H.D. Woodson.

"He be with us next year," Ziggy said as they slow-walked.

"Glad he don't be getting into nothing. Be minding his business like shit," Korey said.

"Peek ain't…you know…" Gino began.

"Gay?" Ziggy asked.

"Nah, nigga. Well…that too…but I was asking if he slow or something," Gino asked.

"Nigga you know he ain't slow. You see he be reading," Korey said, annoyed. Gino was always making little comments that Korey noticed. The kind of comments that reminded him Gino wasn't from Slope. Not *really*.

"I guess slow ain't the right word. You know what it is when a nigga don't connect with other people? Like, if they got it real bad they can't really communicate, but if they just got it a little then they just goofy?"

"Nigga, you talking about being artistic?" Ziggy asked.

"Is that it? Ain't it called something else? Spectrum…something…"

"Ain't nothing wrong with that nigga. He just quiet and mind his business," Korey concluded.

"Aye, I ain't mean no harm," Gino said earnestly. "I just be trying to understand him."

"Well, we understand him fine. It be like that when you really know somebody," Korey said.

Ziggy sighed. If left unchecked, Korey and Gino would fight like cats and dogs.

"Who trying to blaze real quick?" Ziggy offered.

"Shiiiit, me," Gino said. Korey knew Ziggy was trying to defuse whatever this was between him and Gino, so he shut up and went along with the plan to smoke before school.

They cut through an alley about a block before arriving at the building. Ziggy produced a jay from parts unknown, sparked it, dragged, and passed it to Korey. Korey inhaled. Immediately, he relaxed. It seemed to Korey like life didn't need to be as hard as everybody made it. School could start at 10 instead of 8:30—let the mornings be for people who wanted to do other things, like sports, and let the regular kids trickle in. And Peek should come if he wanted to. He was smart enough to tackle the same work. And they should have a daycare in the building for the teen moms and dads. It all seemed clear to him how things could be.

Instead, he got yelled at all day by teachers who thought he couldn't focus. He couldn't, but they didn't have to yell. The city was loud enough. The school was loud enough. Somewhere, desks were always sliding across the linoleum floor, walkie talkies beeped and screeched, whistles blew in the gym, and everybody talked loud, for emphasis, for fun, and for no reason at all. How was he expected to focus on retaining all that information the teachers were constantly throwing at them?

Korey's worries were still there, but he cared just a bit less as he, Ziggy, and Gino sauntered into school fifteen minutes late. The security guards directed them to the attendance counselor, who lectured them about their chronic tardiness. She never noticed their aroma, because it filled the hallways as early as eight in the morning, long before the Slope trio ever made it in the door. After she finished fussing, she wrote tardy passes for all three.

"Ms. de Boer finna be pissed," Ziggy giggled with his eyes half closed as they lurched toward their English II room.

"We ain't that late," Korey debated.

"Just go in there real chill, ya dig?" Gino directed.

"We got this," Korey said. He was getting annoyed with Gino again, this time for being bossy.

Gino slowly turned the doorknob and pushed the door open. Keeping his head down, he muttered "Good morning, Ms. De Boer" to the tall, athletic white woman with the blond pixie cut and deep blue eyes. Ziggy and Korey followed suit.

"Grab your copies of *Julius Caesar,* please," she said dryly. None of them took delight in disappointing one of their favorite teachers, and Korey especially thought things might be different if they'd had her for second period, rather than first, or even better, right after lunch.

They took the weathered, pocket-sized copies of *Julius Caesar* from the blue, rectangular bucket by the door.

"What page we on?" Korey asked a few decibels too loudly. LaKeisha from 35th sucked her teeth and sighed while never breaking her gaze from the text. Korey scowled at her, and for the first time realized the couple dozen students in the room were all reading silently.

"We're reading Act II to ourselves, then reading aloud in a few minutes" Ms. de Boer said.

Korey took his seat at a back table where folders of graded papers from each period were filed neatly in plastic cubbies. Gino and Ziggy took seats in front of him. Other students glanced at them, wiggled out of the way, then got back to reading.

Korey didn't get *Julius Caesar.* De Boer had described it like *Game of Thrones* or *House of Cards,* but there were no dragons, and it was hard to understand. He tried to read it, but his eyes crossed and the words danced on the page.

Ms. de Boer took volunteers to read aloud, and Korey hoped that would break the monotony. He also hoped some other kids would ask questions that might lead him to understand the text better. Maybe that boy who looked like a turtle would ask what was on everybody's minds.

He usually did, and Korey was grateful for that, even if Turtle Boy always seemed to be looking at him with judgment or scorn.

Turtle Boy took Brutus and began reading.

"What, Lucius, ho!" he quoted.

Korey immediately burst into laughter. Ziggy and Gino followed. Turtle Boy and Ms. de Boer scowled at the trio while other students stifled laughter or shifted uncomfortably in their seats.

"Why he call that mans a ho?" Korey asked through tears.

"He wasn't calling anyone a ho," Ms. de Boer explained. "He said 'ho' to mean 'Where are you?' or 'Are you there?' Like how pirates would say 'Ahoy there,' or better yet. 'ThunderCats, ho!'"

"Now she got the ThunderCats in it," Ziggy muttered, making Gino laugh even harder through his clenched mouth.

"I ain't never heard 'ho' used like that. You wild, Ms. de Boer," Korey said.

"Be respectful, Mr. Hoffer," she demanded. Turtle Boy continued and the class settled down. Their peers' slow drones lulled Korey back into a state of semiconsciousness as the words continued to dance on the page. He tried to focus, but the words made no sense, and no action happened. He wanted to believe Brutus was *that* nigga, orchestrating the murder of Caesar, but at this point, Korey just wanted everyone to die so that something—anything—could move him along and out this class.

His eyes fluttered and closed. He was sleepy, but not asleep. He thought about what might happen in chemistry class, and how, at least every now and then, Dr. Igiri would try to blow something up. After chemistry was lunch, and then maybe he could see the girl who always annoyed him. He could tell she liked him, but they didn't have any classes together…

Slam!

"Bitch, are you crazy?!" Korey exclaimed. A few of his classmates laughed, and a few others let out the childish "Aww!" signaling someone had messed up big time.

Ms. de Boer stood over Korey with a heavy dictionary that she had slammed on the table, violently rousing Korey with the sound and vibration.

"Wake up, Mr. Hoffer," she said flatly. She walked back to her desk.

"Don't you ever slam no book in my ear!" Korey yelled, standing up from his seat.

"Korey, chill," Gino said.

"Shut up, Gino. She ain't do that shit to you, she did it to me," Korey said. He'd had enough of everybody, from Gino telling him what to do to Ms. de Boer acting like she was better than everybody.

"Korey, sit down," Ms. de Boer said. Korey walked intently to her.

"So, you ain't gonna apologize for what you did?" he asked.

"Are you going to apologize for coming to my class late, again? For falling asleep, again? For being disruptive, again? I'd say waking you up with a little jostle makes us even-stevens. But you want to call me a bitch. So, get out of my room."

Korey decided, for once in his life, not to argue back and forth with an adult. He needed to cool down for a few minutes. He stormed out, swinging the door with such force that it crashed into the classroom wall. Flabbergasted, the teacher followed him.

He heard Ms. de Boer's footsteps behind him as he tried to walk down the hall. She overtook him and stood in front of him.

"You don't get to call me a bitch, ever!" she shouted, pointing her finger at him.

"And you don't get to slam a damn book in my ear!"

"How else were you gonna wake up and get on task?"

"You sposed to figure that out, not me. Don't slam no book in my ear and get your fucking finger out my face!"

Security came running down the hall before either of them knew it. Mr. Cleveland, the Principal, was close behind.

"What's the problem here?" Mr. Cleveland asked.

"This bitch slamming books in my ear!" Korey shouted.

"Take him down to my office," he instructed the security guards, who weren't that much older than Korey.

"What about her? She the one throwing shit!"

"Shut your mouth until I get to my office, young man."

"How am I supposed to teach kids who are obviously high?" Ms. de Boer asked Mr. Cleveland. Korey never heard the answer. His heart pounded all the way to Mr. Cleveland's office. By the time Mr. Cleveland entered, Korey was once again in possession of his emotions. He accepted his three-day suspension without a fight.

Korey turned sixteen the following February. That's when his real troubles seemed to start. His muscles popped out overnight and he went from looking like a boy to a man. The wispy hairs on his face thickened and his cherubic face hardened into an angular scowl.

It seemed to Korey that the bigger he got, the more the older boys from other neighborhoods tested him. Flipping the brim of his baseball cap on some days, tripping him up the stairs on other days, mumbling slurs under their breath as he walked by—anything to get a rise out of him. What really burned Korey up about it was that everybody seemed to make him the target. It was never Ziggy, who seemed to be everyone's darling. God forbid it be Gino, who could talk his way out of most conflicts. It's like everyone knew that this kid, who looked like a grown man, had the shortest fuse of all.

It took about seven seconds for Korey's life to change. A shoulder bump from one of the boys from Lincoln Heights. A hard shove back. A fall into the elderly music teacher, twisting her ankle. A scuffle leading to an all-out brawl. An accusation that Korey had started it all. A trip to Mr. Cleveland's office. Again.

"You ain't coming back here, Korey," Mr. Cleveland sighed.

"Whatchu mean I'm not coming back?"

"The most I can give you is 20 days for fighting. And you're going to get it. That takes you right to spring break. By the time you get back, it'll be the middle of the semester. You think you'll be able to catch up? Huh? You really think after all that time, you'll be able to just jump back in? I'm not gonna make my teachers plan that far ahead, making packets for you that we both know you wouldn't even finish—if you could. No, Korey. This is over. I'm running down the clock on you. All this smoking in my hallways, disrespecting my teachers, doing what you wanna do? It's over, okay? You are no longer welcome at H.D. Woodson."

Korey sucked his teeth.

"You can't kick me out."

"You don't run me or this school, punk!" Mr. Cleveland slammed both of his palms on his metal desk, making a loud boom that rattled the room. His front office staff stopped what they were doing and preened their necks to see what was going on through the closed door. Through clenched teeth, Mr. Cleveland continued.

"H.D. Woodson is my school, you hear me? Mine. I decide who walks through those doors every day. I watch you and your thug friends walk in and do whatever you want day in and day out, menacing the scholars in here that want to make something of themselves. And you…you just sit up here like nothing. Just taking up space. A waste of biological matter that's gonna end up on the wrong side of police tape. Why don't you make space for somebody that's gonna be something someday?"

"I'm *coming* back at the end of my suspension, fuck you saying to me?"

"I'm saying that if you come back, my security will turn you away at the door. And if you get past them, my teachers will lock the classroom doors on you. The lunch ladies won't serve you. You won't even be able to get a book out of the library. And Korey? If, somehow, you get back into my building and even think about trying me, I have ways of turning your degenerate friends against you, too."

Korey's eyes narrowed to slits.

"Ziggy might be a weed head, but he ain't no dummy. He knows he needs to distance himself from you somehow. And Gino—I like Gino. Even he said you gotta do better. You think I can't turn them against you? You think I can't make you *persona non grata* in your neighborhood? Try me. Come back to H.D. Woodson and see what happens."

Mr. Cleveland slid the suspension paperwork to Korey. "Twenty days," it said. *More like twenty to life*, Korey thought.

He clutched the paperwork and stuffed it into the pocket of his hoodie. He stood up, walked out of Mr. Cleveland's office, and past the nosy ladies at the front. He pushed his way through the people crowding the counter, then left the office. He steamed his way through the security at the front door and left the building.

Tears stained his face a block from the school. He knew Mr. Cleveland had only given him twenty days—a nice time off. But he also knew everything else Cleveland said was true. He could do everything he wanted to—off the books—to keep him out. It *was* Cleveland's school, not Korey's.

He should have knocked over all the shit on Cleveland's desk, Korey thought. Kicked that big ass obnoxious plant. Spat in his face. Kicked in that stupid trophy case. Give him a reason to expel him, for real. Not just for a stupid fight with a boy he didn't even have real beef with.

It was too late. Korey would never step foot in H.D. Woodson again. He woke up every day and walked to the top of the hill with Ziggy, Gino, and Peek, but that's where the walk ended. He turned left on East Capitol Street and found an alley where he smoked weed for breakfast. He walked the streets, generally staying out of everyone's way all day.

He never showed his mother the suspension papers. He didn't want to hear her mouth. After spring break, he continued his phony walks to school, but didn't dare try re-entering the building. He never told his boys what the repercussions of his actions might be. Truth be told, the worst consequence of all would have been losing his friends. He liked them, but knew Gino and Ziggy merely tolerated him, whether out of pity or proximity. He knew they were tired of his quick temper. But they were good dudes and Korey didn't want to lose that.

So, he stopped going to school, even after the suspension was up. Gino and Ziggy didn't question it, and frankly enjoyed the peace of a Korey-free school zone.

By late April, Korey's mother was notified he had been disenrolled from H.D. Woodson for truancy. Korey didn't bother to discuss the suspension or the threats from Mr. Cleveland. Ms. Hoffer wouldn't have known how to fight back anyway. She never fought for her son before, so why should she start now, even if pushing problem children out of public schools was a common tactic of otherwise hopeless educators. Besides, Korey had a reliably unreliable temper which would have led to another long-term suspension anyway.

He heard her screams. He felt the spit from her venomous diatribe hit his face. He had long stopped caring about his mother's opinions and refused to engage with her when she got worked up, which enraged her even more. She pushed him, shoved him, questioned why he had even been born if all he was ever going to do was be somebody's problem.

He wanted to tell her that he hadn't been asked to be born at all, and he'd have been satisfied to have been aborted if that's what she wanted. Who wanted to be born poor, anyway, with a mother like her?

She was a joke to him. Not physically abusive like everyone knew Gino's mother had been. But emotionally unstable and mean. The apple didn't fall far from the tree, and Korey knew it. He took her vitriol and bottled it inside.

He took to sleeping in late rather than walking with his boys, not enjoying his marijuana breakfast until nearly lunchtime. He watched Maury and Jerry Springer and Paternity Court. He made it out of the house in time to link up with the boys again after school.

February 2022 through June 2022

For all intents and purposes, Korey had been living uptown with Kia Grant since well before Gino's death.

Kia was one of the good ones. Although she'd known Korey and the other boys since high school, she had never given them the time of day. Her father had warned her the boys from Slope were bad news, and even though her mother had reiterated that warning, behind closed doors she disclosed that Mr. Grant was merely jealous. The boys from Slope always got the girls.

She noticed when Korey stopped coming to school but had expected to see him again when junior year commenced. She saw Ziggy and Gino return, along with Peek entering for the first time, but also noticed when they, too, disappeared, one at a time. She never suspected they had been pushed out and had presumed they were simply bad eggs. Bad, but cute.

She graduated on time and let Turtle Boy take her to the Prom. She learned on that night that there was no such thing as a "nice guy," only ones who will try to take advantage of you and those who won't. Turtle Boy wouldn't keep his hands off her, even though she'd insisted they were only going to Prom as friends. When he put his hand someplace he shouldn't have, for the third time in a row, she gave him a black eye lasting long enough to ruin his graduation day photos.

Kia got enough scholarship money to be able to go to Montgomery College for two years. It was there that she took up sociology and read books like *Pushout: The Criminalization of Black Girls in Schools* and *Black Boys Apart: Racial Uplift and Respectability in All-Male Public Schools.* She had felt all along, on some level, the world she navigated was a system that she could disrupt if only she had the cheat codes. For Kia, that code was a love of education and a voracious appetite for nonfiction.

Since she was convinced no man was "nice" in a world wholly informed by rape culture and white supremacy, she might as well pursue relationships with whatever man she wanted, including "bad" guys. She had no intention of settling down any time soon, especially not before she got her bachelor's degree. The spring before Gino's death, she'd had an acceptance letter in hand from the University of Maryland and planned to transfer there after completing her associate's degree.

She met Korey at the T-Mobile store in Columbia Heights one busy Saturday. The farmer's market had filled the plaza, and the drunks and homeless people had been temporarily displaced. Kia needed a new case for her phone and since she lived right by 14th and Colorado in a rent-controlled high rise, it made sense to take the ten-minute bus ride down to Columbia Heights. Ellsworth Place in nearby Silver Spring would have similarly been a zoo, but at least this way Kia could also pick up some fresh vegetables for her meal planning.

"Hey beautiful," Kia heard someone say as she walked into the T-Mobile store. She knew how she looked: skin the color of almonds, a slim waist, ample bosom, and thick thighs. Her nails were always done, she always smelled good, and she always wore light, natural makeup. She wasn't one for obnoxiously large false eyelashes for day-to-day living. She wanted to look like the women who got interviewed on MSNBC for being smart—not like a real housewife, although she loved watching those shows as well.

She hoped that the cat caller wouldn't be waiting for her outside the store. He'd probably follow her all through the farmers market hoping to get her phone number or Instagram handle. Kia preferred to do the pursuing, honestly. She knew what she liked, went for it, and usually got it.

Kia found a case, paid for it, and left the store. An average sized man held the door open for her. She thanked him.

"I guess you didn't hear me when I said 'Hey beautiful' earlier," he said.

"I heard you," she said flatly.

"Why you ain't speak back?"

"Because my name is not 'Beautiful,'" she replied, finally looking at him.

"Okay, Kia," he said.

"Wait a minute…" She stopped walking and squinted at the man.

"Korey Hoffer from H.D.?!" She squealed and threw her arms around him. "I've thought about you since you stopped coming to school! How are you?"

For the first time in a long time, Korey blushed. He had become a handsome man, with short dreadlocks, smooth skin, and a full mustache. He was muscular under his jean jacket and long-sleeved t-shirt. He wore a small diamond-like stud in his ear.

"You thought about me?" he asked.

"Why wouldn't I? We were in the same homeroom."

"We never spoke before."

"That doesn't mean you're forgettable. Wow. Good to see you. What have you been up to?"

"Nothing much really. Just out here doing my thing, you know?"

"I feel you, same here."

"You in school?"

"Yup! Up Montgomery. I finish this May with my associates. I live Uptown now."

"Damn. Get it, girl. I knew you'd be doing good."

"I'm trying to."

Kia couldn't help but smile. She truly never thought she'd see bad ass Korey Hoffer ever again. Deep down, she was just happy he was alive— but was happier that he was alive and sexy.

"Hey…you think you could spare 20 minutes for me to take you to this bakery right here? Treat you to a cup of coffee or a cookie or something?"

"Korey Hoffer, are you asking me on a date?"

"Something like that," he said bashfully.

"Why yes, I'd love to have coffee with you," Kia said.

The bakery had a tiny sitting area where Korey and Kia tried scones and *café au lait*. She knew Korey didn't know what he was doing but found it endearing that he tried so hard not to mess up. Their conversation went from current events to "back in the day" gossip, like who dated who behind the scenes. Korey was pleased to learn that Turtle Boy had been a creep all along—he'd never liked him. And Kia was happy to know Korey was at least trying to get his GED. Forward motion was still motion.

They fucked that night. Kia found no reason to waste time when she was attracted to a man with whom she could have a conversation. Korey, she had learned quickly, was especially good at fucking. Not love-making, but actual, down and dirty, oochie wally wally, oochie bang bang *fucking*.

Kia didn't have to worry about faithfulness, as she wasn't looking for a serious relationship anyway. But Korey was soon at her place two nights a week, then three, then four. They didn't have sex *all* the time…but certainly most of the time. Korey was packing a lot, and he knew how to use it.

She knew Korey didn't have meaningful employment, and got a token check every two weeks from Alternative Futures as a form of universal basic income. She also surmised that Korey sold drugs—probably weed based on how little he seemed to be bringing home. Korey didn't spend money on flashy things and was content to just get by.

Still, he treated Kia very well, always spent quality time with her, and took her on cute dates Uptown. Being with him was easy.

There was only one time Korey was hard in Kia's presence. It was June, near the end of the year at Alternative Futures. Though Kia had been doing her best to push Korey toward passing a section of the GED, he kept missing the "likely to pass" threshold on the practice test. He was frustrated.

Then, one very late weeknight, Korey texted Kia to say he was outside and to let him in her building. She put on her fuzzy slippers, took the elevator down, and let him in. He kissed her, hugged her, and held her hand as they went up the elevator. Without time to straighten up, Kia had to move some of her books off the futon to make room for them both. She laid her head onto his chest.

"You gon' tell me what's wrong?" she asked.

"Mmm-mm," he mumbled.

"We are friends first, Korey. You can't come to my house for late night cuddles and not tell me what's wrong."

Korey sighed.

"It's Gino. He keeps…fucking…pissing me off. You wanna know what he said to me tonight? We was on the corner talking. Finished working for the night. Just chillin', dig? And I said fuck it, I'ma tell 'em about you. I don't keep no secrets from my boys, dig? And they started wondering where I been going. So I said 'Fuck it, remember Kia from

H.D.?' And they like 'Yeah.' Well, Peek ain't really remember you, but he was so young. But Zig and Gino did. And I said 'I'm messing with her now.' And you know what the fuck Gino said?"

"What?"

"'What a bad bitch like Kia want with a nigga like you?'"

"Damn! What the fuck did he mean by that?"

"That's what the fuck I asked him? I said 'What's "nigga like you" supposed to mean?' And he just started going in on me! He said I ain't have no high school diploma. I ain't working a real job. Nigga said I can barely read. Said I ain't have no drip. Just went the fuck in. So, I swung on him."

"Oh, babe…"

"I just…blacked out. I mean, how you supposed to be somebody friend and that's what they think of you? That you not good enough and never will be? What kind of shit is that? And honestly, that's what he's always thought of me. As soon as his funky ass came to town, everybody started acting like he was the head honcho. He so smart, why he got kept back, huh? He so smart, why he get kicked out of school just like me?"

"I—"

"Miss Sandra started calling us the Gang of Four and made his ass the CEO. What she call me? The CFO."

"But at least…"

"Gino ain't shit, yo. He ran away from his problems and started over with Slope. You don't get to fuckin start a new life someplace and then be the top dog. Fuck that. I been on Slope my whole fucking life! That nigga is shit! He's dead!"

"Korey! You gotta chill!"

He frothed at the mouth. His heart raced and he was breathless.

"You gotta listen to yourself, boo."

Korey closed his eyes and tried to control his breathing.

"You and one of your best friends had a disagreement. An argument. That doesn't mean you don't love each other. That doesn't erase all the years of good times."

"How you love somebody and you don't respect them? Huh? Gino said that shit like he thought it all along. He think I'm nothing at all. And you know what Peek and Ziggy did? They laughed. They laughed at me even after we finished scrapping. Just cackling like two bitches."

"Well…at least you walked away. Eventually. I know they really upset you, but I'm hoping when you and Gino sit down and talk it out, maybe he can make himself more clear. I know he couldn't have meant to hurt your feelings."

"Ain't no sit-downs, Kia. This shit dead. I don't fuck with them niggas."

"Oh…" Kia hugged Korey. She didn't know Peek, Ziggy, or Gino that well at all, besides what she remembered from high school, so she couldn't say for sure that everything would be okay. It seemed to Kia like Korey might be overreacting to regular jonin' on each other like everybody in DC did to one another. Everybody reaches a breaking point, though, Kia wondered, and she was just glad Korey knew when to finally walk away.

Eventually, Kia noticed Korey had fallen back in with the boys, even though most of his nights were spent with her.

Thursday, August 4, 2022

Kia had been at a book signing for one of her favorite authors on the afternoon of Gino's death. By the time she got home, Korey was sitting in her living room in the dark.

"Why you sittin' here in the dark? You scared the shit out of me," Kia said.

"Gino dead," Korey said.

"What?! When?" Kia exclaimed.

"Earlier today. He got shot."

"Jesus. Do they know who did it?"

Korey slowly shook his head.

"Naw. They don't know who did it."

"Damn."

Korey exhaled.

"We should go to Slope. Like right now," Kia said.

"No."

"Don't you think you should be with your friends?"

"Not tonight. I can't do it," Korey said flatly.

"Okay," Kia said. She never argued with Korey. He was grown. His grief was his own and he'd figure out his own way in his own time. He always did.

Saturday, September 3, 2022: An Evil Child

Kia needed box braids installed, but her regular braider on Kennedy Street had the flu. She decided to trek all the way back to Northeast, for the first time in months, to visit her old braider off East Capitol Street.

The shop was already buzzing at nine in the morning. The television blared with the morning news. Netta—Ziggy's friend—was the receptionist, sweeper, and shampoo girl, as well as the holder of the remote control for the elevated television.

"Turn on cartoons or something, Netta!" a stylist said.

"Chile, ain't no cartoons no more! You think we in the eighties?"

Jerika, the shop owner and lead braider, bemoaned how depressing the news always was as Kia took her seat.

"I know, chile, but we gotta keep up with what's going on if we want things to change," Kia said.

"You just like you used to be as a little girl," Jerika said. "I remember when your momma used to bring you in here with your little books, waiting patiently while she'd get her tracks installed."

"You remember that?" Kia asked.

"Of course I do," Jerika said as she prepared her tools. "I'm not that old."

Kia laughed.

"You caught an Uber down here?"

"Yeah, chile. But I know you do good work."

"You like it Uptown, though?"

"Yeah, it's aight. Closer to school. Same drama up there as down here, though."

"Drama everywhere," Jerika sighed as she began separating Kia's pre-washed hair.

"You heard about Gino, right? Y'all was in school around the same time."

"Yeah, I heard. Sad. And they still don't know who did it."
Netta laughed.

"Oh, they know, hunty. Everybody knows."

"Oh." Kia shifted in her chair as Jerika pushed her head slightly. She applied cool gel, moisturizing her hair as she braided it, adding strands of human hair as she went.

"That boy was always bad news." Jerika shook her head.

"Real nasty children grow into real nasty men," Pam, a stylist, said from the back of the salon. The patrons and other stylists grunted in agreement.

"Thank God it wasn't Peek, chile," Jerika said.

"Oh, please. Peek wouldn't hurt a fly. And Ziggy too spaced out to think about killing nobody," Pam declared.

Kia tensed up and closed her eyes.

"Don't be talking about my man like that," Netta said with a faux attitude.

"You know when God was giving out brains, Ziggy said 'Naw, I only need half—I'm watching my figure.'" Pam's joke made the salon erupt with laughter.

Netta rolled her eyes.

"That's okay, though. I can think for the both of us," Netta laughed.

Kia's head swam with suspicion. They were going down the list of Gino's friends but had left one off. Nobody there knew Kia and Korey had been dating. Why wouldn't they say his name?

"Too bad it wasn't no cameras over there. Would be an open and shut case," Jerika said.

"It was witnesses, though. At least one," Pam revealed.

"You know Slope don't snitch on they own," Jerika countered.

"Things change," Netta said. She rose from the reception desk and walked to the back. She retrieved a broom and swept around the booths. When she got to Jerika's area, Kia locked eyes with her.

"So…who did it?" Kia asked. Netta froze.

"Korey, of course," Netta whispered.

"Just evil," Jerika muttered. "An evil, evil child."

Kia's throat went dry.

"How…how do we know that?" Kia stuttered.

"We know cuz Korey *been* had a bad temper. Plus, the person who saw him do it finally told somebody," Netta said while she swept.

"But…why?"

"Chile, why does anybody kill? Knowing Korey, he was prolly jealous Gino was doing something for hisself. Did you know he was finna go to UDC?"

"No. I didn't know that."

"Mmm-hm. Well, that's that. And you ain't heard none of that from me. I hope the police finally catch his ass. It'd be the first damn good thing they did all year."

"Korey's on the run now?" Kia asked.

"Ain't seen him since a few days after Gino died. He ain't even come to the funeral. But I guess he wouldn't have…"

Kia became nauseated, but she kept calm for the six hours it took for her to get her braids complete.

Kia's hands shook as she unlocked her apartment door. Korey was there, as he had been for the past few weeks, eating her food and running up her electric bill.

"You gotta go," she announced as she put her purse on the kitchen counter. She propped the door open and stood beside it.

Korey stared at her in disbelief, then he laughed.

"Oh, you funny," he said. He resumed his game on the PlayStation 5 Kia had bought.

"I am not kidding. You need to leave right now."

"The fuck is this about?" he asked.

"You know exactly what the fuck this is about. You need to leave right now before I call the police."

"What would you need to call the police for? I've never done anything to you. You trippin'."

"You killed that boy," Kia said.

"What?!"

"You killed Gino."

"Who told you that?"

"Everybody's talking down Slope. Whole salon full of bitches with your name in their mouth. It was an open secret, Korey. Everybody saying you did it."

"I bet that tranny freak Netta was in the middle of it, too. Why you go down there anyway? I thought you got your hair done down the street?"

"Netta wasn't even in the salon," Kia lied. "But I know you killed that boy because you ain't deny it once! Get out!"

"Lower your damn voice, Kia!" Korey boomed. He rose and approached the door. He tried to kick away the triangular block holding it open, but Kia got in the way.

"Don't touch my fucking door, Korey. Get your shit and get out of my house."

"You don't understand what's going on," he hissed.

"I understand enough. You killed somebody and decided to hide out in my house. Get the fuck out, Korey."

"You don't know what happened. That nigga been jealous of me since he first knew me. He took my spot. He took everything from me."

Korey put his shoes on and stuffed his clothes into his backpack.

"He didn't take anything from you. He showed up in your life right on time. He was the glue that kept y'all together. Think back on everything you ever told me about him. Every good memory you ever had, he was there. He never turned his back on you, even when you was acting crazy."

"Bitch. Don't call me crazy," Korey growled through gritted teeth.

"Oh, I'm a bitch now? Bet. Watch me call the police if you ain't out of my house in thirty seconds."

"Pussy wasn't that good no way," he mumbled.

"Now we both know that's a damn lie. But that's your problem. You don't know how to have a disagreement with somebody without thinking you gotta end them. Your biggest enemy was never Gino. It was you! Gino had nothing but laughs. Light. You just a dark cloud until you get what you want. But you gotta work for it, Korey. You gotta pay your dues. You could have learned something from Gino had you paid attention."

"If you love him so much, why don't you go to hell and fuck him yourself?" Korey spat as he crossed the threshold into the hallway. The door slammed behind him.

Saturday, September 3, 2022: The Crow

Korey's first gun was at the bottom of a sewer off East Capitol Street. He kept a second one in his bookbag while he was at Kia's place, but transferred it to his pants in the elevator on his way out. He was so angry that he was muttering to himself.

His first halfway real relationship was over, thanks to Gino's dead ass. And Ziggy. And Netta. And Peek. Especially Peek. He'd known Peek since he was born, and they both knew the code: Slope don't snitch.

But there Peek was. Snitching. And he had to be dealt with.

Caw! Caw!

A black bird had landed on the bus shelter at 14th and Colorado. Korey guessed it was a crow.

"Shut the fuck up, dumb bird," he mumbled.

Caw! Caw!

The bird never moved, mocking Korey as he walked closer to the bus shelter. If he had a rock, he'd have thrown it. But he continued walking. When he was about six feet away, the crow finally flew out of sight.

Korey walked for blocks. He passed the bus barn, then the sorority building with the green awning. He was still so very mad, like the fire that had been lit in him at his birth had been doused with lighter fluid, and instead of the constant smoldering, had engulfed his insides with flames. He passed a school and remembered how much he hated school when he was young. He couldn't focus, and every last fast-talking teacher got on his nerves. They never slowed down long enough to get him to understand and were so boring that his attention always drifted to the windows.

He started conversations constantly, even at five years old, with any peer who would listen. Mischief was always his idea, from stealing paperclips, one at a time, from his teachers' desks, to peeing on the lavatory walls.

He remembered a bunch of acronyms during one meeting when he was in sixth grade: ADD, ADHD, ODD. He knew what ADHD was, and that his mother forbade any sort of medication for him, instead putting the onus back on the teachers. "You the teacher. You can't deal with a little boy?" she would ask.

But Korey wasn't an ordinary little boy, and he knew it. He was bad. That's what everybody called him, so why be different?

Korey, Gino, Peek, and Ziggy were four different kinds of people entirely, but they were all labeled "bad," mainly because of Korey. He was the bad apple, the troublemaker, the ringleader who invariably led all four of them into some sort of shenanigans. He was the leader of the Gang of Four. But Gino had the gift of gab. He talked his way out of as much trouble as they got into. He could talk smooth, negotiating an expulsion to a suspension, a suspension to a detention, and a detention to a stern talking-to. Korey envied that about him.

Gino was a little taller, a little more handsome, a little smarter, a little more. Everyone knew it, and Korey most of all.

Caw! Caw!

Korey blinked and was near the Ethiopian coffee shop in Columbia Heights. His daydreaming caused him to miss most of the walk so far, but that damn crow snapped him out of it.

"Another one? Same one?" he said to himself. He couldn't tell—the bird was across the street, perched on a light post near a Vietnamese restaurant.

"Get the fuck outta here," he whispered.

A crew of four gorgeous, curly haired Latinas in short black dresses walked around him on the way to a bar. Two of them batted their eyelashes at him, while another looked at her phone. The fourth looked him up and down and then scoffed.

"Bitch," he mumbled.

Women were all the same, especially Kia. Nasty attitudes. Don't know a good thing when they see it. He had money—just as much as the rest of his squad. He looked just as good. Everybody he knew wore fake drip, so who cared? Nobody in the hood had real gold or diamonds unless they stole it. Korey felt he was trying, and that should count for something. He was in school just like everybody else, trying to get the same credentials.

He crossed Park Road, the street that would have taken him to Alternative Futures. Mr. Towers had his favorites there, too. He knew Towers liked Gino best because he got his GED first. So many folks loved Alternative Futures, but to Korey, it was another legal scam with fake ass teachers collecting a paycheck. He didn't feel like he'd learned anything new since enrolling, except how to hustle a sucker out of their stipend.

Caw! Caw!

The stupid crow was on the Starbucks sign now.

"What the fuck do you want from me, bird? Shit!" Korey said aloud. People on the sidewalk glanced at him, then minded their business once more. It was Columbia Heights. It wouldn't be the first or last time somebody talked to a bird.

A woman stopped in front of Korey and blocked his path.

Dana. Gino's girl. Her teeth were clenched under her lips. Her nostrils flared and her chest heaved with a rush of adrenaline.

Caw! Caw!

The crow taunted Korey, daring him to say something, anything to the woman that he'd made into Slope's latest widow.

Silence.

"When we get together, in silence, whether it's hot outside or cold, we wait. We wait for God to talk to us. We don't do things like we used to. Can't no preacher tell us something God told him to tell us. God can tell us hisself. Why you think that church building been empty since the 60s? We don't need that here. If we listen for God, he will talk to us—if we wanna hear him." Korey's grandmother told him this at a very young age.

So he waited.

And tried.

And prayed.

And begged.

But he never heard God when he sat in worship with the rest of Slope.

And he didn't hear God on this busy street, with nothing but space and opportunity for Dana to end him, if she wanted, or he her.

There was no God telling him to repent or to beg for forgiveness.

Just him and Dana and the crow.

Dana waited expectantly for Korey to do anything, to say anything, even if it was just "Move, bitch." But Korey said nothing. He stared at Dana as intently as she stared at him.

A crowd of a few dozen people exited DC USA, the shopping mall in Columbia Heights, surrounding both Dana and Korey. In the sea of people, they were separated. Korey pushed forward, against the crowd, and eventually ended up at the corner. He crossed the street, entered the Metro station, and got on the next train headed home to Slope.

Sunday, September 4, 2022

The sun rose over Slope.

Miss Sandra put on her floor-length dashiki, sipped a cup of coffee, and read the Bible on her phone to get ready for worship.

Jordan and Rahman took a shower together, taking turns scrubbing each other's backs, and getting more playful than the time would allow.

Ziggy woke up as the big spoon to Netta's little spoon, with his head nuzzled in the nape of her neck.

Dana hadn't gotten much sleep at all, save for a few hours where she dreamed of Gino, woke up, fell asleep, and dreamed of him again.

Peek had woken up before the sun, and he prayed, thanking God earnestly for another day to try to honor everyone who believed in him.

Pops didn't come to worship. He didn't want to miss a second of the baseball game between the Cincinnati Reds and the Washington Nationals. He carefully bathed himself and put on his Nats jersey and cap, before sitting in his easy chair. He smiled and waved at his family as they marched out the door to the intersection.

Ziggy and Netta pulled out the barriers from their normal spaces between the houses on the North side; Jordan and Rahman handled the barriers from the South side.

There seemed to be more gathered at worship than usual. Something in the air pulled the families together under the hot sun. This was their ritual, performed time and time again for decades, with few knowing why or how the tradition had come to be, despite worshiping in the shadows of the burned-out shell of Pleasant Stream, that had never been repaired, and had been overtaken by wildflowers and graffiti.

At the appointed time, Peek rose.

"Slope gathers here, at this intersection, in a neighborhood that belongs to us, to worship the Creator of all things. We decided long ago that we are the preachers and the teachers that we have been waiting for. We decided that God will take care of us, if we listen. You are welcome to listen with God, with us, in silence. And if he tells you to speak, then please…"

Peek heard a door slam from Korey's house up the block. It was him, emerging from his family's home as though he'd always been there—not at all like he'd been on the run for the past few weeks.

"If he tells you to speak…" Peek said again, distracted. Scared. But resolute.

"If he tells you to speak…then speak." Peek locked eyes with Korey, who sped up his gait as he entered the circle of families and folding chairs.

All were frozen as Gino's murderer reentered their circle for the first time since his death. Rahman noticed the glint of Korey's weapon from his waistband first. He nudged Jordan, whose eyes widened as he saw the gun as well. Without alarming the worshipers, they tried to get Peek's attention with his eyes, but he was laser focused on Korey.

Sweat beads formed at Korey's temples, and he reached for his weapon. Peek stood stiff as a board as Korey approached.

"Korey, no," Miss Sandra whispered.

He raised his gun and pointed at Peek's chest, three mere feet away from him. His finger hovered over the trigger.

Peek lifted his head to the sky and closed his eyes.

The clatter of a dropped metal folding chair startled everyone. A blond, blue-eyed child froze and turned red. His mother hushed him and picked up the chair herself as everyone in the intersection, save Peek, looked in their direction.

Korey, confused, lowered his weapon. The woman was flanked by about a dozen other white folks of various ages. Many were middle-aged and elderly, but a few were younger, like her. They walked toward the intersection, oblivious to the action.

Jordan and Rahman rose and went to Korey as the new tribe approached.

"Who are they?" he asked.

"Don't know," Rahman said. He stretched out his arms and encircled Korey in an embrace. Miss Sandra rose from her seat, approached the men, and hugged Korey as well.

Jordan placed his hands on Korey's hand and carefully took the gun from him. Dana approached, and took the gun from Jordan, stowing it in her cross-body bag.

Peek's eyes opened and he lowered his head once more. Ziggy tearfully approached him and threw his arms around him.

"We got you, Peek. And you got this," he whispered.

Korey's muscles tensed up under Rahman's embrace. He struggled.

"No, friend," Rahman whispered. "We got you, too. We got you."

The white woman with the child placed her folding chair on the asphalt and took a seat, creating a new row in the worship circle. On this new adventure east of the river to a newly discovered Quaker community, they remained blissfully unaware of the almost-murder they could have witnessed. After a few moments of rustling, the white visitors settled into the silence.

Primordial floodgates inside of Korey broke open. Rivers of sobless tears flowed from his eyes as he took ownership for what he did and who he was: a child of rage. For all the windows broken and tires slashed…for all the bruised and bloodied nerds he'd bullied…for all the holes punched in walls…for all the times he called a girl or woman a bitch…for all the bones he'd broken…

For the bullets he'd shot.

For the lives he'd taken.

For the rage that seemed to be part of his DNA…for the relationships he'd broken…for the families he'd shattered:

He was sorry.

The rage gave way to shame.

Rahman felt his shoulder become moist with Korey's tears.

"Let it out, little brother," Rahman said, gripping Korey tighter.

Korey wailed.

For the childhood lost.

For the opportunities squandered.

For the life he took.

"He gone…" he sobbed.

"I know, buddy. I know," Rahman said as he cradled Korey's head.

"Come here," Peek said. In one arm, he held Ziggy by the shoulder. His other arm was outstretched, waiting for Korey. His eyes, red and watery, welcomed Korey back into the circle, despite what he had done.

"I can't." Korey shook his head.

"Yes, you can," Rahman whispered. "These are your brothers."

"Come here," Peek repeated. Korey obeyed, loosening his grip on Rahman and walking to Peek and Ziggy. They pulled him into their embrace.

"Is this part of it?" an older white man in a wide-brimmed straw hat whispered to his wife. She shrugged.

"Maybe it's like altar call, but we missed it?" she whispered back.

Miss Sandra, Rahman, Jordan, Netta, Dana, and a few others surrounded the boys, shielding them from the onlookers.

Korey struggled to catch his breath.

"Where's Royce?" he asked.

"I'm right here, friend," she said, appearing from the throng.

"Let's go, okay?" he said.

"I got you, friend," she said. Ziggy and Peek let go of Korey but touched him for as long as they could before Royce led him away, to the inevitable justice waiting for him.

Peek sat back down in the front row, and, one by one, everyone else did the same. The remainder of the hour was totally silent. At the end, Peek shook hands with Ziggy. All those assembled followed suit.

Peek didn't understand exactly who the white people were who had descended upon their meeting, how they'd heard about it, or whether they would return. He didn't know what they meant by Quaker, or why they were so quick to call him "Friend." But he knew, somehow, that they would be back, just as sure as the first white woman jogging in the hood signaled irrevocable change in any other DC community.

The sun hung high over Slope.

Miss Sandra finished cooking her Sunday meal and served it to all who were hungry, including Dana, as she had been led to do years before, and she would do for years to come.

Jordan hugged his husband from behind as they crossed the threshold into their forever home. All this was his.

Rahman's phone vibrated in his pocket. For the first time, a group chat had begun between his children, and they had included him.

For the first time, Ziggy and Netta held each other's hands and went for a walk. They paused at the footbridge over Watts Branch, remembered Gino, and decided to keep going and discover what was on the other side.

Denise drove to the station, where Royce was holding Korey, determined to defend him as she'd defended every other boy from Slope, despite how hard it might be.

Pops sat in his easy chair with his eyes permanently closed as the Nats/Reds game played on the family's big screen television. He had finished his leg of the relay race that Jennie Mustapha had handed to him decades ago. The race was not yet won, but his leg was done.

Epilogue:
Sunday, October 16, 2022

"It's been six weeks since my Pops died. Six weeks since my best friend was arrested for the murder of my other best friend. Five weeks since Pops' memorial service. A month since I got back in school. And a week since I got my GED. The first at my school for the year. I'm sad. I'm happy for myself, but I'm still sad. Pops ain't with me to see it. Gino ain't here to see it. Korey ain't around to see it either. We were all supposed to be here. Now it's me and Ziggy.

"I been silent this whole time, like I always be. But I can't be silent no more. Life ain't easy here. It ain't right to lose somebody because of a gun, or jealousy, or whatever makes people kill each other. It ain't right to own a house but be afraid that you ain't gon' have enough money to take care of it. It ain't right to have to catch two buses to get to a grocery store that you can't hardly afford no way. And it ain't right that despite all the shit we gotta go through here, in DC, that it's a million times worse in them places Black folk really shouldn't even go to if they can help it.

"But…despite how crazy this world is…despite not having a father around, God gave me Pops for as long as he did. And before Pops left this world, God sent me father figures and big brothers for me to look up to. They ain't show up how I expected. And I damn sure ain't know they was gonna be married to each other. But they here. Amen."

"My name is Peek. Peculiar Tyrone Jones. Son of Jacquetta. Grandson of Earnestine. Great-grandson of Pops. Descendant of free people of color and enslaved Africans and white people in Westhampton County, North Carolina. My people come from towns with funny names like Howgill and Nayler and Goodaire. But my town? My town is Slope. Not DC. Not Northeast. Not even Grant Park.

"In my town, we come together on Sunday mornings—outside, usually—and we sit in silence waiting for God to talk to us. Sometimes He be whispering, and I gotta struggle to sit stiller and stiller so I can really hear Him. Sometimes He be loud and…unrelenting. Like a drum line. Like a thunderstorm.

"Recently, I learned that the way we do what we do makes us Quakers. Quakers. Like my ancestors in North Carolina. Like the man on the oatmeal box, I guess. Whole time, I thought I was just following what my mom and grandma be doing. And Pops. And everybody I knew and loved. Ain't nobody ever said nothing about being no Quaker.

"But the name we always heard about was Miss Jennie. I guess she was a Quaker. But the way she was a Quaker ain't stick with us here in Slope, I guess. It make me wonder, how much of her did Pops really know? And why didn't this thing, this big part of her life, have a name that stayed with us?

"And what did them Quakers really know about her? Did they know she spent every Sunday night in Slope, having dinner with us? Did they know that besides who she loved in Slope that she loved her some Delta Sigma Theta? What part of her got erased by white folks, just like most of who I am get erased when I'm anyplace else in this city?

"Miss Jennie died before I was born. I'm the fourth generation of my family to pray like she taught us to. I guess someday I'll have kids and I'll teach them to pray like I do, too. That'll be the legacy I pass down, just like she passed down to my Pops.

"I look out on us, and I see we got something good. Something strong. Something powerful. Something that can keep us alive, even after death. Pops is here. I see him nodding and grinning. Gino is here. I see him smiling and trying not to crack jokes on me. I see Miss Jennie and I know she proud of who we became. And I think—maybe—maybe she want me to not be afraid of all these new people who here. Maybe she want me to know these white folks showing up don't mean us no harm. Maybe they appeared because we ready for them, and they ready for us and how we do things.

"So…I don't know…maybe God just want me to say, 'welcome to Slope.' We been doing a whole lot of living before you got here and we plan on doing a whole lot more. Just don't put no labels on us. We got this."

Postscript

"…it is the Voice which spoke to Abraham, to Isaac, to Jacob, to Elijah, and the prophets which spoke through the 'last despairing cry' on the Cross, which speaks today through the eyes of the wordless and the mouths of the saints. It is a voice of warning, and at the same time a voice of hope. It cautions against pride, it points to love as the redeemer of knowledge. All man's glory has not silenced it. We need to listen to it at this moment, on the threshold of man's greatest glory or his greatest disaster."

Kenneth E. Boulding
From *The Quaker Reader*

Queries for Worship Sharing

How is God equipping me to free myself from generational trauma?

How does the faith of my immediate ancestors look different from my own faith journey?

How are the stories from the members of my community lost because of bias and privilege?

How does God demand that I see the Light in others of totally different experiences?

How can I share my spiritual journey with others who may have been harmed by religion?

Book Club Discussion Questions

How would you describe the socioeconomic status of Slope?

Do you feel that the residents of Slope are impoverished?

What do you think *A Peculiar Legacy* is saying about generational trauma?

Do you think that Pops' migration to the north was ultimately a good thing? Why or why not?

Do you think that Slope has a crisis of absent fathers?

Royce mentions envy that she was never chosen by Miss Sandra as a leader. Is this envy warranted?

How does fraternity membership influence Jordan and Rahman's sense of self?

What role do you believe the Gaffney-Bruces will play on Slope in the coming years?

Also by Rashid Darden

The Potomac University Series
Lazarus (2005)
Covenant (2011)
Epiphany (2012)

Men of Beta
Yours in the Bond (2019)

The Dark Nation Series
Birth of a Dark Nation (2013)
Children of Fury (2020)

Dark Nation Stories
Thunder Rolls: A Dark Nation Story (2020)
Pascal: A Dark Nation Story (2020)

Anthology:
Time (2019)

Poetry:
The Life and Death of Savion Cortez (2011)

Coming Soon:
The Testaments I-VIII

Rashid Darden is an award-winning, best-selling novelist of the urban LGBT experience, a seasoned leader of Black fraternal movements and nonprofit organizations, and a professional educator in alternative schools. He is from Washington, DC, and is based in Conway, NC. He is a Quaker and worships with Friends Meeting of Washington.

Rashid won Honorable Mention in Genre Fiction in the North Street Book Prize for *Children of Fury* in 2020. In 2017, Rashid's play "Message from 'The Legba'" was selected as a winner of the OutWrite DC and Theatre Prometheus One Page Play Competition. It was staged in 2018. Rashid won the Elite 25 Award in Literature from *Clik Magazine* in 2006.

Rashid believes wholeheartedly in living an authentic, intersectional life at all times. He is an out, black gay man who has experienced chaos and order, wealth and poverty, urban bustle, and rural peace. He brings to his novels as well as his own life a sense of thoughtful disruption. Ultimately, he believes in the principles of everyday brotherhood—that is, the parts of ourselves which keep us connected to one another in meaningful ways.

Connect with him at
www.RashidDarden.com

and @rashidipedia on social media.

www.ingramcontent.com/pod-product-compliance
Lightning Source LLC
Chambersburg PA
CBHW040530170726
48295CB00012B/414